THE GREEK WAY

Pausanius pressed a hand against Hector's naked, trembling chest and ran it down to his stomach, stopping just short of his dick. The captain's rough touch and his lust were like heat. Pausanius bent slowly forward and put his lips to Hector's neck. Hector closed his eyes, as the captain's tongue grazed against his throat, as the hand moved down from his stomach and caressed his pubic hair, brushed almost imperceptibly against his cock. Pausanius lifted his face, and slowly kissed Hector's lips. Hector responded, opening his mouth, allowing the captain's tongue to slip inside. He tasted the wine on the captain's breath.

Pausanius pressed his mouth against Hector's ear and whispered, hotly. 'You have to beg me, Hector. Beg me for my cock.'

THE GREEK WAY

Edward Ellis

First published in Great Britain in 1999 by
Idol
an imprint of Virgin Publishing Ltd
Thames Wharf Studios,
Rainville Road, London W6 9HT

ISBN 0 352 33427 4

Cover photograph by i-2-i images

Typeset by SetSystems Ltd, Saffron Walden, Essex
Printed and bound in Great Britain by
Mackays of Chatham PLC

The Terrence Higgins Trust ♡

SAFER SEX GUIDELINES

These books are sexual fantasies – in real life, everyone needs to think about safe sex.

While there have been major advances in the drug treatments for people with HIV and AIDS, there is still no cure for AIDS or a vaccine against HIV. Safe sex is still the only way of being sure of avoiding HIV sexually.

HIV can only be transmitted through blood, come and vaginal fluids (but no other body fluids) passing from one person (with HIV) into another person's bloodstream. It cannot get through healthy, undamaged skin. The only real risk of HIV is through anal sex without a condom – this accounts for almost all HIV transmissions between men.

Being safe
Even if you don't come inside someone, there is still a risk to both partners from blood (tiny cuts in the arse) and pre-come. Using strong condoms and water-based lubricant greatly reduces the risk of HIV. However, condoms can break or slip off, so:
* Make sure that condoms are stored away from hot or damp places.
* Check the expiry date – condoms have a limited life.
* Gently squeeze the air out of the tip.
* Check the condom is put on the right way up and unroll it down the erect cock.
* Use plenty of water-based lubricant (lube), up the arse and on the condom.
* While fucking, check occasionally to see the condom is still in one piece (you could also add more lube).
* When you withdraw, hold the condom tight to your cock as you pull out.

* Never re-use a condom or use the same condom with more than one person.
* If you're not used to condoms you might practise putting them on.
* Sex toys like dildos and plugs are safe. But if you're sharing them use a new condom each time or wash the toys well.

For the safest sex, make sure you use the strongest condoms, such as Durex Ultra Strong, Mates Super Strong, HT Specials and Rubberstuffers packs. Condoms are free in many STD (Sexually Transmitted Disease) clinics (sometimes called GUM clinics) and from many gay bars. It's also essential to use lots of water-based lube such as KY, Wet Stuff, Slik or Liquid Silk. Never use come as a lubricant.

Oral sex
Compared with fucking, sucking someone's cock is far safer. Swallowing come does not necessarily mean that HIV gets absorbed into the bloodstream. While a tiny fraction of cases of HIV infection have been linked to sucking, we know the risk is minimal. But certain factors increase the risk:
* Letting someone come in your mouth
* Throat infections such as gonorrhoea
* If you have cuts, sores or infections in your mouth and throat

So what is safe?
There are so many things you can do which are absolutely safe: wanking each other; rubbing your cocks against one another; kissing, sucking and licking all over the body; rimming – to name but a few.

If you're finding safe sex difficult, call a helpline or speak to someone you feel you can trust for support. The Terrence Higgins Trust Helpline, which is open from noon to 10pm every day, can be reached on 0171 242 1010.

Or, if you're in the United States, you can ring the Center for Disease Control toll free on 1 800 458 5231.

One

———

The temple of the Oracle at Delphi was not what Orestes had expected. People came from as far away as Egypt and Persia to ask the Oracle for her famous prophecies, to hear the words of the god who spoke through her. All the great heroes had been here, from Herakles to Jason. Orestes had followed the path, the very stones and earth, that demigods had trodden before. Now he was here, in this divine place, on a mission of his own.

At the portal to the shrine, Orestes had been disrobed. His cloak, tunic and sword were taken from him by silent, lean youths, who then bent down to untie his sandals; he was dressed now only in a simple loincloth. From there he was led through a gloomy passageway, which grew darker with each step. The floor of the temple was soft against his naked feet: animal furs covered the stone tiles.

He didn't know now what he had imagined, but certainly not this. As he passed through veiled curtains into darkness and smoke, the scents of Babylonian oils and Nubian spices, the atmosphere trembled dizzyingly with sex. The sweat of anticipation, and a little fear, gathered under Orestes' arms; his biceps felt heavy; a drop of moisture slipped from his armpit down his slender, contoured torso to his waist. He ran a hand through the

1

thick curls of his black hair, and wiped sweat from his lip, where a day's rough stubble had grown.

In the shadows of the long corridors stood naked men, the pale smoky light of candles playing on the sweat that ran down their rippling chests. He could smell them, the fresh moisture of their supple limbs, the scent of semen. Orestes was a tall, imposing figure; but these men seemed inhumanly big, like bronze Titans gleaming in oil. There was the strange sound of singing and incantations from somewhere deep in the temple, as if from the centre of the world.

Torches, glowing in reds and greens and blues, lit the way through the corridors. Silk passed across his face as he moved, nervously, shivering in excitement, towards the heart of the ancient mystery. The naked men followed him, almost hidden in the shadows, and always out of reach, moving like centaurs. Occasionally he saw the glint of eyes. For a moment he stopped, suddenly afraid, as a man like a statue of Poseidon backed off into the darkness of an adjoining corridor, gripping his bloated cock. It was as if the walls of the corridor were male flesh; if only he dared risk the anger of the God, he could reach out and feel the warm hardness of a demigod's erection in his hand. Orestes swallowed, his own dick hardening, the soft cotton cloth folding around it, gently squeezing his balls.

He had reached the core of the temple. The light was a little brighter from a row of torches, each one a different colour: saffron, emerald, turquoise. A curtain of almost transparent fabric hung across an alcove, filled with smoke, or steam, or supernatural vapour, in which crouched a dark, silhouetted figure. The hum of voices was louder. The breathing of men, the smell of their groins, was close around him. His cock was rigid now, pushing at the soft loincloth. He could hardly speak. His sturdy thighs trembled slightly; he could feel the sweat drip between his round, hard buttocks.

Then, abruptly, there was silence. The singing stopped. There was not even any echo. The air seemed dead.

The figure before him remained perfectly still. Orestes wanted his erection to go; it seemed disrespectful, even sacrilegious, to be in this place with a hard cock, wanting these powerful, sweating bodies, now quite still and silent in the darkness. His throat was dry.

Her eyes seemed to see through him. They were dark, smouldering coals in her strange face. For a moment he thought of Perseus and the Gorgon, with her head of writhing snakes, who could turn a man to stone with a glance. He was afraid. He could see his own face, incredibly, reflected in each gleaming eye: the tousled hair hanging over his forehead, the strong cheekbones and trembling, anxious lips, the thick, black eyebrows which almost joined above his straight, sharp nose.

Then the Oracle spoke. Her voice was low, as if it came from far beneath him, from Hades itself. And it didn't sound like a woman's voice, nor, for that matter, a man's. It was like the voice of an old, wise beast.

'What do you seek from the Oracle, traveller?'

Orestes gathered his wits. He cleared his throat, horribly conscious of his urgent erection, surely visible even in the poor light. When he spoke, his voice was hoarse.

'I want to know if my mission will be successful, Wise One.'

There was a long, flat silence. The only sound was the faint breathing of the naked men pressing against the walls. Orestes found himself counting them: ten broad, muscular chests slowly rose and fell in the room. Near the light of a torch, he could see a large, proudly erect cock. It throbbed as he looked at it; his own cock pulsed as if in response. His breath was short, now. He wanted to sink to his knees before these bodies, and worship their stiff, beautiful cocks. He wanted the come of Olympus to rain down on his body in the eerie, magical darkness.

Then suddenly the Oracle screamed. It was a sound like a hawk, high and piercing, from as far above him in the firmament as the voice before was far below. The scream seemed to last for ever, until it hurt his ears.

Just as suddenly, it stopped. The Oracle spoke again.

'You will travel far, and find many things you do not expect to find. And in the end your search will lead you back where you began.'

The Oracle rose. Smoke enveloped her, and she disappeared, abruptly and absolutely. The torches flared. Orestes' cock was hard enough to burst; he felt his knees buckle, and sank down on the warm, soft floor of the temple. Around him, a moan began: a human sound, perhaps, yet close also to the growl of an animal. The naked bodies surged forward from the shadows into the vague, flickering, many-coloured light.

He could hardly keep his eyes open. The figure that stood before him was a huge, male shape, its head and face all but invisible. It was just powerful thighs, with dark hair glistening with sweat; a wide, wrestler's torso covered in a thick mat of hair, almost fur; and a giant's cock – heavy, solid muscle – thrusting towards his mouth.

Orestes surrendered to his lust. He moaned, and sank his mouth over the monstrous dick, which plunged to the back of his throat, choking him. Rough, large hands were caressing him, firmly stroking down his back, seizing his arse, his thighs. His balls ached with longing, as the God's cock surged into his mouth, fucking his face. He moaned, violently, desperately, and yanked his hard, urgent dick from his loincloth. No sooner did he touch it than he came, his body convulsing as his sperm shot across the hides scattered beneath him. He felt the cock in his mouth surge to even greater volume, as hot, sweet spunk hit the back of his throat. Around him, the dark shapes were shooting come over him from all directions, beside him, behind him.

The God pulled his cock from Orestes' lips, and he fell forward, on to his hands, swallowing the spunk, savouring its divine flavour. He was drenched in come. He began to sob, helplessly, ecstatically, his body still in spasms, his prick still dripping semen on to the holy ground.

When Orestes awoke, he was outside the temple, quite naked, his belongings tied in a bundle beside him. The portal to the temple nestled in the side of the hill above him beside a little theatre; below him the road led east to Athens, from where he had come. A few huts were scattered across the valley. The sun was directly overhead, burning into his neck. The iron hilt of his sword was hot to the touch. He pulled a fresh tunic from his leather pouch; the clean, white linen felt cool and good against his skin.

Orestes struggled down the hill to where his horse was tethered. It was many leagues to Sparta. He was nervous, but not afraid. Not yet. He was proud to have been chosen for this mission.

He climbed on to his horse and rode with some haste towards the sea. Cedar trees baked in the heat; the shadows of the late afternoon formed deep, black shapes on the earth. Orestes cut an imposing figure: tousled, raven-black hair, a lithe brown body on a powerful horse, galloping south to the distant hills of the Peloponnese.

Two

_____

Orestes shielded his eyes with the flat of his hand, and looked down from the top of the hill. Below him sprawled the city of Sparta. In the distance behind it were the mountains; around it were farms, olive groves and small woods. The city itself seemed from here to be like an overgrown village of wooden huts. At its centre was a sizeable area of stone buildings, but nothing of any grandeur. There were a few temples, some villas, and what he guessed to be public buildings; but none of them were beautiful. Orestes clicked his heels against his horse and galloped across the fields.

Farmers looked up from their work and watched suspiciously as he approached the perimeter of the city. It was not a welcoming place.

Somewhere nearby, in a hidden valley, the Spartan army would be in training for the war. He remembered his first sight of their phalanxes of shields, the sound of their bloodthirsty war cries, and tried to forget how afraid he had been. Now, riding into the city of Sparta itself, he needed all his courage.

Soon the fields gave way to paved but dirty streets. Low stone buildings, simple in design and construction, lined the roadside. Everywhere was the stench of rubbish. Children played; small boys pretending to be warriors, with little wooden swords, yelled belligerently in their harsh local dialect. Women thrashed linen sheets and hung them up to dry in the hot sun. Chickens clucked and screeched in back yards.

Orestes found himself in a busy marketplace. In Athens the market served also as a forum for philosophers to engage in dialogue and debate; here there were only merchants selling their goods – rough fabrics, basic foodstuffs like fruit and the occasional sheep, none of the exotic foreign merchandise one found at home. Orestes climbed from his horse and led her by the reins.

Market traders shouted out their prices, trying to entice him to buy. Orestes stopped at a stall selling oranges, and paid a few drachmas for several. The merchant was a burly, hairy man who looked like he rarely washed.

'Friend,' said Orestes, 'I'm looking for somewhere to stay.'

The trader looked at him doubtfully. 'There's an inn in that street.' He pointed a little to the south. 'Ask for Ariadne.'

Orestes thanked him and led his horse away. He peeled an orange, which was sweet and sticky; he buried his face in it, sucking up the juice, enjoying the taste after his long journey.

He found a narrow, cobbled street, a drain running down the centre – cleaner and better smelling than before. An old woman in black passed him, on her way to the market, and Orestes asked the way to Ariadne's inn. She pointed to a villa on the corner.

Orestes tethered his horse, pushed open the gate to the villa's courtyard, and went in. It was a wide, stone rectangle with a little fountain in the middle which no longer worked. A slave woman was sweeping to one side, in the shade, with a coarse broom.

'I'm looking for Ariadne.'

'I'm Ariadne.' Orestes turned to see a woman standing in the doorway to the house. She was perhaps forty, an elegant, tall woman with her hair tied up, in a long, vermilion dress, her eyes bright and intelligent.

'I was told you might have a room.'

Ariadne looked him up and down. 'Five drachmas a night. You look like you've been travelling for days.'

Orestes nodded, smiling. This woman was not so different from an Athenian; even her dialect seemed softer, more educated, than those he had heard in the streets. Ariadne turned, evidently intending him to follow her. She stopped to ask the slave to water Orestes' horse and take it across the street to the stable.

'We don't get so many travellers these days,' she said softly. 'War isn't good for business.' She led Orestes into the cool interior of the house.

It was a simple enough place, but clean and with its own elegance. Fine clay pots lined the walls, some filled with flowers. In the centre of the main room was a long dining table. Ariadne turned to face him.

'Where are you from?'

Orestes put down his bag. 'Syracuse.'

Ariadne raised her eyebrow slightly. 'Indeed? It's a long time since we've had visitors from so far. Most of my guests are from the coast. Sailors, sometimes. Merchants occasionally. I like people who have widely travelled.' She smiled, in genuine welcome, and beckoned Orestes along a shaded corridor.

His room was small, with a bed, a jug of water, a towel and nothing else.

'If you'd like to eat with us, lunch is in an hour,' said Ariadne. 'Perhaps you'd like to wash and rest a while.'

Orestes thanked her, and she left him.

Lunch was pigeon with olives and bread, and some wine, which was rich and potent. Ariadne's only other guest, it seemed, was a ship's captain from Pylos, a city on the west coast most famous for its glory in the days of the Trojan War. His name was Nekos, and he was a heavy, rugged man in his thirties with a slight beard and large, powerful hands which ripped at his bread heartily. He did not say much, but during the meal occasionally caught Orestes' eye. Orestes felt a slight stirring in his loins.

He liked Ariadne. She was a dignified woman, who plainly

wished the war would end. It was bad for business, she repeated. And also she was worried about her son.

'He's a soldier, of course. I worry what will happen to him.'

Orestes had heard strange stories about the ways in which Sparta had perfected its war machine, her soldiers' strict and incomprehensible codes of honour. It had never occurred to him that behind each one of those ferocious warriors was a worried mother. He looked at Ariadne. 'You must be very proud of him.'

'Oh yes.' She looked down and stoned an olive. 'Any mother would be proud of him. He's won honours in the war.' There was a flicker of doubt, perhaps cynicism, in her smile. 'And nothing means more to a Spartan.'

Nekos chewed a large mouthful of meat, and grinned slightly at Orestes. 'Spartan men don't know how to make their women happy,' he said. 'Whether they're mothers or wives.'

Ariadne ignored him, and poured some water into her wine.

Nekos looked hard into Orestes' eyes, and he leant forward, laying a hand almost protectively on Orestes' arm. 'They're strange here. The men. Not like in my city. Not like in Syracuse, either.'

Orestes shifted uncomfortably in his seat. Nekos glanced uncomfortably at Ariadne, as if worried about speaking in front of a woman.

'Just . . . be careful,' said Nekos. 'You're very pretty. Delicate hands.'

Orestes cleared his throat. Ariadne didn't seem to be paying attention. He nodded at Nekos, not sure he understood.

'It is hard, being a Spartan woman,' said Ariadne. Orestes looked at her: she was smiling, but somehow melancholy. 'My son was taken to train as a soldier when he was a child. He's grown up now, and visits me sometimes. But his real mother will always be the army.' Orestes nodded, sympathetically. 'And in Syracuse. Do you bring your children up for war?'

'No,' said Orestes. 'We're a commercial people.' There was a brief, heavy silence. Orestes changed the subject. 'So where should I visit in Sparta?'

She looked at him oddly, knowingly, and for a moment Orestes was afraid she could see right through him. 'I think you'll find there is plenty to interest an attractive young man in Sparta,' she said. 'Unless you are as puritanical as our sailor from Pylos.' Orestes grinned, shyly.

The hoplites trained all day in the sun, and were tanned and hardy. They were the Spartan heavy infantry, pledged to a military life in this martial city-state. They dedicated their lives to the preparation and execution of war.

Hector wrestled, naked and sweating, with his friend and comrade, Epharon. Around them, others were grunting with effort; a short distance away, pairs of soldiers honed their skills with swords.

But it was fun, this training. The two of them panted and grunted and laughed, as each attempted to knock the other off his feet.

Kicking at the back of Epharon's leg, Hector tried to unbalance his friend. Epharon shifted his weight, laughing, as he gripped Hector's arm, trying to find the purchase to get his neck in an armlock. Epharon struggled against him, pressing his leg inside Hector's thigh; he felt the soft weight of Epharon's cock squash against his hip.

Hector enjoyed the straining of his muscles, his biceps, his powerful legs. He enjoyed the warmth and sweaty solidity of Epharon's body beside him. Epharon's face was red with the effort of fighting. Their strong arms gripped each other's body.

Epharon almost kicked Hector's foot from under him: for a second, he tottered. Hector gritted his teeth, annoyed with himself. He leant all his weight into Epharon's torso, pushed with his hip, dragged at the firm calf of his friend's right leg. Then, unexpectedly, he gripped Epharon's arm and pulled him off his feet, lifting him over his shoulder.

He threw Epharon to the ground, where he landed on his back, scattering dust. Epharon rolled away, trying to scramble to his feet, but Hector was too quick: he jumped on him, knocked him forward and grabbed his arms, tightly, pulling them behind

10

his back. Hector's soft dick was crushed against Epharon's buttocks.

With a cry, Epharon surrendered. Hector let him stand, and they both laughed, punching each other lightly on the chest.

There was the sound of another laugh, behind him. Hector turned to see Pausanius, their commander, applauding them. Pausanius was in his armour, his breastplate polished to shine brightly in the sun. Hector and Epharon were reflected in it: for a moment, ashamed of the vanity but unable to resist, Hector admired his own and his friend's bodies, glistening with sweat and oil. For a second he imagined seeing himself through Pausanius's eyes: powerful, contoured body a little stockier than Epharon's, cropped hair slightly fairer than most, large green eyes under delicate lashes. He straightened his back, and stood proudly with his legs apart, facing Pausanius.

The captain stepped forward, and put a calloused hand on Hector's shoulder.

'You'll be a champion wrestler next, Hector,' he said.

Hector glanced at Epharon. 'A lucky throw, commander,' he said. Pausanius was staring at him, gazing into Hector's eyes. There was a small flutter under one of the captain's eyes from an old war wound, but his face had lost none of its vitality. Perhaps thirty-three years old now, Pausanius was a handsome man. For a moment his gaze dropped to Hector's crotch; he turned away, a little awkwardly.

'Carry on.' Pausanius strolled off, with long, powerful steps. Hector watched him go.

Laughing, Epharon grabbed Hector from behind, and tipped him over. Hector tried to resist, but lost his footing, and landed with a thud on his knees. Epharon laughed, loudly and with good humour; Hector rolled over and looked up at him, scowling playfully. Epharon was almost silhouetted against the bright sky. As he turned, Hector could see that his cock was swelling slightly. He scrambled to his feet, and charged at Epharon, knocking him flying.

Hector pinned Epharon to the dirt, knees holding down his legs, hands gripping his arms. Epharon struggled, still laughing, his prick surging to a full erection, pressing against Hector's balls. Hector bit his lip, enjoying the helplessness of his friend, who wasn't strong enough to throw him off, and the pressure of his hard-on; and Hector's dick rose triumphantly between his thighs.

Pausanius called from a distance. 'Come on, lads. No time for that! You're meant to be training.'

Grinning, Hector climbed from Epharon, his erection bobbing as he walked away. Epharon climbed to his feet.

'Race you!' shouted Epharon, and he ran off in his bare feet towards a nearby hill. Instantly, Hector chased after him. Straining every muscle in his body, he soon caught up. He sped past his friend, his dick now comfortably shrinking as he concentrated on sprinting as fast as he could. Speed was Hector's greatest pleasure, after sex; battle, if he was honest, was a poor third. The whip of the wind around his naked flesh, through his hair, across his smooth face, was what made him feel most alive. He easily beat Epharon, and turned to face him, leaning cockily against a cedar tree.

Panting, Hector and Epharon collapsed in the shade, where it was cool and pleasant.

Epharon grinned at Hector. 'Captain Pausanius wants you,' he observed.

Hector shrugged. 'No, he doesn't.'

'He can't keep his eyes off your prick.'

Hector scowled at him. 'Epharon! How can you say such things?'

Epharon laughed. He had a hearty, wicked laugh.

'You have no shame, Eph.'

Epharon looked down, intimidated by the intensity of Hector's gaze. He shook his head, embarrassed. 'Sorry.'

Hector clambered to his feet, holding out a friendly hand to help Epharon to his. He had immediately forgiven him, and Epharon smiled at him, happily.

They walked back towards the low wooden huts where the hoplites lived. Epharon threw an arm round Hector's shoulder. Hector could tell how much his friend adored to touch him: at any opportunity, Epharon would try to make contact. If he made

Hector laugh he would giggle delightedly; if he made Hector angry, he would blush. It happens, Hector thought as they strolled towards the barracks: men get these crushes. Epharon had a crush on him; but it would pass.

The hut was simplicity itself. Ten beds – five on each side of the single room, each covered with a rough blanket for the colder nights – and a couple of circular tables were the only furniture. Each soldier jealously guarded and polished his armour and his weapons, which were usually a sword and spear, although occasionally a soldier would learn to use an axe or a bow. They were proud of their breastplates, shields and plumed helmets: each detachment of the army had different-coloured feathers.

Hector sat on his hard, crude bed. The others were out, still training. Epharon crossed to the table where slaves had left some grapes and bread and a few olives. He broke a loaf in two and handed a piece to Hector. Hector chewed at a large chunk, hungry after their exertions, as Epharon sat facing him. Epharon had an erection again; but Hector was preoccupied, and didn't feel like sex.

'The commander is an honourable citizen,' Hector said suddenly. 'You should be careful not to start vicious gossip, Eph.'

Epharon nodded, sheepishly. His cock was straining for attention, but Hector concentrated on his food. Epharon lay back on the bed, and fondled his hard-on, glancing over hopefully.

Hector decided to say no more on the subject of Pausanius. It was not that he wanted to make Epharon feel guilty. He loved Epharon as one of his dearest comrades. It was simply that he admired the commander above all other men. They all did: loyalty to the commander was a matter of principle. But Hector's fidelity went further. He was bound to Pausanius by a moment in the heat of battle.

Epharon slowly drew back his foreskin, the head of his cock red and bulging, and glanced over again at Hector, as if he might have changed his mind. But Hector shrugged, apologetically, demonstrating that there was no sign of movement in his own dick. Epharon sighed, softly.

Abruptly, the door burst open, and two more of his comrades

came in, naked and gleaming with sweat. There was tall, slender Severon, the best javelin thrower in their group, his dark hair curling down over his eyes, and Gatha, the shortest of the company, but with a bronzed, muscular body and a delightful shock of black hair around his soft, pink cock.

They laughed when they saw Epharon, his erection in his hand, plainly frustrated with Hector.

'You never stop, Eph,' said Gatha, dropping on to his bed, tired from a day in the sun. Epharon grinned, his cock flexing.

Severon sat beside Epharon and playfully tickled his balls. Hector watched them, feeling strangely uninterested. Gatha's cock was starting to stir.

Hector finished the bread. He smiled warmly at his comrades and stood. Gatha reached up to fondle Hector's cock, but Hector pulled away. He winked at them, and headed for the door, seeing the disappointment in Epharon's face. But then Gatha sat astride Epharon's chest and thrust his dick into his mouth, and the young Spartan was happy.

Hector walked out into the gathering evening. He didn't feel like it tonight. He would return later, when his friends had spent themselves. For now he wanted to watch the sky grow dark and fill with stars.

By the side of the temple of Aries, god of war, was a little tavern, the moon rising directly above it. Ariadne had told Orestes that an old man served expensive wine here to Sparta's most important citizens. He approached, nervously. There were a few men inside, but it was yet only early in the evening. Orestes noticed a muscular Spartan with a proud face, sitting by the window with a carafe of wine, who looked up when he saw him. The Spartan was perhaps approaching thirty, dressed in a tunic with gold edges; his bearing and clothes suggested a member of the city's oligarchy.

Orestes nodded in greeting. The Spartan looked at him. His neck was thick; his arms solid and strong.

'Stranger.' It was hard to tell whether this was a welcome or a warning.

Orestes stepped into the café and sat at a table near to the proud Spartan. The old man brought him a carafe of red wine, without being asked. It seemed the Spartans had only one type of wine.

Orestes sipped his drink. He was a little woozy from the alcohol at lunch, and wasn't sure he wanted to drink much more. He smiled at the fierce aristocrat.

'My name is Orestes,' he said.

'You have a strange accent,' the Spartan noted, suspiciously.

'I'm from Sicily. The colony of Syracuse.'

The Spartan stared at him for a moment. Then, as if making a decision, he pulled his chair over to Orestes' table.

'Cleomenes.' He took Orestes' hand, shaking it firmly. 'What brings you to Sparta?'

Orestes shrugged. The Spartan's handshake had hurt slightly. 'I hope to see everywhere before I die.'

Cleomenes laughed, his face brightening, as if he thought this was the strangest ambition he had ever heard. He glowered, momentarily, then laughed again. 'Not Athens, I hope.'

Orestes smiled. He steadied his nerves. It was hard to gauge the Spartan's manner.

'What do you think of Sparta?' Cleomenes looked deep into his eyes, and Orestes' heart fluttered slightly. Close to, he could see Cleomenes more clearly. He had strong brown eyes, with heavy dark lashes, and a face that was strangely beautiful, a strong jaw and a proud aquiline nose. His forearms were heavy and covered with black down, and his chest swelled under his tunic, tufts of hair visible at the neck.

'It's my first visit,' said Orestes. He gave a little shrug, spreading his hands, and noticed the Spartan's eyes dwell briefly, as if surprised and enchanted, on his fingers. He remembered Nekos's comment that his hands were delicate, and was suddenly awkward, embarrassed, as if his hands had undermined his masculinity. 'I'd like to see more of it.'

Cleomenes grinned, and clapped Orestes on the shoulder, shaking him. 'Well, then, Orestes. Consider me at your service!'

Cleomenes beckoned over the old man and paid for both

carafes of wine. Then he led Orestes out into the street, where now it was quite dark. Stars were thick in the sky above, but a few clouds hid some of them, and the streets were treacherous, littered with unseen potholes.

The Spartan had a long, athletic stride which Orestes found a little difficult to keep up with. He asked Orestes about his travels as they walked, but it was clear that this was a man to whom the outside world was little more than place names, and his sense of geography was vague. He had fought in battles, and knew roughly where they had taken place, but even then his knowledge was inexact. He was more interested in the details of the battle.

And he was proud of his military successes. Orestes discovered that Cleomenes was a high-ranking officer in the Spartan army, the son of an 'ephor', a magistrate. The ephors were the governing body of the city, more powerful in reality than its king. In other words, Cleomenes was a very important Spartan. Orestes was delighted: it seemed his mission had started well.

But it was difficult to listen to Cleomenes' tales of battles against Athens.

'We will smash the Athenians, in time,' said Cleomenes with gusto. 'They're soft, like women. If it wasn't for the cities they have compelled into their service, we would have smashed them already.'

Orestes resisted pointing out that if Athenians were so weak they would not be able to compel anybody into anything.

'Imagine if all of Greece was like them,' Cleomenes went on. 'Wasting their time in ridiculous discussions and writing poetry!' He grunted, as if he could think of nothing worse.

There was, Cleomenes admitted, apparently unaware of any irony, little to see in Sparta, and soon they had run out of sights – a few temples and a plain, unimaginative public building, and all of it obscure in the shadows of the gathering night. But he was evidently enjoying himself, showing off to his guest like a little boy.

'Perhaps you would care to join me for a wrestle?' he said suddenly.

Orestes looked at him. Cleomenes seemed frighteningly powerful. It occurred to him that in a wrestling match he might get a broken neck.

But he smiled nervously, and said: 'If you promise to remember that I am a mere Syracusean, and don't kill me.'

Cleomenes laughed, clapping Orestes again on the shoulder, finding this hilarious.

His home was bigger and better furnished than Ariadne's inn, befitting a high-ranking noble in Spartan society. In fact it was the house of his father, the ephor. But, apart from a few slaves, there seemed to be nobody about.

'Today was my leave from military duty,' Cleomenes explained. 'I'm glad I met you, or I would have died from boredom.'

He led Orestes through the house into a courtyard out the back. Here there was a small pool of fresh water, and a jug of olive oil.

Grinning in anticipation, Cleomenes stripped off his tunic, and began to smooth oil on his limbs. Orestes followed his lead.

Naked, Cleomenes was impressive indeed. His torso was well defined and broad, his legs pure, solid muscle. His soft cock, which he also smothered in oil, was big, fat, with tight hairy balls. Orestes forced himself not to look at it, and to concentrate on his undoubted trepidation at wrestling with such a man. He was sure it would be something of a disgrace to get an erection. Orestes gritted his teeth: he knew Cleomenes expected this to be easy, and was determined to prove him wrong.

Cleomenes finished oiling his body, and looked at Orestes with pleasure. They began to circle each other, bending forward, arms ready to grab, bodies coiled to spring. Cleomenes lunged for Orestes, who skipped backward, avoiding him, so that the Spartan nearly lost his balance. Cleomenes laughed, as if pleased this wasn't going to be too easy after all.

Then he lunged again, this time grabbing Orestes' neck in a vicelike grip. Orestes flailed his arms, trying to break free, but Cleomenes pulled him to the ground. Orestes struggled not to cry out. He wriggled, the oil slippery between their bodies. Swinging his legs around, he managed to turn Cleomenes over, and pull out of his grasp. For a moment, Orestes seemed to have the advantage, but Cleomenes was terribly strong.

Suddenly he found himself on his side, completely trapped in a powerful hold which pinned his arms, Cleomenes behind him, breathing down his neck. Orestes strained every muscle, but simply could not move.

To his amazement, he felt the Spartan's cock press into his buttock. It was hard, pulsing, and Cleomenes' breath by his ear was heavy, and getting shorter. The wrestling hold was hurting, but the firmness of Cleomenes' grip, and the oily pressure of his muscles, the urgent stiffness of his warrior's prick, sent tremors of excitement through him.

His own cock swelled to erection. Cleomenes kissed his neck, roughly, with the scrape of stubble against his skin. He wrapped a leg around Orestes' thigh, pushing his hard-on, slippery with oil, against Orestes' arse.

The Spartan loosened his grip, slightly, slithering a hand down Orestes' chest, grasping hungrily at his straining cock. Cleomenes gripped it, painfully, running his oily hand up and down the shaft, covering the head and squeezing it. With his other hand he pinched Orestes' nipple, and Orestes whimpered softly in pain. Cleomenes moaned, lustfully. Orestes tried again to break free, but still he couldn't move. The Spartan sank his tongue into Orestes' ear, wanking him, harshly dragging back the foreskin, rubbing his own hard, needy dick against Orestes' buttock.

Cleomenes' cock slid between Orestes' arse cheeks. 'I'm going to fuck you so hard you'll beg me to stop,' the Spartan whispered. Orestes swallowed; he was shivering with excitement. His cock was ready to burst; his balls contracted. The rough Spartan hand was gripping his shaft in a strong, tight fist.

Orestes seized a moment when Cleomenes' grip loosened to slip out of his arms. He forced the Spartan on to his back, and, without giving him the chance to act, descended on to Cleomenes' rigid, throbbing cock. For a second he just stared at it. It was incredible: long, hard as stone, thick veins bulging along its shaft, wet and sweet from the oil. Panting, breathless with excitement, Orestes peeled back the foreskin to reveal the red, hungry head, and sank his mouth over it, drawing it right into his throat. Cleomenes gasped. His cock was warm and salty. Orestes sucked fiercely, gripping Cleomenes' balls in his fist.

Cleomenes yanked Orestes' head away, and pushed him over, trapping him again in a wrestling hold, his arms under him. Orestes' cock was proud and stiff above his stomach. Again, he could not move, but this time the Spartan could reach his aching hard-on with his mouth. He devoured Orestes' cock, very hard, grunting with lust. It hurt: there was absolutely no tenderness to this act, only a base lasciviousness, the purest abandonment to carnality. Cleomenes wanted Orestes' cock, and he wanted it badly.

Orestes struggled, afraid he would come. Using all his strength, he freed his arms, and pushed the Spartan away, leaping on to him. They rolled across the gravel courtyard; Orestes felt his skin graze, as little stones tore his flesh. Their cocks mashed together, hard and oily.

Cleomenes seized Orestes' hips and rolled him, violently, on to his back, lifting his thighs, pressing his pulsating cock against Orestes' balls. Orestes found his arms pinned to the ground. He tried to struggle, but he was helpless. And the sensation of the Spartan's hard-on roughly rubbing against his balls drove him wild. Orestes' cock swelled to bursting point, lifting from his stomach; the tip was drooling pre-come.

Staring up at Cleomenes, Orestes knew he was beaten, knew he had surrendered. Cleomenes was trembling, his cock pulsing eagerly against the muscle between Orestes' balls and his arsehole. The Spartan hitched Orestes' legs over his shoulders. Orestes could feel the gravel under his back, as rough and painful as the soldier looking down at him, face screwed up with frantic lust, hair hanging slightly over his eyes. His own dick strained, as rigid with desire as he believed it could be, the long dribble of pre-come seeping from its tip to his stomach. Every vein in his cock was bulging. His heart was pounding in his chest. His breath was short.

He felt the head of the Spartan's cock press against his ring, and his arsehole puckered, his rectum flexed with anticipation. With no consideration or gentleness, Cleomenes plunged his shaft, slippery with oil but engorged and fat, into Orestes' arse.

Orestes screamed in agony, but Cleomenes seemed not to care, and just thrust hard into him. Orestes could not resist: the thick rod filled him, plunging deep inside, a burning rock of muscle. Orestes' body tensed, strained. But the pain soon melted into the most intense, almost frightening pleasure as Cleomenes' cock glided over his prostate.

Growling like a lion, Cleomenes gripped Orestes' hard, hard prick in his hand as he fucked his arse. Orestes wailed, surrendering completely to this savage debauchery, flailing his head on the ground as the Spartan impaled him with his incredible weapon. He tightened his rectum around the cock inside him, wanting to feel every inch of it, groaning as it forced its way ever deeper. The Spartan's stomach bashed against Orestes' balls, the sac tight against his groin; Cleomenes' balls hammered against Orestes' arse, already sore. But this was overwhelming: he had never been fucked like this.

Orestes couldn't take it. He shot warm spunk over his chest, hitting himself in the face. Cleomenes moaned with excitement. His cock reached its full, thrilling size, and Orestes' arse muscles tightened, in time with his orgasm, around it. Cleomenes emptied his load into Orestes, panting, his body in spasms, his face contorted with passion.

Cleomenes fell on top of him, gasping, and Orestes wrapped his arms around the Spartan's powerful body, his legs around his quivering, solid buttocks.

Pulling out, the Spartan bent to lap the sperm off Orestes' chest, as if eager to drink it while it was still warm. Orestes looked down at his head, vaguely surprised by this. Then, while Orestes was still flat on his back, exhausted, Cleomenes forced his dick back in to the Athenian's arsehole. Orestes gasped in amazement and pain.

Effortlessly, Cleomenes lifted Orestes from the ground, some-
how managing not to remove his cock. It was difficult, and the
Spartan had to bend his legs, but he managed to carry Orestes
into the house, his hard-on massaging the sensitive spot inside
Orestes' arse as they moved, teasing Orestes with delicious pain.
Cleomenes threw him on his back on a table.

Orestes did not believe this would be possible, but the
sensation of the hard cock refusing to shrink, and refusing to
leave his still-tightening, pulsating rectum, was impossibly arous-
ing. His own cock was also still hard, aching. He wanted to
weep in pain and ecstasy and lust. He didn't want to go on,
didn't know if he could take it; but Cleomenes was not finished
with him yet.

Gasping with exhaustion and disbelief, Orestes lay back on the
wooden table, as the Spartan started to fuck him again, his cock
now slippery from spunk as well as oil. Orestes' dick strained,
throbbed, painfully. It was like being fucked by a wild animal. It
hurt, but it was incredible, the roughest, most reckless sex he
had ever known.

He moaned, almost pleading, part of him wanting the Spartan
to release him, but most of him just wanting Cleomenes' cock
still deeper inside. Cleomenes' chest was tight, every muscle
stretched to the limit. They were both dripping with sweat. He
gazed at Cleomenes' strong body, his lips pursed in a lascivious
expression of raw, brutal lust.

In that moment, Orestes knew there was only one thing he
wanted more than to be fucked again like this. He wanted to
turn the tables on this savage, brutal Spartan warrior, and to fuck
Cleomenes' arse as ruthlessly as he had fucked his.

Taking Cleomenes by surprise, he pushed forward and knocked
the Spartan backward; the massive, engorged cock slipped from
his arsehole as Cleomenes fell on to the tiled floor. Orestes leapt
from the table on to Cleomenes, who was startled. As if this were
still a fight, Orestes lifted the Spartan's legs, pressing his cock
against Cleomenes' puckering ring. For a moment Cleomenes
struggled, but then his face went almost white, and in a dry
whisper he said, 'Oh yes, fuck me. Fuck me hard!'

21

Orestes thrust his cock into Cleomenes' arse, just as the Spartan had done to him. The rough, powerful warrior wailed with pleasure, his cock flexing, as stiff as it could be above his flat, muscular stomach. He spread his legs impossibly wide apart, to allow Orestes to ram deeper and deeper inside him. Orestes fucked him with utter abandon, his body surrendering to instinct, entering a faster and faster rhythm, independent of his will. Cleomenes gripped his own cock and wanked like a madman.

'Fuck me!' he shouted. Orestes gripped Cleomenes' chest muscles in his hands, squeezing the nipples, hard, until Cleomenes shouted out. The Spartan was moving his arse to the rhythm of the fuck, his legs wide apart, his body covered in sweat, his face a wanton grimace.

This mountain of hard male flesh, so utterly at his pleasure, was almost too much for Orestes. Sweat dripped from his forehead, splattering on to Cleomenes' chest. The Spartan lifted his arse higher, wanting Orestes to plunge in even deeper. Orestes' cock was sore from fucking this tight arse so soon after orgasm, but he had to go on. On and on, ramming his balls against the Spartan's cheeks.

Cleomenes was almost sobbing. 'Deeper, deeper! I want your cock as deep as it will go!' And, as Orestes forced his cock into him, the Spartan pummelled his rocklike, straining dick with his fist, the hairy balls bouncing at the base. Fast, faster. The veins on his neck were taut, bulging along the edges of the broad muscles; his face was a tight scowl of lust, as he gritted his teeth, and grunted in time with the movement of Orestes' cock.

Orestes emptied what spunk he had left into Cleomenes' arse, and the Spartan, contracting every muscle tight around Orestes' shaft, shot more spunk than Orestes would have thought possible over his chest, into his hair, and on to the floor. Cleomenes let go of his cock, and beat his fists against the floor, as more globs of white fluid dripped out.

Orestes pulled out quickly, now very sore, and dropped the Spartan's legs. He sank to the floor, exhausted.

For a while neither of them spoke. Their chests heaved, as they waited for their heartbeats to slow. Orestes was sore all over. His dick was red and raw, his arse burning from the ring to the depths of his rectum; his muscles ached from the wrestling and the exertion. He was covered in sweat and drying spunk.

Cleomenes looked at him, smiling. 'You know how to fuck, stranger,' he said, with admiration. He laughed, lustfully.

'You too,' said Orestes, with a gasp of amazement.

Cleomenes scrambled to his feet, his cock finally beginning to shrink but even now bloated, little drops of spunk still dripping from its tip; Orestes' own cock was dwindling to its normal size. For an awful moment he thought Cleomenes might want to do it again.

But Cleomenes ran outside into the courtyard and plunged into the pool of water. Orestes followed him, slowly: walking was painful. Carefully, he stepped into the cool water, sinking down to his waist. Cleomenes splashed him, and began to wash his chest and neck for him.

'You have the best cock I've ever seen on a non-Spartan,' said Cleomenes, his eyes wide with a surprising innocence. Orestes smiled, too exhausted to speak. The Spartan's face broke into an excited grin. 'I must introduce you to my friends.'

Orestes made his way back to Ariadne's inn. Every inch of his body hurt; he felt as if he had spent a week in the hardest athletic training. But even as he walked his cock stirred slightly, as he thought of the animal pleasure in which he had just indulged. He knew what Cleomenes meant: he was going to be having a lot more such encounters before his mission was complete. His throat was dry at the thought of it, his aching penis already eager at the prospect.

He forced himself to remember that there was something more important here. Cleomenes' friends were the cream of Spartan society. He had found the very people he needed to befriend to find the military secrets it was his mission to discover. He had made great progress.

Whether he would survive even a few days of sex like this was another matter. But, if this was the price for saving Athens from her enemies, it was his duty to pay it.

Three

The dawn spread like a mist across the hills around the
Spartan military camp. As soon as the light touched the
edges of the barracks windows, and the distant warmth of the
sun began to hit the hard earth floor, Hector and his fellow
hoplites were waking, stretching their muscular arms and reaching for pitchers of water to dispel the tastes of sleep.

Epharon, as usual, was first of the ten soldiers out of bed, the
clear morning light caressing the sinews of his back and buttocks
as he splashed the water, still cold from the chill of the night,
across his chest. He turned to Hector and grinned. Hector leant
on one arm and watched him for a moment, let his gaze linger
on the clump of fur at Epharon's groin, the dick dripping with
water running down from his stomach. Hector had woken with
an erection. He stroked it now, vaguely, and scratched his balls.

Around the room, his comrades were climbing from their
bunks, tipping jars of water over their dark hair, shaking their
heads like puppies. Almost immediately, as the room grew
brighter with the rising sun, they were laughing playfully.
Epharon ran to Hector's bedside, and grabbed the earthenware
pot beside it, giggling, threatening to drench Hector if he didn't
get out of bed.

'Come on, lazybones!' He tipped the jar within inches of

24

emptying its contents over Hector's head. But, as his eyes lingered on Hector's hard cock, his own lurched a little in excitement.

Hector jumped from the bunk, and wrestled the pot of water from Epharon's hands. As soon as they made contact, Epharon's dick swelled to full erection. He grinned again, a little sheepishly.

Hector looked down at his friend's stupidly stiff penis, bobbing in anticipation, and hurled half the contents of his water jug at Epharon's groin. Epharon yelled happily. Now he was awake, Hector wasn't in much of a mood for sex, and even the sight of his friend's straining hard-on left him unexcited; his own erection was starting to droop already, to Epharon's evident disappointment. Other hoplites around the dormitory were busy getting ready, indulgently watching Hector and Epharon play, but anxious to get out into the sun.

'You only think about one thing, Eph,' Hector scolded, emptying the rest of the cool liquid over his own head. He closed his eyes for a moment, enjoying the water on his body, feeling it run down his neck, his back, his hard, strong chest. Drops of water ran between his thighs and his testicles.

Gatha's hearty voice forced his eyes open. 'You two! You're like a couple of girls sighing at each other.'

Hector laughed, and for a moment considered jumping on Gatha and making him take that back. But Epharon did it for him. He leapt across the room, and hurled himself on to Gatha's back, forcing the stocky discus thrower to stumble and topple forward. Pinning his arms, Epharon tried to hold him down, but Gatha swung around, knocking Epharon under him. Hector smiled: both of them had healthy, firm hard-ons. Across the room, Severon, who had started to oil his limbs in preparation for the day, gripped his own cock in his hand with a kind of nonchalant lust. The other soldiers glanced over; Hector noticed a few more dawn hard-ons rising to attention, but he concentrated on his closest friends.

'There's no time for that,' said Hector, feeling somehow like an older brother. 'We'll be late. I'm sure none of you want to make Captain Pausanius angry.'

Gatha clambered off Epharon, who looked over at Hector and pulled a face, as if Hector were the world's worst killjoy. Epharon climbed to his feet, his cock bobbing freely as he did so.

Hector regarded his young friend with mock criticism. 'What use would you be in the midst of battle? You'd be too busy stroking your cock to kill anyone.'

'Be too busy sucking the enemy's dicks, would Eph,' growled Gatha. He bent down to his jar of oil, and began to smooth it over his arms. Epharon giggled wickedly, and crossed back to his bunk.

In silence, now, the seriousness of the day's training ahead of them, the dormitory of young warriors began to prepare. Hector slid his hand into the oil, and rubbed it over his chest, smoothing the viscous unguent down his stomach, then around his thighs. The sun was beating through the windows now, bright and hard. Steam rose from the floor where water had fallen. Hector turned his face to the light, and closed his eyes again, warm sunlight against his eyelids.

Suddenly, he felt apprehensive. This was not a normal day. Something strange, perhaps even dangerous, was about to occur. He felt a beat of excitement in his stomach, like the feeling just before going into battle, almost like the moment before sex. He slipped his fingers, smothered in soft olive oil, up the crack between his buttocks.

'Put some on my back for me, Hector,' Epharon said suddenly, breaking the silence.

But Hector did not respond. He opened his eyes and looked at his youthful comrade, but did not move, just continued smoothing the oil into his own skin. For a second, Epharon seemed hurt, unable to understand why he was ignoring him. Then Gatha stepped forward, vigorously rubbed some oil between the palms of his hands, and slapped it on to Epharon's back. Epharon remained facing Hector as Gatha went to work, roughly covering the muscles to protect them from the sun.

Eventually, Hector smiled, and as soon as he did so Epharon's face broke into a grateful grin. Hector watched as Gatha playfully finished off by rubbing oil on Epharon's balls. When Epharon's cock surged instantly to erection again, Hector burst out laughing.

Severon was the quickest to get ready, and was already halfway through the door. He stopped to look back at Gatha, his cock at half-mast, pretending to be uninterested, and at Epharon, still with a burning erection, and shook his head in fond disbelief.

Hector watched Epharon follow Severon outside. He felt a strange detachment from his friends at this moment. Perhaps it was his premonition about the day to come, his excitement at a possible adventure. But also, he realised, the routine of sexual horseplay seemed oddly uninteresting to him. It was the normal thing: all day, fooling around, each one of them getting probably hundreds of hard-ons during the course of their exercises, knowing they couldn't satisfy their lusts until training was over and the sun had set. By then, they would be overcome with desire, and the daily orgy with which they finished their exertions would be a bacchanalia to rival the most drunken religious feast.

Yet today Hector felt very little sense of anticipation of the night that lay ahead. He loved his comrades, loved their bodies, loved to hold them and take their cocks in his mouth, loved burying his dick in Epharon's eager, squirming arse. But they suddenly seemed such children.

Epharon was their little plaything, the boyish soldier who adored being fucked, one after the other, by his comrades. But the prospect, for the first time, filled Hector with no excitement. Epharon was lovable, but like a favourite pet dog. Gatha was exciting, experimental, his stocky body hard and manly, his equally sturdy, thick cock a pleasure to hold and taste; Severon's lithe, slim frame was a delight to have standing over him, his small, round testicles resting on Hector's mouth. But it seemed, in the light of this day – a day he knew carried with it some portent, perhaps of glory – to be so much less than he wanted.

Hector followed his friends outside into the burning heat of the morning sun.

When Orestes awoke it was mid-morning. His room in the inn was cool and shaded. He washed, and made his way downstairs.

He was surprised to find the inn had been transformed overnight, or he had not noticed the changes the day before when he was still sore from his wrestle with Cleomenes. Garlands decorated the courtyard. A sheep was in a small pen, waiting to be slaughtered, bleating stupidly, oblivious to its fate. Bowls of fruit had been arranged under the verandas, no doubt smaller than they would have been in peacetime, but impressive nonetheless. The slave girl was watering the plants.

Ariadne emerged from the shade of the main room, in a dark-green gown which reached down to the ground.

'The place looks nice,' said Orestes simply.

She nodded, gratefully. 'The preparations for the Feast have begun,' she said.

Orestes smiled. He wasn't sure what to say. The Festival of Dionysus was the best time of year in Athens, when poets produced their plays and the real genius of their civilisation displayed itself in all its magnificence for the world to see. He wondered what it would be like in primitive, uncultured Sparta.

'Do you celebrate the Feast in Syracuse?' Ariadne asked.

Orestes laughed. 'Of course.'

'A pity we have to be at war.' For a brief moment, Ariadne seemed to hold him with a gaze of frightening intuition, as if she understood everything. He held her gaze, refusing to react. 'So little fruit.'

Orestes laughed.

Ariadne led him back inside for breakfast.

In the house, Nekos, the burly sailor from Pylos, was already tucking into bread and eggs. He looked up at Orestes as he took a seat opposite him at the table. Orestes helped himself to water, fresh from the well. The sailor watched him, inquisitively, over his food, and his gaze unsettled Orestes, who tore himself a piece of bread.

The bread was rough, but fresh. Nekos grinned, his mouth full of food. 'Did you enjoy your first day in the capital of war, then?'

Orestes shrugged, a little uncomfortably. 'It was interesting.'

Nekos laughed, spitting bread slightly across the table. 'These

Spartans, eh? Mad, the lot of them. Different breed from Syracuse. Or Pylos. We're both sailing peoples, yours and mine. Peoples of the sea.'

Orestes nodded, smiling.

Nekos grinned, tearing off another piece of the coarse bread. 'Miss the sea, do you?'

Orestes nodded. The eggs were fried in olive oil, and slightly cold because they had been standing a while.

Nekos mopped up egg with his bread. 'Different breed,' he repeated.

Naked, the warriors practised their sports in the boiling heat. The day began with javelin throwing. Severon was the expert in this field from Hector's little company, one of the best throwers in the army. Each barracks competed with the others in a daily contest, which Severon usually won. Hector watched with pleasure as Severon hurled the little spear through the air, every muscle in his body tight like a spring.

Hector's speciality was sprinting, in which, last year, he had won a prize at the Games at Olympia. Even in the middle of this long, bitter war, there was time for the Games. After javelin practice, and a brief meal of bread and sweet black grapes, Hector raced a couple of hoplites from a rival barracks across the flat plain between two hills, and beat them easily. He knew Captain Pausanius was watching, and enjoyed the sensation of that great soldier's eyes burning, admiringly, into his back. He loved the softness of the dust beneath his naked feet as he flew across it, like an arrow, bronzed beneath the sun. He loved the way, as he ran, his cock rocked from one thigh to the next, how as he sailed through the wind he felt light, almost the purest energy, but then, when he stopped, the sweat drooled down his neck, the warmed oil seeped into the crevices of his naked loins.

But all day he continued to feel that something strange was in the air around him, that today was different from every day that had preceded it.

Towards the middle of the afternoon, with the sun high in the sky and fiercely burning up the hardened earth, Pausanius approached Hector and his comrades and asked them to meet him in their barracks.

It was cool inside. Hector, Epharon and the rest of their company sat on their bunks, covered by their tunics for the first time that day, and watched Pausanius expectantly. He had brought with him a clay carafe of watered-down wine and some rough goat's cheese.

Pausanius's eyes lingered always on Hector. Hector knew, of course, that Epharon's guess was right: the war hero wanted him badly. Pausanius was far too honourable a citizen to try to act upon his desires, but this knowledge excited Hector. He could flirt – slightly, never enough to be obvious – with Pausanius, and enjoy the wickedness, the childlike daring, without ever entertaining any risk. Looking at the captain now, Hector thought how handsome he was, only slightly scarred by his many battles: the old wound just below his right eye made him blink more than was normal, and there was a deep scar on his left forearm from where he was once badly hurt. Hector stared into Pausanius's deep, almost soot-black eyes, and his mouth twitched in the barest hint of a smile.

'I've called you in for a matter of the greatest importance,' said Pausanius. The hoplites all stared at him attentively. Pausanius had a rough, slightly gravelled voice, like a man who has lived and drunk hard. His manner, like his looks, was earthy; he was a man of the people in every way, likeable but still commanding, a man to fear.

'None of you need telling how long this bloody war has gone on. Some of you weren't born when it started, or were still sucking away merrily at your mother's tits without a care in the world. You've grown up thinking that war with Athens is normal. A normal state of affairs, Greek against Greek.'

They nodded. Hector was fascinated, but puzzled. There was an unexpected note of sadness in the captain's voice.

'It wasn't always like this, as you know. When I was a lad, the stories we told each other were about a time when Greek fought alongside Greek, Spartan alongside Athenian, against the might of the Persian army. How a handful of brave hoplites, like yourselves, held off the Persians at the pass of Thermopylae, and died, every one of them, in glory.'

They nodded again. They had all heard this story a thousand times, but never tired of it.

'How Athens, then on our side, sank the Persian fleet at Salamis. They were great days, glorious days. I think our grand-children might look back and wonder what our generation was playing at, don't you?'

Hector, like his comrades, wasn't sure how to react to this. What was Pausanius building up to? He was alert, anxious to know what was leading his brave hero to utter such dangerous words.

'War is always glory, don't get me wrong,' the captain went on. 'But some wars are more glorious than others. And this one – this one has gone on too long. We've lost too many brave, handsome soldiers in a war with fellow Greeks.'

Pausanius paused, and sipped some watery wine. 'So, if we can end it, that's no bad thing. Are you with me?'

Nervously, the small company of hoplites nodded their assent.

'You lot are very privileged, you see. Because you're going to play a part in ending this miserable, wasteful war. The final reckoning is due.'

He gazed around the barracks, fixing each attentive face individually, before coming to rest on Hector's. For a moment he just stared at Hector, as if forgetting who or where he was. Hector shifted uncomfortably under the stare, and looked down.

'Let's just say there are some Athenians who've finally seen sense,' said Pausanius. Hector breathed a quiet sigh of relief. It seemed there was no flavour of treason in the captain's thoughts. If there were Athenian traitors, that was different. That was fine.

'But you don't need to know the details,' Pausanius continued. 'All you need to know is that you should be very proud. You've been chosen to be at the vanguard of a special mission. A mission which will end the war, and secure our glorious city's victory.'

Hector leant forward to speak. 'You mean . . . some kind of surprise attack, sir?'

Pausanius looked at him for long, difficult seconds, his eyes

31

flitting from Hector's forehead to his mouth. 'That's very perceptive of you, Hector.' His voiced lowered a little as he said Hector's name. 'But, like I say, you'll know all the details in good time. This is secret, remember. You're not to breathe a word to anyone about what I've said. For now, all you need to do is get ready for the battle of your lives. Train harder than ever. Glory or death awaits you.'

He stared for a moment longer at Hector, then suddenly got to his feet. He threw his arm up in a salute, and the company of hoplites jumped to their feet to salute him back. Then Pausanius strode vigorously from the room.

The preparations for the Festival of Dionysus were making even Sparta a place of some beauty. The flowers that hung from every window made Orestes sorry that he was visiting at such a time, and for such a purpose. It showed another side to these people: a carefree, colourful side. Orestes found himself thinking how similar they were, in some ways, to the people of Athens. Of course, simple people the world over have much in common, and the Spartans, however strange and coarse their ways, were at least Greeks. But, still, he was surprised to discover how comfortable he felt, watching the preparations for the Feast he so loved, honouring the same god he worshipped at home.

It was with some apprehension, nonetheless, that Orestes arrived at Cleomenes' porch, and was taken in by the household slave. As he sat waiting for the Spartan, Orestes' loins started to stir. He wondered whether he would be invited again to share in such unrestrained physical pleasure, and whether it wouldn't be advisable to refuse. His task in Sparta was to find information, not to indulge his basest lusts. His mind wandered to the previous day's torrential fuck, and Orestes' throat began to tighten and dry.

When Cleomenes walked into the room, smart in his tunic, his body like a wall of hairy muscle, and shook Orestes' hand with that powerful grip, the Athenian trembled slightly in anticipation. Cleomenes raised his eyebrows suggestively, and, without warning or grace, suddenly gripped Orestes' balls. The

Spartan laughed, and took his hand away. Orestes was embarrassed, because his cock was so clearly erect, and there was something humiliating in allowing his desire to become so apparent to a man who was, after all, his enemy.

'No time for that now,' said Cleomenes with a hearty clap on Orestes' back. 'I want to introduce you to one of my friends.'

Throwing his arm around Orestes' shoulder, he led him out of the house.

As soon as Pausanius was gone, the barracks exploded into excited chatter. Hector lay back on his bunk, delighted but still puzzled.

'What do you think he meant?' Gatha sat beside Hector on the bed, chewing an olive. Hector shrugged. All around, the same conversation was taking place. Hector felt as if he was in some kind of magical bubble, and the noise of his comrades' eager talk around him was a million leagues distant. His premonition had been right. This was not a day like other days. A special mission to secure Sparta's victory? What greater honour and glory could he hope for? Yet it still did not seem right. It did not seem complete, as if this was not what his premonition was about. This was all a matter of war, the business of soldiers, and a mission, a task, whether special or not, was not what the Fates had been whispering to him since that morning. Hector felt this, the force of some kind of prescience, almost overwhelmingly, as if a god were hiding under his bed and singing him some strange, incomprehensible song. He had to admit, as a mere hoplite unused to the power of prophecy, that it scared him.

Then he was pulled out of his private thoughts by Epharon, who was running around the room with a new flagon of wine (which, he promised, was wholly uncontaminated by water, and which he had been hiding for a special occasion), tipping sweet red liquid into his comrades' goblets. Gatha clapped Hector on the thigh, and grasped his hand to pull him to his feet.

'This,' said Gatha with a wide grin, 'calls for a celebration.'

Soon the ten of them were beginning to get drunk, and the lascivious conclusion of the festivities was already in preparation.

Epharon was encouraging his fellow soldiers to toss their tunics aside and feel the warm evening air against their limbs. Outside, the sun was beginning to set, and the light in the barracks was a deep, mellow bronze, the colour of the soldiers' flesh.

Hector, his vision already a little hazy from the wine, followed Epharon's suggestion and dropped his tunic from his shoulders. Playfully, Epharon poured him some more wine. Gatha was entertaining three dark, sinewy Spartans by flexing his biceps and allowing them to measure the girth of his arms with their fingers.

Epharon giggled, and addressed the whole company. 'Did you see,' he laughed, 'how Captain Pausanius gazes so lovingly at our little Hector?' He flashed a cheeky smile at Hector, as soldiers burst into laughter. Epharon grinned, with a hint of nervousness, and adopted a posture mimicking their heroic captain. 'Oh, Hector!' he growled, in a fair imitation of Pausanius's voice. 'If only I wasn't a captain, I could – oh, the things I could do!'

Hector looked at Epharon scoldingly. Then he burst out laughing. The barracks all laughed. Epharon strutted, naked, blinking excessively in parody of their commander. His cock was inching its way up to erection as he turned to face Hector, who was sitting on his bunk.

For a moment, they stared at each other, Epharon laughing, still a little nervous, afraid of offending Hector, but excited now, as his rigid dick made perfectly clear.

'What do you mean, Captain?' said Hector, joining the game, and pretending to be blushing.

Epharon stepped towards him. 'Lie back, soldier, and let your commanding officer show you what a thousand battles can teach.'

Dutifully, Hector lay on his back. His comrades were gathering round, surrounding his bunk, most of them naked, their cocks hardening deliciously. Hector had a firm erection himself now. Epharon gazed at it, blinking frantically. Gatha laughed, and punched Epharon on the shoulder.

'Excuse me, soldier,' said Epharon. 'But a hoplite may not punch an officer!' The crowd of horny hoplites burst out laughing again.

'Captain, what do you want with me?' whispered Hector, his cock flexing in anticipation.

Epharon bent down, his face close to Hector's groin. In a low, hoarse voice, he growled, 'I want to break every code in Sparta.' The hoplites laughed again, as Epharon edged his mouth closer to Hector's dick.

Hector was laughing, but he had to admit, this game was very exciting. He imagined that it was, indeed, the earthy captain bending down beside him, Pausanius's warm, wine-drenched breath he could feel tickling the hair on his balls.

Epharon looked up at him, and blinked again in his right eye. He pretended to be panting with uncontrolled excitement. 'I want to lick your little hoplite balls,' he said. And he did so: he gently ran his rough, warm tongue around Hector's balls, then dropped his head to kiss the place just under Hector's tight scrotum, next to his arsehole. Hector's cock flexed again. A tiny droplet of pre-come oozed from the tip.

'Oh, Hector. Your cock smells fantastic. It reminds me of . . . of corpses on the battlefield.' The soldiers laughed again, but now they were all leaning forward eagerly, their erections in their hands. Hector closed his eyes, and felt Epharon's tongue run up from his arse to the tip of his dick. There was no pretence now in the young soldier's urgency: he was trembling slightly, as he adored Hector's cock.

Suddenly there were arms under Hector's knees, and others under his shoulders. His comrades lifted him from the bed and held him in the air, level with their chests. Opening his eyes, he could see nine greedy faces gazing longingly at his hard, pulsing cock.

'It's your duty to give the captain his pleasure,' said Gatha, beside Hector's face. Epharon gripped Hector's dick in his hand, hard, and stuffed it into his mouth like a man who hadn't had sex in his life. Hector sighed. He imagined the handsome captain, really like this, desperate to worship his cock, eagerly taking it deep into his throat. Somehow, the soldiers around him continued to hold him aloft, as arms pulled his legs apart, and a tongue forced its way into the crack of his arse, while Epharon, leaning on his stomach, continued his fast, almost frantic sucking. Hector's body began to rock as hoplites took one hand away from supporting him to grip their own cocks and wank.

Then he found himself being turned over, still held safely in his comrades' arms, but dangled now over Epharon's hard, needy cock.

'Suck the captain, Hector – it's your duty,' whispered Gatha into his ear. Hector was sure that Pausanius's cock looked nothing like Epharon's – which was young and silky, where as he imagined the captain's had a battle-seasoned roughness to it. But he closed his eyes again and continued in his dream, sinking his lips over Epharon's erection, lowered down on to it by the hard, muscular arms of his hoplite comrades. He imagined the powerful, broad body of the war hero, the thick, mature cock with bulging veins sinking between his lips.

Hector's ankles were wide over the shoulders of two men, while a third, squatting under his thighs, was thrusting his tongue in and out of his arse. His cock was hanging under him, but nearly horizontal, rock-hard. Everywhere Hector looked, now, he could see an athletic body with a massive erection, hands reaching out to grab something to fondle, fists wanking madly, balls bouncing. Gatha ducked under Hector's body to smother his cock with his mouth.

Hector gorged himself on Epharon's dick, in his mind giving Pausanius every manner of pleasure. Epharon was quivering with lust; Gatha slavered, grunting, over Hector's cock.

Then Epharon pulled away, afraid of coming. He bent down to Hector's ear. 'Fuck your captain, soldier,' he growled, his imitation of Pausanius less convincing now his desire had taken over. 'I want to feel the full length of your hard hoplite cock in my arse.'

Hector found himself with his feet on the ground, Epharon bending forward, inviting Hector to spread his, Epharon's, arse cheeks. Gatha whispered in his ear, 'Take him, Hector . . .' Hector pushed his dick against Epharon's arse. The soft, young body was so different from Pausanius's, or how he imagined Pausanius's to be: but as his cock pressed against the pliant arse ring, and he pushed harder, and felt Epharon's body yield to his masculine power, it would do well enough in his imagination. Gatha walked round to offer his fat, bulging dick to Epharon.

Epharon almost cried out, although his mouth was full of Gatha, as Hector plunged inside him. Hector gripped his friend's torso in his hands as he sank in, deeper, faster, his balls colliding with Epharon's arse. All around him, hoplites had started to suck or fuck each other. Whoever it was — he guessed it was Severon — was still ramming his tongue into Hector's arse as he fucked Epharon, conjuring the powerful body of the captain, at his mercy like this, grunting like this, surrendering to him utterly like this. Hector reached around Epharon's hips to grasp his straining dick in his fist, gripped tightly on Epharon's balls, wanked him, felt the cock harden to the point of eruption. Epharon's arse, as ever, was soft, juicy, tight, the muscles of his rectum squeezing Hector's shaft as he impaled him with it. Facing Hector, stocky Gatha screwed up his face in obscene pleasure as he thrust his dick into Epharon's mouth.

Then there was a cock pressing its way into Hector's arse as he continued fucking Epharon. This wasn't part of the fantasy. But by now Hector's body was in spasms of lust, and he could not protest. And Severon's ironlike muscle pressing against him was too spine-tinglingly marvellous to protest against. He put up no resistance, and Severon pushed almost painlessly inside him.

Fucking and being fucked, Hector was in a delirium of pleasure. A youthful, athletic body in front, a hard, lean, athletic body behind, he was out of control, just sliding back and forth. Hector cried out, screwing shut his eyes. It was as if their three hard cocks had become one muscle, stretching from Severon through him into Epharon. He opened his eyes to see Gatha shooting come all over Epharon's face. Epharon's cock, in his hand, spat a load across the ground. His balls tightened, his cock strained, and, in time with the pulsing of Epharon's rectum, he ejaculated, gasping, as Severon's cock seemed to fill his arse utterly, and came inside him.

Hector's cock, still hard, slipped out of Epharon, and behind him Severon pulled himself free. Gradually, the passionate groans were growing softer, as one Spartan warrior after another reached orgasm and sank, exhausted, to the ground.

Hector fell to his knees. Epharon turned and buried his face in Hector's groin, still wanking, eager for a second orgasm. And Hector realised that nothing would provide more inspiration for it than his own cock: Epharon couldn't get enough of it. As Epharon came again, his face creased into a grimace of ecstasy that looked like the most terrible pain, Hector understood that, indeed, it was pain of a sort. Whereas for himself Epharon's body had been a receptacle for a fantasy, a convenience for his real desire for the captain he could never have, Hector was all Epharon wanted. Hector felt a terrible sadness at this thought. Epharon's orgasm was a sob of unrequited love; when he dropped his head to kiss Hector's softening cock, this was no fantasy for him.

For a moment they stayed like that, Epharon with his face in Hector's groin, his eyes closed, Hector gazing into space. But then Epharon opened his eyes and grinned, somewhat bravely. He climbed to his feet, and looked at Gatha.

'I'm so lucky,' said Epharon. 'My friends have the juiciest pricks in the Spartan army.'

Hector laughed, and touched Epharon's hair. Epharon stood, wiping spunk off his chest with his hand, and reached for the flagon of wine. The orgy was over. Soldiers were caressing each other, tenderly, but everyone had come now. Severon was drying himself down with a towel.

Gatha grinned. 'I think we need some food,' he laughed.

But, as his comrades began to pass around bread and cheese, Hector felt completely disengaged from them. With a certain horror, he realised he didn't want to be with them at all. He sat on his bunk, crumbling bread into his hand, ignoring the conversations that surrounded him like a buzz in his ears.

Suddenly, Hector stood, pulled his tunic around him, and draped a cloak over his shoulders. As he tied it at his throat, Epharon looked up. He was eating an orange, and the juice seeped over his chin.

'What are you doing, Hector?'

'I'm just going out for a while.' Hector smiled at Epharon, but was seized by a sudden, inexplicable need to escape. 'I won't be long. I'll see you later.'

Hector walked swiftly across the near darkness around the barracks to where the horses were tethered. Not sure what he was doing, or why, he took a horse, quickly threw a bridle on it, and leapt on to its back.

He galloped through the gathering darkness, possessed ever more strongly by the sense that some strange destiny was calling him.

Four

The house Cleomenes took him to belonged to a certain Lyador, a man in his thirties with huge hands and a voice that seemed to emerge from his chest without travelling through his throat. Lyador was an officer in the Spartan army, like Cleomenes, and therefore also from a prominent family. He led them into a plain antechamber where a couple of slave girls were dusting the simple earthenware pots. Garlands for the festival were hanging over the stone walls.

'You've journeyed all over the world, then, Orestes?' Lyador asked him. This was a feature of Spartans, Orestes was starting to realise: a stern hostility to outsiders and fierce pride, coupled with a fascination about the world which was almost palpable in its eagerness.

'Not all over. A few places.'

'Have you been to Persia? To Egypt? Lydia?'

Orestes fought not to laugh. Lyador's excitement just at saying the names was charmingly parochial. 'Persia, no, unless you count Phoenicia. Egypt, yes, to Memphis. Lydia, yes, and around the coast of Asia Minor.' He observed the apparent confusion in his host's eyes, and wasn't sure which part of what he had said had confused him. Lyador sent one of the slave girls for wine, and they sat on the plain wooden benches, without cushions, which the Spartans seemed to consider cosy. Orestes sat beside Cleomenes, who was uncomfortably close, his knee resting against Orestes'.

'I would like to go to Persia. To Babylon. I've heard they have excellent astrologers.'

'So they say,' said Orestes. He wondered if Lyador actually thought Babylon was in Persia itself, but decided against commenting on this. There was a moment's pause. Orestes looked between Lyador and Cleomenes. 'What would you ask an astrologer?'

Lyador shrugged, mildly, his eyes searching Orestes' face. It occurred to Orestes that everyone in this city, Spartan or not, seemed to have eyes that were unnervingly knowing.

'Ever been to Delphi? To the Oracle?' asked Cleomenes abruptly.

Orestes was briefly surprised by the question, but he quickly recovered his composure. 'No,' he said.

'It would be good to know the future,' said Lyador, still searching Orestes' face. 'After all these years of war.'

Orestes hesitated, unsure how to proceed with this train of discussion. The slave girl returned with a large pitcher of wine, and poured some for him into a clay goblet. It was, again, that rough Spartan wine which tasted as if it had been fermented in a hurry.

'What do people say, in those distant lands, about our war?' Lyador asked him. Orestes glanced down, very slightly nervous, at Cleomenes' thigh, beside his. It was so thick and powerful, and once again he remembered the extraordinary sex they had had. He thought of Cleomenes on his back as he, Orestes, penetrated him, grunting like an animal as he pummelled his hard cock.

'I think most barbarians find it hard to understand,' Orestes answered his host.

Lyador frowned. Cleomenes leant forward, the whole length of his firm thigh now pressing against Orestes'. Orestes' dick stirred under his tunic. He realised Lyador was waiting for him to explain.

'To the Persians, or the Egyptians, it is incomprehensible that we Greeks have independent cities. They only understand empires.'

'Empires are an excellent idea,' said Cleomenes suddenly. Orestes laughed, a short burst of a laugh which he didn't know whether to continue.

'The Persian empire is vast, I believe,' said Lyador. He gulped some wine, then fixed Orestes with a stare which was quite inscrutable. 'Surely nobody in the world thinks the Athenians can defeat us.'

Orestes held his gaze. 'No,' he said eventually.

'They're living in the past,' observed Cleomenes. 'The Persians and the rest.'

Lyador nodded. Orestes nodded back, not fully understanding. 'You see,' Lyador explained, 'of course we have dealings with them. Persians, Lydians. Egyptians even, sometimes. Perhaps they will be our allies. Perhaps not. But they never tell us what they really think. It's all politics, obviously.'

He leant forward to pour Orestes some more wine. The wine was strong, and Orestes was warm inside from what he had drunk already.

Lyador smiled. 'That is why you are of interest to me.'

'Oh?' Orestes glanced down, still distracted, at Cleomenes' thigh.

'Since you have no axe to grind, the barbarians will be honest with you. That's why I want to know what they have told you.'

Orestes cleared his throat. In fact, the firm, wonderful body of Cleomenes beside him and the memory of their intense sex was unsettling him more than Lyador's questions. But he knew this was a difficult moment, and he had to tread carefully. 'I see. You understand, I'm sure, that to the best of my ability I try to keep out of political discussions on my travels.'

'Of course,' said Lyador.

Cleomenes suddenly gripped Orestes' knee, very firmly. 'But they all believe, don't they, that Athens is as it was? They all live in the past.'

Orestes swallowed. He still wasn't sure what Cleomenes

42

meant. 'The Persians, say,' Cleomenes went on. 'They think these are the same Athenians who slaughtered them at Marathon and humiliated their fleet at Salamis. They don't understand how decadent the Athenians are these days, how –' he searched for the word '– how putrid their ways have become.'

'They are a wealthy people, the Athenians,' Lyador went on. 'Wealthier than us. With different problems.'

'They buy their allies,' Cleomenes grunted. 'Trade is what does it. Trade and history.'

'We, as I'm sure you know, have constant problems with our helots, our slaves.'

'Everyone has problems with their slaves,' Orestes ventured. Lyador and Cleomenes both burst out laughing, as though Orestes had told a great, worldly joke. He laughed with them, all the time more unable to keep his mind from the prospect of sex again with Cleomenes. And now, for the first time, he noticed how handsome Lyador was, with his broad chest and supple arms. Orestes found himself wondering if his hospitality extended to more than coarse wine.

'You seem frustrated by the war,' said Orestes suddenly. They both looked at him, a little surprised perhaps by the audacity of the question.

'Of course,' said Lyador eventually. 'We are the greatest soldiers on earth, we Spartans. We live our whole lives for combat. Yet we have been unable to defeat Athens, simply because they have money. And, with money, influence. It is frustrating.'

'We detest them,' added Cleomenes. 'With their poetry and philosophy and prancing around on stages with masks, and singing songs about . . . what? Who can understand them? Men dressed as women. It's revolting.'

Orestes nodded. Finally, Cleomenes moved away from him, as he stood, evidently to pace the room and gesticulate as he warmed to his theme.

'By now, by rights, we should have slaughtered every last one of the miserable wretches in their soft silk bed sheets.'

Orestes was entranced by the fiery passion in Cleomenes' dark eyes as he spoke. He wanted simply to sink to his knees and seek out the Spartan's thick cock under his clothing, forget this chatter and gorge himself on that sweaty warrior's body. But he had a job to do. He must not forget why he was here.

'How do you think you can defeat them, then?' Orestes asked.

There was a moment's utter silence. Cleomenes looked down at him, still with that anger in his eyes. Lyador glanced, with the merest hint of anxiety, at his compatriot.

If Orestes could have torn his eyes from Cleomenes' thighs, he felt sure, he would have been able to gauge this conversation properly. But he felt as if he were improvising stupidly, unable, as he usually could, to keep a hold on where things were, to grasp every nuance of the situation. He was blundering around, confused by the most intense lust. It was appalling, pathetic. Not only would he fail in his mission if he couldn't manage to clear his head: he would end up killed.

'We have a plan,' Lyador said abruptly.

The words did the trick. Orestes stared at him, his mind finally clearing of these absurd, lascivious thoughts. Again, there was a heavy silence, until Orestes laughed, managing well to sound as if he didn't really care.

'Of course, you're not going to tell me the plan.'

Lyador laughed with him; Cleomenes was still seething, but wordlessly now.

'No,' said Lyador. 'Of course not.' He got to his feet. 'Let's eat, shall we?'

During dinner, the two Spartans entertained Orestes with tales of their military adventures. Some Cleomenes had already told him, but like all soldiers they never tired of hearing the same stories. In return, Orestes told them of his travels to far-off countries. He had seen the pyramids, the statues of Rhodes, had once, as a child, even been to Carthage, and to Italy; he had, indeed, lived in Syracuse for some years. His tales, therefore, were largely true.

Inevitably, however, the conversation returned to more pertinent matters.

'You haven't told us,' said Cleomenes suddenly, 'if you have ever been to Athens.'

'Actually,' Lyador added, 'given that your travels have been so wide, it is almost as if you were hiding the fact.'

Orestes shrugged. 'Of course I've been there,' he said simply. 'And I didn't mean to hide it. It just seemed . . . impolite to talk about it.'

Lyador smiled, as if this satisfied him.

'What did you think of the place?' Cleomenes asked him.

Orestes looked between them. 'It's a remarkable city, I have to confess.' They waited for him to go on. 'Beautiful temples, gardens. Close to the sea, and I love the sea.'

Lyador gestured for a slave girl – who was hovering so much in shadow that Orestes hadn't even realised she was there – to refill his goblet of wine. Orestes wasn't sure how much he had drunk, but it must have been a lot, now, and his head was cloudy.

'Tell us honestly,' said Lyador. 'Who do you want to win?'

Orestes sipped some wine, and looked at his host very seriously. 'This war has been going on my whole life, Lyador. It seems like part of nature, like the beach beside the sea. It seems like it won't ever end. I can't think about winners and losers.'

He was aware of Cleomenes shifting on his bench beside him. 'But do you *like* Athenians, Orestes? That's the question.'

Orestes looked at him. He stared for a moment at the jutting hardness of Cleomenes' jaw, and wanted to kiss him. 'Look,' he said eventually, 'you've been very generous to me, and I'm from a city which is far away. And neutral. I want it to stay that way. Your war is none of my business.'

'Well put,' said Lyador. But Orestes knew this hadn't answered his question.

'How much does it matter to you?' Orestes asked. Cleomenes leant across him to help himself to some bread, and his arm brushed Orestes'; and he felt himself shiver.

'It doesn't matter.' Lyador leant back, and belched, signalling the end of the meal. 'You're my guest.'

For a while the Spartan stared into Orestes' eyes, and he felt a thrill of excitment, tingling his loins.

'I would be delighted if you would be my guest again, tomorrow,' said Lyador.

Orestes' penis swelled slightly. 'I'd like that,' he replied.

Cleomenes walked with him through the streets, dark now and lit only by the moon, which was a distant, cold, silver crescent. They reached Cleomenes' house. The Spartan turned to him, and gripped his hand in his customary firm grip. Orestes wasn't sure what to say: he wanted Cleomenes to invite him in more than anything in the world at that moment. The war, his mission, everything, seemed irrelevant, too far from where he was to care about. He just wanted to suck the Spartan soldier's cock dry. His own cock was hard; the softness of his clothing against the moist tip of his dick was exciting in itself.

Cleomenes held his hand for a few more seconds, then released him. 'I'm tired,' he said. 'Tomorrow, I have training.'

'Oh.'

'I would ask you to enjoy more wine with me. And perhaps . . . But I need my rest.'

'I understand.' Orestes wanted to seize him in the street, pull his legs apart, and fuck him till he screamed. Or be fucked, taken, there, without regard for anything or anyone who might be passing.

Cleomenes suddenly leant down and gripped Orestes' yearn-ing cock through his tunic. He laughed, and squeezed it. 'Another time.'

Before Cleomenes could turn away, Orestes lunged for his cock. It was stiffening, but far less hard and eager than his own. He took his hand away, feeling foolish. Then he managed to laugh also. He knew he was blushing, and grateful for the dark.

Cleomenes turned to go. 'By the way,' he said, stopping suddenly to look back. 'Lyador found you most appealing.' He grinned, with a sudden, unexpected naughtiness, and disappeared into his house.

★

Orestes walked through the streets. It was late, and there were few people around. A woman, weighed down by years of childbirth, was hanging out washing. An old man sat in the curb with a carafe of wine, humming to himself.

Orestes' erection was aching horribly by the time he arrived back at Ariadne's inn, and all he wanted was to get into his quarters and relieve himself. He was surprised to discover that the lamps were still shining in the courtyard, and Ariadne was serving crushed oranges to a young visitor.

Ariadne looked up as Orestes came through the gate, and smiled welcomingly. Her guest was hidden in shadow, but his eyes caught the light from one of the lamps, and shone, almost luminously, like the green eyes of a cat.

'Orestes, good evening. I believe I mentioned my son to you before. This is Hector.' In the corner of the courtyard, the sheep, still waiting for slaughter, bleated pitifully.

Hector stood to shake his hand. He was slightly shorter than Orestes, his shoulders covered in a dark cloak of some kind of animal skin. Under that he had a plain white tunic tied at the waist. His face was contoured by the light of the lamp and the pressing shadows, a soft curve down to his chin, which was speckled with dark stubble. It was a face on the cusp of manhood, still with the clarity of youth. His smile could melt snow. Orestes gripped Hector's hand in both of his, delighted to meet his landlady's son.

'I thought you were off training in the hills.'

'I am,' said Hector. 'I mean, I was. I'm going back tonight.'

'He decided to drop in on his mother.'

Orestes stared for a moment at Ariadne, observing her pride and her sadness. She gestured for him to sit, and he did so.

'Orestes is a traveller. From Syracuse,' said Ariadne, turning to her son, again with that discomforting knowingness.

Hector leant into the light, smiling at Orestes with what seemed like genuine interest and pleasure.

Ariadne yawned, covering her mouth with her hand. 'It's late.' She stood. 'I'm afraid I must be going to bed.' She bent down and kissed Hector on the forehead. 'Please. Don't leave it so long this time.' She nodded to Orestes and walked towards the house, vanishing suddenly in the shadows.

Orestes glanced nervously at Hector. It was as if he could feel the warmth coming off the Spartan's body.

Hector fidgeted slightly. 'I suppose I should be going, too,' he said. But he didn't move.

Orestes couldn't think what to say. He gazed at the Spartan soldier in the dark: he was excruciatingly beautiful, sturdy and powerful, his body rich curves of muscle, yet also, somehow, soft. His face was smooth, and clear.

Hector grinned, a bit shyly, and still didn't move.

'What's it like, then?' Orestes laughed at the stupidity of his question. 'Living your life as a Spartan soldier, I mean.'

Hector grinned and shrugged. 'It's all I've ever known.'

'Have you seen any fighting?'

'Oh yes. Once I was awarded a prize. I rescued my captain from certain death.'

Orestes stared at him, uncertain whether there was any irony in this comment, said with such ordinariness. But there seemed to be none. 'I hope your captain was grateful.'

Hector looked down, and Orestes wondered if he had said the wrong thing, hit some kind of raw nerve. 'He's a great hero. Pausanius. That's his name.'

His green eyes burnt in the light of the lamp. Orestes felt a twinge of absurd jealousy. 'You respect him a lot, I imagine. Your commanding officer.'

Hector nodded. He played with his hands for a moment, rubbing one thumb against the palm of the other hand. Orestes watched the light on his strong forearms, the delicate gossamer hairs. 'And how do you like our city?'

'It's fascinating,' Orestes said honestly. 'I've never been any-where like it.'

'Where have you been?'

Orestes smiled to himself. Again, that Spartan assumed non-chalance about the world beyond their tiny state.

'Egypt, Lydia . . .' Orestes went through the list, all the time watching the slight widening of Hector's eyes as the names worked their spell. Eventually, Orestes stopped speaking. Hector was visibly entranced, imagining those faraway citadels with their monuments and hanging gardens, and sights, Orestes assumed, that were a blur of unlocatable magic. 'Tell me about being a Spartan soldier.'

Hector shrugged, and didn't answer for a moment, as if he didn't understand the question.

'How do you train? I mean, is it all swordcraft, or do you have other – ?' Orestes trailed off, once more feeling his question was stupid, and also afraid to continue unless he trapped himself into comparing his own training at the gymnasium in Athens.

'Running, wrestling, javelin, discus. And swordcraft, obviously.'

'What do you like best?'

Hector hesitated. 'Every martial art is an honour and a duty.' He pulled a slight face, as though aware, for the first time since Orestes had met him, that there was something mechanical and learnt in his answer. 'I like running. I'm the fastest runner in my company. I won a prize at the Games last year.'

'Really?'

'Were you there?'

'No. I was in – I was in Syracuse then.'

They held each other's eyes in the meagre light. Orestes was lost for words. He had never seen a face so earnest, so lacking in guile. Yet the green eyes twitched with a kind of repressed curiosity. Hector's simplicity masked a keen intelligence. He must be careful not to be lulled into giving away secrets. He felt this was a face for which a man might give away the greatest secrets of his soul.

'Why –' Orestes ducked his head apologetically. 'Forgive me. I was about to ask something which is none of my business.'

'Ask. I can always refuse to answer.'

'I wondered why you came to visit your mother tonight.'

'I don't know.' Hector looked away, briefly. 'I missed her. I was lonely.' He turned back to Orestes. 'Suddenly, I needed to talk to her. I don't know why. Does that sound . . . childish?'

'Not at all. I miss my mother, too.'

'Where is she? In Syracuse?'

Orestes almost told him the truth. 'Yes, in Syracuse.'

Hector drained a jug of wine into two cups; one had been Ariadne's, but he offered it to Orestes. 'I was there, surrounded by all my friends. We're very close in the army. And I love my comrades. I'd die for them.' He looked into Orestes' eyes, searchingly, as if worried he would see scepticism or condescension. 'But suddenly I needed to be away from them for a while.'

'Nothing wrong with that,' said Orestes. He took the cup, his fingers lightly brushing against Hector's as he did so. His eyes wandered down Hector's chest, the swell of his muscles beneath the cloth. His legs were apart slightly, and he was jogging his knee with a hint of nervousness. Hector glanced over at the house, as if checking his mother was there. Orestes noticed the sinew of muscle at the side of the Spartan's neck, and wanted to lean across and gently caress it. Hector turned back to him.

'Maybe I needed a woman's company for once,' said Hector. Orestes only grunted in reply. 'I think it's difficult, sometimes, only being around men all the time.'

'Surely the army provides you with – you know. Women.'

Hector looked at him with an expression of immense puzzlement, and then burst out laughing. He had a soft, musical laugh which didn't seem to fit his physical appearance. 'For sex, you mean? Oh, we manage all right on that score.'

Orestes tried not to look too curious, but Hector's eyes saw through him, and he laughed again.

'I suppose you'll think it odd, you Syracuseans, or whatever we should call you.' He stared at Orestes with renewed earnestness. 'We believe that our soldiers fight more bravely if they're lovers. An army of lovers. Every hoplite in my company is my lover. Does that shock you?'

'No.' Orestes laughed. 'It sounds wonderful.' His heart missed a beat, and his cock started to grow. Its tip was already well lubricated from the impossible erection he had had all night, and the foreskin slipped back easily over the moist head. He leant forward to hide it from Hector. It seemed to Orestes that so far Sparta had been one long hard-on, which was not what he had expected when he had set out on his mission. But now, with this beautiful young man, he wished it had been different. It seemed sordid. To be sitting here with an urgent erection after a long night of unsatisfied lust for Cleomenes reduced the pleasure of the moment. It made his desire for Hector merely lust.

Hector swung around closer, more confidential, and he spoke more softly, perhaps afraid Ariadne might overhear. 'Tonight, for example. We had sex. Fucked each other, you know. As usual. And I enjoyed it enough. It's always enjoyable. But it wasn't – I don't know. It wasn't enough.'

'What else did you want?' said Orestes, yearning to bend that little bit further so they could kiss.

But Hector leant back. 'I don't know. The rules are very strict. We're forbidden to do it with anyone outside the company. To have sex with a commanding officer would be a terrible dishonour.'

'So that's what you want.'

Hector momentarily glared at him, but he was visibly unsettled that his desire was so obvious. They held each other's eyes. 'Sex with an outsider,' said Hector. 'A non-Spartan. That would lead to banishment.'

Orestes caught his breath. This was said with such abruptness, verging on cruelty, that his eyes smarted. Yet he could not be sure if Hector meant anything by it, if the young hoplite was even vaguely aware of how badly he wanted him, if it had even occurred to him. The thought was crushing.

Yet then, so briefly he might have imagined it, he thought he saw a look of sadness and sorrow in those beautiful eyes.

'I think Pausanius wants me. You really can't imagine the dishonour it would mean.'

Orestes nodded.

'It must never happen.' Hector seemed to stare deep into his soul, and Orestes felt quite overwhelmed, as though his heart would break. 'Anyway. I'm not sure that's what I want. I don't know what I want.'

Suddenly, Hector stood. Orestes looked up at him.

'I must be going. I've been gone from the company too long

already.' He bent down to shake Orestes' hand, and gripped it tightly, but there seemed no hint of sexual interest in the gesture. Hector seemed altogether more casual, harder, than he had a moment before. He said goodbye to Orestes in a businesslike manner.

And then he was gone, slipping into the shadows. Orestes heard the sound of a horse, whinnying softly, the thud of galloping hooves, and then silence.

Orestes crossed to where the sheep was penned. It looked up at him with slow, doomed eyes, and bleated. He leant across and touched the sheep on the head, and for a moment fondled its ears, absently, for no reason. The animal seemed to accept this; but then it trotted away to where there was a water trough.

Orestes walked away through the house into his quarters. Before he had arrived and met Hector, he had been desperate for this privacy, so he could relieve the urgent lust he had felt all evening, enjoy a slow, indulgent hour of masturbation. Now he lay on his hard bed, his cock rigid with painful desire, but he was unable to wank. He wanted simply to remember the encounter with Cleomenes the day before; for some reason he could not clearly define, he didn't want to think about Hector. But, every time he tried to fix the image of Cleomenes, it dissolved, replaced by Hector's solemn face, the thought of his orgies with his comrades, and of the faceless Pausanius; and, hungry as Orestes' cock was, hard as it was, he couldn't make himself come.

Hector galloped into the night, towards his barracks. Above him the stars peppered the black sky, the constellations of all the great heroes. He allowed himself to enjoy the vibrations of the horse's back against his balls. The man from Syracuse had intrigued him. Imagine: to have seen all those places. And he was so beautiful. Hector had been entranced by him, by his strange accent, the soft, musical tone to his voice. He had wanted to reach out a hand to smooth the curls of his dark hair, caress the thick line of his eyebrows, which almost joined above his nose.

All through the conversation Hector's heart had been loud in his ears. He had been captivated by the stranger's lips as he spoke, by his white, even teeth, thrilled by way he moved his hands, by his long, almost delicate fingers. He had wondered what luscious orgies Orestes had been to in those far-off places, what sultry brown-skinned boys he had ravished; and he had glanced down at the firm cushions of his thighs and wanted to sink into them.

Hector could not stand all these thoughts and feelings colliding in his brain. He wanted Pausanius, his war-hero commander. And he wanted, he knew, this visitor to his mother's house. And both of them were forbidden. Yet all the soft caresses and hard cocks of all his comrades were suddenly no longer enough. Something was missing in Hector's life.

He thought of his premonition that morning, but still had no idea what the portents were about. The future was a strange and frightening mystery.

When Hector arrived back at the barracks, he crept into Epharon's bunk. He needed a body beside him. Epharon murmured sleepily, his cock springing to erection as if by habit. Under cover of darkness, almost in his sleep, Hector curled up and gently took his friend's cock in his mouth. He sucked it for a while, tasting its salty flavours, feeling Epharon's body writhe beside him, too exhausted to wake, all the while his own cock refusing to stir. And then he fell asleep, with Epharon's furry balls resting against his lips.

Five

———

Orestes watched the market traders in the centre of Sparta. There was a sense that the place had seen better times: stocks were depleted, the chickens and sheep were skinny, and the fruit was bruised and sometimes rotting. There was a faint aura of decay. Yet still the Spartans were thriving the best they could. What Cleomenes and Lyador had told him was certainly true: Athens had much stronger trading partners, and, even after all these years of war, the agora at home was awash with exotic colours. But Orestes had to admit: there was a simple charm to this market, its rough-voiced vendors, the plainly dressed women buying onions.

It was hot, and Orestes was hiding his face under a wide-brimmed hat. Even so, when Lyador saw him, he recognised him immediately. The Spartan strode forward and shook his hand vigorously.

'Cleomenes is training today,' said Orestes, as if he felt the need to explain why he was wandering the streets alone. Lyador nodded.

'I know.' Orestes felt there was a twinge of suggestiveness in Lyador's expression. 'I hope you haven't forgotten you're my guest again tonight. A group of officers will be there. You might find them interesting.' He took Orestes' hand, and the Athenian felt his pulse quicken with a throb of excitement. An evening with Spartan commanders offered a tremendous opportunity to learn their secrets.

Orestes nodded, allowing the Spartan to hold his hand a moment longer. 'I'm looking forward to it,' he said.

But, as he left Lyador and wandered through the city streets, he had to ask himself exactly what was exciting him. Was it that he might have the opportunity to extract information from important Spartans? Or was it the thought of a drunken evening with these hard, fascinating soldiers?

Orestes was so absorbed in his thoughts that, when he looked up, he realised he was lost. He stopped at the intersection of six crudely cobbled streets. Looking back, he wasn't even sure which one he had come down. They wound away, low stone buildings on either side, little puddles of mud collecting between the paving stones. Orestes felt a sudden and foolish sense of panic quicken in his chest. He fumbled at his waist for the handle of his sword, as if he thought some bandit might leap from the shadows and attack him. But the streets were deserted.

He chose a path and walked up it. There was very little movement in the small houses on either side of the road. Cats lay in the shade. A slave girl scrubbed linen in a back yard, but ignored him as he passed.

Then, at the corner of the next street, Orestes found a little temple, a simple structure of flat stone walls and a square portal. From inside there was the scent of some kind of burning incense. The only marks on the building were the words, over the door: APHRODITE GODDESS OF LOVE.

Orestes hesitated for a moment, then took off his hat and walked through the portal into the temple.

Inside it was dark except for the soft glow of torches. It seemed to be a single, square room. In the shadows he could see a statue at the centre, and as he stepped towards it could make out its shape more clearly. It was a representation of the goddess, of course, chiselled with little art: perhaps a cubit higher than a man, an image of an almost naked woman with exaggerated breasts. Her eyes were studded with red stones, garnets rather than rubies, which glinted in the light of the burning fires.

Orestes stood in front of the statue, looking up at her glistening eyes. He didn't know why he was there, but he was briefly transfixed, unable to move. Then he heard a rustle of movement behind him, and turned to see a hooded silhouette standing in the portal.

'Hello,' said Orestes. His voice echoed slightly in the stone building. The figure stepped forward into the darkness. Orestes strained his eyes to see, but there was only a deep shadow in the glimmering dark. 'I'm a traveller. I was lost.'

The figure passed by a torch, burning low and casting little light. But Orestes caught a glimpse of the face: it was a young man, a dark, beardless face which did not seem Greek.

'You don't have to explain being in the temple of Aphrodite,' said the stranger. His voice had a trace of an accent, but Orestes couldn't place it. The young man stepped closer. He was dressed in a cloak which he had thought to be black but was, he could now see, a deep green. He lifted back his hood to reveal a head of cropped black hair.

Orestes laughed nervously. 'Maybe not.'

The stranger bowed, rather oddly. It occurred to Orestes that this was the first greeting of its kind he had encountered in Sparta; normally, the strong Spartan men would grip his hand with fierce, firm shakes.

'You're not from Sparta, either,' Orestes noted.

The young man smiled, vaguely, as if searching his mind for a memory. 'No. I am from Egypt. I came here some years ago.' He spoke Greek very well, and what gave him away was a slight hardness to his intonation, that sound the Egyptian language had that smelt of their religion, their obsession with death. Orestes wondered if the man was older than he looked. He would have guessed, in this light, that he was in his early twenties; but he could have been one of those people who seem never to age. 'I became a priest of the Goddess. I take care of this little temple.'

Orestes frowned. This seemed an extraordinary fact: an Egyptian, priest to a Greek goddess, and in Sparta, of all places. He found it hard to believe. Or, if it was true, it suggested some extraordinary story.

'You don't seem to have many worshippers,' said Orestes, trying to laugh. The smile died on his face, and he looked away.

'No. That's why I am here, in Sparta. You see, none of them know how to love. It is my mission – to find the places where the light of Aphrodite has never shone, and push away the shadows.'

In the shimmering light, the young priest licked his lips with his tongue. The wet spittle glistened briefly, like a magic trick. He stepped beside Orestes and looked up at his Goddess.

'Sparta is full of shadows.' The Egyptian leant up and touched the statue tenderly on the hip, as if caressing a lover. It seemed to Orestes the strangest gesture of religious devotion.

Now he was close, Orestes could see how beautiful the Egyptian was, with his dark, brooding eyes with long, curling lashes, his soft neck with a prominent larynx, his wet lips. He was so different from the Spartan men he had met: not feminine, but softer. His flesh was brown, much darker than Greek skin.

'Tell me,' said the Egyptian. 'Do you also worship the goddess of love?'

'Of course.'

'And now? Are you worshipping her now?'

Orestes laughed. The priest was looking at him, his eyes glowing in the light of the torches. He smiled.

'Come. Let us see.'

The priest walked away, past the statue, turning to wait for Orestes, who followed, unsure. Behind the statue was a silk curtain, which Orestes had not noticed, leading into a small antechamber, where there was an altar. In the middle of the flat wooden table was a bowl of burning incense, and here its smell was very strong.

The curtain fell behind them. The priest seemed almost otherworldly in this dark, torchlit room. He dropped the cloak from around his shoulders, to reveal that he was wearing nothing but a small cloth around his waist, hiding his genitals. His chest was smooth, and brown, and dappled with little dark hairs around the gentle curve of his pectoral muscles. No warrior, to be sure: but this was an athletic, strong young body.

'Who do you love?'

Orestes laughed, his voice catching slightly. 'I don't think I love anybody.'

The priest looked at him, his deep, smouldering eyes filled with benevolent tolerance. 'Of course you do.' He took Orestes' hand. 'And you want to be sure that Aphrodite is with you in your love. You want to know if she sanctions it.'

Orestes didn't know what to say. The Egyptian held his hand gently, with little more than the light touch of his fingertips.

'You must make a sacrifice to her.'

'What kind of sacrifice?'

The priest turned to face him head on. He was a little shorter than Orestes, and had to look up into his eyes. Gently, with fingers brushing against Orestes' throat, he lowered the Athenian's tunic over his shoulders, lifted it down from his arms and let it fall to the floor. Orestes was naked underneath except for his loincloth. As the priest gently caressed his chest, stroking the muscles down to his stomach, Orestes' cock stirred, jerking to erection, pressing a tent into the cloth around him. The priest rested one hand on the mound of Orestes' erection, so gently he could hardly feel it, yet at the same time feel it absolutely, a soft, divine pressure. Orestes' heart began to beat very fast.

The Egyptian's cock was upright, forcing aside his loincloth. His dark balls were perfect little secrets in the darkness. As the priest leant forward to touch Orestes' nipples with his soft tongue, he slipped a hand inside Orestes' clothing, loosening the cloth so it fell on top of his tunic beneath him.

Then, kissing with a moist, tender mouth, the priest lowered his head towards Orestes' cock. He pulled back the foreskin, slowly, tickling Orestes' balls with the other hand, then covered the head with warm, wet lips. Orestes gasped. Nobody had ever sucked his cock with such gentle, delicate strokes, so teasingly, so delightfully. It was the opposite extreme to the hard, aggressive passion of Cleomenes, that urgent, almost painful lust. Orestes' knees trembled.

The Egyptian sighed, taking Orestes' cock as far into his mouth as it would go, gripping his balls in a gentle, cool hand. Orestes slowly lifted his head, and gazed down in wonder at the rigid hard-on reaching up from the Egyptian's thighs. It was circumcised, long and perfectly thick, the veins along its belly throbbing impatiently.

Orestes put his arms around the Egyptian's waist and lifted him on to the altar. He gazed for a moment longer at the dark, silky cock, than dropped in worship to his knees and swallowed it right up to the base. There were tears in his eyes as he buried his head in the priest's groin, the hard, deliciously sweet shaft of muscle thrusting inside him, grazing the back of his throat. It tasted of exotic, sensual scents. It filled his mouth, like warm, soft rock, a muscle throbbing wonderfully against his tongue, the dark, hard balls colliding with his chin. With his other hand he grasped his own, pulsing, wet cock and pumped it, gripped it hard, dragged back his foreskin and tightened his fist around the shaft.

The priest was murmuring, and Orestes realised it was a prayer. He heard the Goddess's name, Aphrodite, Aphrodite, like an incantation. The priest's voice rose to a moan – until, suddenly, he felt the body stiffen from neck to ankle, the hot shaft in his mouth expanded to its limit, and sweet, salty sperm exploded against the back of his throat. Orestes drank and drank, as though it were nectar from Olympus, as he came himself, huge spurts of come he could feel shooting from the heart of his balls, covering the floor of the temple in patterns of milky liquid.

Eventually, the Egyptian grew still. Orestes didn't want the gorgeous cock to leave his mouth, and gripped his gums around it, gently, delighting as it flexed again, emptying its last drop of spunk into his throat. But then the priest lifted his head away.

As Orestes stood back, still trembling, his cock red and still drooling come, the priest fell to the floor, gathering Orestes' sperm into a cloth. Then he placed the cloth, filled with the odour of sperm, on the altar of Aphrodite.

Orestes' cock was still hard. Tenderly, as though in reverence, the priest bent down and took it in his mouth again, but briefly, licking off what was left of his semen. Then they kissed. The priest's hard yet delicate body pressed against him; their still-hard cocks squashed moistly against each other; Orestes could taste his own spunk on the Egyptian's breath.

The priest pulled away, and knelt down before the altar of his Goddess, closed his eyes and muttered some quiet prayers. Orestes watched, his cock finally starting to soften. In the darkness, he pulled on his clothes.

They returned to the main part of the temple, the Egyptian once more wrapped in his cloak. 'The Goddess is with you, traveller. She has gazed on your penis and wanted it, tasted your sperm and liked it. Today you have entered the Goddess's vulva and swum into her womb. She will be with you, and she thanks you for your gift.'

Bemused, Orestes walked away, towards the sunlight. Reaching the portal, with the blinding light of the sun outside, he looked back. But he could no longer see the priest in the darkness, and something deep in his soul advised him not to go back. He walked out into the street.

Hector ran. He preferred to sprint over a short distance, but this was a long-distance run, across the dry hills. Already he was far ahead of his competitors, his bare feet sweeping across the dusty earth. He was naked, and the hot sun was burning on to his shoulders; the wind was wiping sweat from his back but still he could feel it, dripping between his thighs. Normally, when Hector ran, it cleared his mind. But now his thoughts were full of the traveller from Syracuse, his strange, eloquent accent, his soft, forgiving mouth.

The ground was hard beneath his feet, but his soles were rough from a lifetime of running. The muscles in his legs were straining with effort, but he enjoyed the slight pain, the tensing of the flesh around his thighs and calves each time he lifted his leg to run on. He looked down, briefly, to observe the swell of his thighs, all sinew and no trace of fat, as he ran. He liked the power in his arms, swinging in time with his movement, the ripple down his back as he raced.

He noticed, ahead of him, a figure on a horse, at first just a black shadow against the harsh blue line of the sky. As he drew closer, he realised it was Captain Pausanius.

Pausanius drew level with him as he ran, the horse trotting casually beside him. He leant down with a flask of water, and Hector took it, still running, and drank. The water was warm, but delicious in the heat. He handed the flask back, and for a while they continued, side by side, runner and horseman.

'You're a fine athlete, Hector,' said Pausanius suddenly.

'Thank you, sir.' He panted a little, finding it harder than he had expected to run and talk.

'A firm body.' Pausanius hung back very slightly, and Hector wondered if he was admiring his buttocks. He clenched them, enjoying this.

'Thank you, sir.' Hector felt a twinge of excitement. He wondered, and it nearly made him laugh, if he could still run with an erection. There was part of him that wanted to tease this stern captain, to offer what he knew he could never have. But then he thought of the dishonour this would mean, and ran harder, as if he could outrun the horse.

Pausanius trotted beside him. They were silent for a while. Eventually, Pausanius said, 'I wanted to talk to you about young Epharon.'

'Sir?'

Pausanius was thoughtful. 'He worships you, Hector.'

Hector laughed. He laughed because it was silly, the idea that anyone worshipped him. And also he laughed because the note of jealousy in the captain's voice was not difficult to hear.

'I don't . . . think so, sir. It's just . . . you know. A boy's crush.'

'Tell me.' The captain rode on, beside him, doubtfully. 'When you . . . when you lads get up to your tricks, when it's dark and you're all fucking each other . . .'

Hector glanced up, and grinned. Pausanius seemed quite uncomfortable, and Hector wasn't sure why. There was no secret or disgrace in sex between the hoplites: it was not only expected but encouraged, to strengthen their bonds.

Pausanius went on. 'You don't think Epharon especially likes you.' Hector didn't answer. 'It's your cock he wants to suck, isn't it? You he wants to fuck him up the arse?'

'I suppose so, sir. Yes. But it's nothing to worry about.'

Pausanius was silent again for a while. Then: 'And how do you feel?'

'I don't understand, sir.'

'When you're fucking his juicy young arsehole and gripping his rock-hard cock in your hand. When you come over his face and he drinks your spunk as if it were wine. When he sucks your cock as though the world would end without it. How much do you love him?'

Hector finally stopped running. His rivals were far behind: he could hardly see them in the distance. Pausanius seemed very agitated. Hidden under his military tunic, Hector knew, was a burning erection; and now he had stopped running, now there was no breeze to cool him, and, standing naked in front of the captain he so badly wanted, Hector knew what would happen. His cock surged to erection, and quickly he ran on, praying to Zeus it would soften and not disgrace him. Pausanius rode beside him, looking down at it as it bobbed from side to side, lust in every corner of his face. Hector blushed, still running. The captain cleared his throat; but one hand left the reins of his horse and gripped his erect cock; he tried to hide this from Hector, but Hector knew.

'Sorry, sir.' Hector was very upset. If anyone should see him, aroused like this with a captain, he would be in terrible trouble. But Pausanius, alarmingly, was determined to draw attention to it.

Pausanius's voice was trembling slightly. 'What's done that to you?' he said, attempting a tone of rebuke. 'Thinking about Epharon's delicious young dick, no doubt.'

'He's my comrade, sir.'

Pausanius galloped ahead, angrily, then stopped his horse to wait for Hector to catch up.

'I need to know, Hector. I need to know if Epharon's love is more than befits a soldier.'

Hector ran past him, afraid, and not sure how to respond. The captain called after him. 'I need to know, Hector. I'll have to see for myself. You know that, don't you?'

The young Spartan ran on, as fast as he could, leaving the captain behind. His heart was filled with worry. He needed to speak to Epharon, to warn him of the danger that lay ahead.

Orestes arrived at the entrance to Lyador's house. It was near the centre of the city, a short walk from Ariadne's. After his encounter with the Egyptian priest, Orestes had quickly found his way back to a main street. He had been gripped by the strange feeling that, if he were to try to rediscover that simple stone temple, he would not be able to. As he walked, as fast as he could, afraid but unable to decide what had frightened him, it had felt as if the streets were closing in on themselves behind him, covering themselves in their own stones. He had been unable to look back, and had pulled the brim of his hat down around his ears and ploughed on, relieved more than he could understand when he had found a familiar landmark.

He knocked on Lyador's door, the memory of the afternoon still burning at the back of his mind. A silent slave girl, one he had seen before, opened it and waited for him to enter.

In the shady inner chamber, lit by perhaps a hundred candles, which flickered in a gentle breeze, were six Spartans, including Lyador. They were all in their casual aristocratic evening tunics, edged with gold braid, and the room smelt of scented oil. Lyador stood to welcome him, and Orestes sat between two men on a wooden bench as the slave girl served him the rough, sweet wine.

The men were all Spartan officers, colonels or thereabouts, none of them older than forty, the youngest, Endrocles, under thirty. Plainly, every one was a seasoned soldier. They each had that remarkable Spartan hardness, virile faces and strong limbs, and bodies with little excess fat. Their sandals, laced up to the knee, emphasised the power of their calf muscles. When they shook his hand in those firm, almost painful grips, their palms were rough. He noticed battle scars on their arms. One of them,

Aganos, had lost an eye and wore a patch over it; but it did not detract from the angular symmetry of his face; it seemed to add a depth of experience and wisdom. Orestes was instantly enchanted by all of them.

They asked the routine questions about his travels, and displayed the typical Spartan suppressed delight in listening to his stories. In turn they commented on what a fine fellow Cleomenes was, and how lucky Orestes was to have discovered such a host on his first visit.

Then the conversation drifted to more warlike topics. These men were soldiers, frustrated by the current stalemate in the war. They were anxious to see fighting, as none of them had been engaged in battle for some months, and their warriors' arms were twitching.

'What would you do,' Orestes asked in the midst of this talk, 'if you defeated the Athenians?'

Aganos fixed Orestes with his one eye. 'What would you want us to do?'

Orestes tilted his head, thoughtfully. 'I'm not a soldier.' Nobody seemed prepared to answer his question. 'But what would you do? Slaughter them all, men, women and children? Make them your slaves? Force them to pay tribute?'

The silence that greeted this question made Orestes wonder if any of them had thought about it. Perhaps winning the war was enough; what that meant, or what came afterwards, was as mysterious to them as it was, at this moment, to him. Like him, they had known this war most of their lives: like the beach beside the sea, as he had said, it seemed almost like a law of nature. It occurred to him, as he waited for them to speak, that he also could not have answered the question on behalf of his own citizens. He knew, he thought, what his own policy would be: peace, and perhaps some tribute to compensate for the years of trouble they had caused. But could he be sure there was not, in Athens itself, a faction that dreamt of wholescale massacre? It alarmed him to think this. He wondered, suddenly, who the slaughterers might be, which politicians sought this conclusion.

The ghastly thought quickly passed. No, Orestes thought. We

are a city of poets and philosophers, lovers of wisdom, not war. We have been fighting this war against our will, not out of choice or ambition.

'Slaves are a lot of trouble,' said Lyador.

But Endrocles, the youngest colonel, leant forward, his face full of anger. 'It's obvious, surely. We would destroy them, raze their city to the ground and scatter its miserable ashes. Bring down the walls of their pretentious Acropolis, tear down the temple of Athena, drop the remains of their arrogance into the Aegean Sea, and leave the survivors to wander through the ruins, weeping.'

Orestes looked at him, fascinated by the ugliness spewing from such a handsome face. He glanced around at the others, trying to gauge whether this was some kind of joke.

'Tribute would be better,' commented Lyador.

Aganos looked at Orestes seriously, and Orestes sensed a certain embarrassment in his eye. He, Orestes, was, as far as they knew, a visitor from an exotic Greek colony, and perhaps his hosts were anxious not to appear the crude barbarians their reputation suggested. 'Forgive Endrocles his youthful – vigour,' the soldier said, stiffly. 'But, you see, the Athenians are such an arrogant people. They see themselves as somehow chosen by the gods. They look down their noses at us. Can you blame us if we want to wipe the smugness off their smirking faces?'

Orestes looked directly into the Spartan's glinting eye. 'I have to be honest, Aganos. I mean – I'm sure you understand – no disrespect. But the Athenians, it must be admitted, have a lot to be proud about. There is nothing in my own city, which I love dearly, to rival the splendour of their architecture alone.'

He looked around, wondering how this comment would be received. Orestes was playing a dangerous game. It would have been simpler, for the purposes of spying, to act the part of a vicious enemy of Athens. But he had felt from the outset, and each encounter with Spartans had only confirmed his suspicions, that he was more likely to gain their trust if he seemed honestly neutral. This, now, was a moment that could determine whether his strategy had been right.

'Are you fond of architecture, Orestes?' It was Lyador speaking to him, his face mature and handsome in the candlelight.

'Not especially,' said Orestes. 'But if you visit Egypt, the pyramids and the ancient temples are wonderful to see. If you go to Rhodes, or Parnassus, you can't help but be amazed by the daring of their buildings and statues. Athens is like that.' He paused, and looked at Endrocles. The young Spartan was staring at him, curiously. Orestes felt a beat in his gut as he gazed on the young man's brittle beauty. 'It would be a pity to destroy such beautiful things. That's what I feel, if you want my honest opinion.' Some of the colonels around him nodded, and Orestes felt encouraged to continue. 'Frankly, it wouldn't reflect well on Sparta, either. You don't want the world to see you as vandals, do you – burning to the ground every work of art you can get your hands on?'

'No, of course not,' said Aganos.

Orestes was uncomfortable, every one of the Spartans around him gazing at him inquisitively.

'Is that how you see us?'

Orestes turned to look at Lyador, whose face seemed genuinely interested, even worried. He hesitated for a moment. 'No.'

There was a long pause in which, it seemed to Orestes, he was under the careful scrutiny of each one of these fearsome warriors. He wanted not to be the centre of attention, but could think of no way to deflect their interest.

But then Lyador, surprisingly, climbed to his feet. He staggered, very slightly, from the effects of all the wine he had drunk, but was still in control of himself. Orestes looked up at him.

Lyador smiled. 'You are a good soul, honourable visitor from Syracuse,' he announced. Then he laughed, and added, 'Wherever the hell that is.'

His guests all laughed their hearty Spartan laughs. Orestes realised how drunk he was: he had been guzzling wine from anxiety, not paying attention to its effects. Now he felt woozy. Suddenly he was acutely aware of the hard, powerful bodies that surrounded him, and there seemed to be – although maybe it was his imagination – a charged sexual tension in the room. He looked up at Lyador, his broad chest and thick, powerful neck; then he glanced over at Endrocles, lounging provocatively on his wooden bench, his tunic curling up his leg, tantalisingly suggesting the mound of his crotch. To steady his nerves, Orestes slugged back some more wine.

Lyador lifted his goblet, as if in a toast. Around him, the other five colonels lifted their wine. Orestes lifted his, vaguely aware that there was something happening he didn't understand. 'Cleomenes is most upset he can't be here tonight, Orestes,' he said, grinning at his visitor. 'He tells us you have a fantastic cock.'

Orestes wondered if he had heard correctly. He gazed at Lyador.

Lyador lowered his voice, speaking either confidentially or as if he imagined some eavesdropper. 'You might think this quaint,' he said, addressing Orestes directly. 'Or stupid. Or superstitious. I don't know what you'll think. But we in the Spartan army have a –' he struggled for the word '– a belief. A tradition, you might say.'

He spoke in a strange, urgent whisper. 'We believe that our victory depends upon our manhood.' Orestes nodded, not understanding, although his cock was already starting to swell in excited anticipation. 'And occasionally we need to replenish our manhood.'

Orestes stared at him. Through the corner of his eye, he noticed that Endrocles was fondling his own groin. He almost dared not glance over. 'We believe this,' Lyador went on. 'We know from experience that it's true. That the gods will enter us and make us stronger.'

Orestes cleared his throat. His cock was straining, erect, although he did not know what Lyador meant; he knew only that the moment was charged with a palpable sexual intent.

Aganos looked at him seriously, his eye twinkling. 'The more semen that enters our bodies, the greater warriors we will be.'

Orestes' cock throbbed helplessly. He dared to look around now and saw, to his quickening excitement, that each of the six Spartan colonels was coaxing his dick to an eager erection.

Endrocles, opposite him, stretched his legs apart, and pulled his prick from under his clothes, gripping it in his hands. It was not huge, but solid and inviting; Orestes stared at it, anxious to have it in his mouth.

'Please.' Lyador spoke to him with an urgency contained by curious politeness. 'You would do us a great honour if –' He seemed lost for words. Orestes could see the vein in his neck throbbing.

'Foreign semen is especially potent.' It was Endrocles speaking, a droplet of pre-come beading from the slit at the tip of his dick. Orestes' heart was racing; his cock was as solid as a stone club. 'It symbolises the draining of your fertility,' Endrocles added, as though this were something he barely understood himself, but was in any case not greatly concerned by it.

'You would do us a great honour,' Lyador went on, 'if you would fill each one of us with your sperm.'

They were waiting for his answer. It crossed his mind that it was surprising, if they wanted him, that they didn't simply take him whether he agreed to it or not. But they seemed to require his consent.

Without saying another word, thrilled to please his hosts, Orestes stood, lifted his tunic over his head and tore off his loincloth, exposing his stiff, eager dick to their delighted eyes.

Lyador was first. With a groan of the purest pleasure, he bent forward and sank his lips over Orestes' pulsating hard-on. It was not a gentle suck: like that of Cleomenes, his passion was aggressive, almost violent. As Lyador sucked tight on Orestes' cock, the other Spartans cast off their clothes.

They surrounded him, six toned, military bodies with taut, wonderful cocks, and each one of them seized by his duty to fellate Orestes until his balls were empty. For a while they simply took it in turns, lined up to tantalise and tease him, one rough mouth engulfing his straining hard-on after the other. Orestes reached out to grip their cocks, tingling with excitment as he fondled the warm, needy flesh.

Endrocles, with something to prove, was the roughest of all, seizing Orestes' solid shaft in his hands and smothering it with his mouth. In his eyes Orestes could see the crudest, most insatiable desire. Orestes thrust his hips forward, burying his dick in the young Spartan's mouth, enjoying the idea of this arrogant soldier serving him like this; Endrocles grunted, almost retched, controlled himself and gripped Orestes' balls so tight it did actually hurt, then gasped, leaning back for a moment to feast his eyes on Orestes' thick, wet shaft.

One-eyed Aganos pushed Endrocles aside, and with his own enormous dick in his hand, buried his face in Orestes' groin. The Athenian arched his back, his whole body shaking with exhilaration; he grasped hold of Aganos's shoulders, which were wide and strong, with a thick layer of hair, and lunged into the warrior's throat. Around him, the rest were doing their best to restrain their excitement, slowly wanking their cocks.

Then teeth were softly biting his nipples, and a tongue lunged eagerly up his arse. Endrocles seized his face in both hands, his eyes burning with lust, and begged: 'Fuck me . . . Fuck me.'

Endrocles bent forward, his arse ring pink and dilating. Orestes gripped him by the waist and forced in his cock. The Spartan was surprisingly soft and moist, as though he had carefully prepared for this by lubricating himself with oil. Endrocles' arse muscles tightened triumphantly around Orestes' rigid, iron-hard cock, and Orestes started to fuck him. Endrocles moaned in pleasure, wriggling his body to intensify the sensation, as Orestes plunged into him, grasping his waist to keep his balance.

Lyador whispered lasciviously into his ear: 'Fuck me, take me, I surrender.' Powerful arms gripped him around the thighs, and Orestes found himself lifted away from Endrocles, rough, soldier's arms under his thighs, then taken to Lyador, who was bending forward.

His cock pierced into the Spartan, who sobbed, perhaps in pain. The Spartan colonels gently lowered Orestes' feet to the ground. He flailed around, and found Endrocles' dick: he pulled the young colonel around, and sank his mouth over his avid, drooling cock. Lyador was under him, lifting his arse so Orestes could penetrate deeper, deeper; Endrocles' thick, dark, salty cock was lunging into his mouth; around him, four more solid, rock-hard cocks were eager for his lips. Orestes' body was contorted by spasm.

And suddenly he was pulled away from Lyador, on to a carpet of warm, hard bodies and rigid cocks. As he shot spunk, high into the air, Lyador and Endrocles competed to catch it in their mouths. Then Endrocles sank forward and drank the dregs of Orestes' spunk from its source.

His cock was aching now, but the Spartans hadn't finished with him. Immediately, Aganos was upon him again, coaxing his dick back to its fullest erection, smothering his tired balls with spit, sucking at him as if his life depended on it. The other Spartans were eager for their chance, worshipping his cock from every side. Two of them slavered over it, as he lay back, as if in a perfect dream. They wanted every drop of semen his balls could give them. But also they were loving it. Every one of them was grunting with unbridled passion, fighting for possession of Orestes' cock. Lyador and Endrocles, having drunk their fill, had started on each other. Endrocles was on top: they were tasting each other's cock, their eyes closed, their faces filled with an easy rapture. Orestes looked down at Endrocles' hard, round buttocks as he buried his tongue in the older man's arsehole.

A tall, thick-chested colonel whose name Orestes could not remember was sucking ferociously on his cock, now, muttering prayers, and wanking himself furiously. Someone else – he couldn't even see who it was – was standing over him, a long, wide hard-on lifting before his eyes. Orestes stared at it, then grabbed it greedily with his lips. The warm, hard muscle against his face, the oily, musty smell, the huge balls ramming against his chin: Orestes knew he had gone to Heaven. They called it Sparta, but it was Heaven.

He came again, vast spurts of come, and the Spartans shared it, moving their mouths to catch some of his spunk on their tongues. Beside him, Endrocles stared at him as Lyador started to fuck him. Orestes gazed, almost stupefied now, at Endrocles' lithe, athletic body, his cock hard enough to burst, as Lyador grunted and strained and ravished him. Still on his back, with the others still devouring his raw, bruised cock, Orestes reached

out to caress Endrocles' hard, throbbing shaft, leaning forward
and taking it in his mouth at exactly the moment that Endrocles
came. The spunk hit the back of Orestes' throat, as he felt both
bodies, Endrocles' and Lyador's, hit orgasm. He gulped down
Endrocles' sperm, felt it hot and viscous as it slipped down his
throat.

Spunk was raining down on him from all directions. Everywhere he turned there were luscious cocks disgorging come,
powerful men in paroxysms of pleasure, wide thighs trembling,
chest muscles bulging, necks taut, at the moment of release. He
kept Endrocles' cock in his mouth, wouldn't let go, and then
came again, a third time. Spartans surrounded him, lapping up
his sperm, moaning in a frenzy of adoration.

Back at the barracks, Hector hurried to find Epharon. He was
sitting by the side of the shack, watching the sun go down.
When he saw Hector, he smiled happily and got to his feet. He
was wearing his tunic, but it was wet for some reason, and every
contour of his body was clear; there was a dark smudge at his
groin, and his dick, soft for once, was the shape of a bloated fig
under his clothing.

'Eph, we have to talk.' Hector seized Epharon's hand and
pulled him away from the barracks. Not far off was a small copse
of cedars, shady during the day, pitch-black at night.

'Hector! What's wrong?'

Hector waited until they were hidden from the world by the
trees before beginning to explain. But it was hard to explain.
And, even in the darkness, Epharon's tender face melted his
heart. He wished he could love his young friend the way he
wanted to be loved. He wished he could force from his mind
the forbidden desires that plagued his heart: an officer and an
outsider.

'The captain thinks you're in love with me,' said Hector,
straightforwardly. 'Tell me it isn't true.' He stared at Epharon,
thinking this was the most difficult thing he had ever had to do.
The codes of the army were simple. They were an army of
lovers; but an *army*: it was considered quite indecent and

improper for a hoplite to fall in love with one of his comrades in preference to, or to the exclusion of, others. Love of that sort was a womanly virtue.

Epharon laughed, nervously. 'Of course not, Hector.'

Hector stared at him in the moonless darkness, waiting for him to go on. He knew, of course, that it was quite true, that Epharon was indeed in love, helplessly.

Epharon shuffled his feet. 'I don't know what you're talking about, Hector. Of course I love you. And I love your cock. And I love it when you fuck me. But –'

But even in the heavy shadow Hector could see that Epharon was hard. His wet tunic clung to the shape of his erection. Epharon glanced down at the bulge.

'Oh, Hector. You know me. I'm always ready for sex. It doesn't mean anything.'

But it did mean something; and Hector felt so sorry, so frankly miserable. He wanted to kneel before Epharon and suck him, to show his affection. He felt a faint twinge of lust at the idea. But not enough.

They looked at each other for a while. Epharon flexed his cock under the wet clothes, and giggled guiltily.

'How did you get so wet?' asked Hector suddenly, as if noticing for the first time.

'Gatha pushed me in the brook.'

Hector laughed mildly. Then he stepped forward and took Epharon firmly by the shoulders. 'Eph, listen to me. Tonight, I think the captain will be watching us. I *know* he will.'

'How do you know?'

'He told me.'

Hector was awkward for a moment. He knew this was a strange revelation; it was odd indeed for an officer to have told him such a thing. It implied a dishonourable intimacy. The image of Pausanius gripping his erection under his uniform flashed into his mind.

'You must be careful, Eph. I want you to promise me something.'

'Of course.' Hector could have wept. In Epharon's voice,

which he tried so hard to keep steady, was a note of the most terrible despair. He wished they could kiss. But it would have been the worst thing to do.

'Ignore me. That's all you have to do. Pretend I don't exist. Share yourself as much as you can. Suck every cock that comes near your mouth. Let everyone fuck you. I don't care what you do, as long as you ignore me.'

Epharon was silent for a while; then: 'If that's what you want, Hector.'

The pain in his young friend's voice was more than he could stand. 'Please, Eph. Understand. If Pausanius thinks you are in love with me, you know what will happen. He'll report it. You'll be expelled from the company.'

He pulled Epharon to him, and immediately the younger Spartan's arms wrapped around him, clinging to him as if this were the last time he would ever be able to do this. His tunic was cold and clammy with water; the rigid rod of his hard-on dug into Hector's stomach.

'It's not what –' Hector fell silent, and pulled himself away. 'This is a serious business, Eph.'

Epharon nodded. Even in this darkness, Hector knew he was crying.

'It's more complicated than you can imagine.'

Epharon struggled to control his tears. 'I don't understand.'

'He's jealous, Eph. He wants a reason to destroy you. He thinks – he thinks I'm in love with you, too.'

Hector turned away. He knew what Epharon was about to say, and wished with all his soul he wouldn't say it. 'And . . .' Hector forced himself to turn back and face his friend. 'But you're not, are you?'

Hector shook his head. 'No, Eph. No, I'm not.'

For a moment, Epharon tried to be brave. But, however courageous a soldier he might be, Hector knew that this moment was too much for him. He wanted to soothe him, to make the pain go away. But too much was at stake now.

'That's the truth, Epharon. I don't love you. Not in the way you want. And I won't.'

Epharon cried, audibly, now. Without speaking again, he walked away. Hector watched him pass out of the darkness of the trees, into a shaft of moonlight as he headed for the barracks.

Under his breath, amazed at what he was thinking, Hector cursed Pausanius.

Orestes' senses were still reeling as they ate dinner, sitting around a low table. He was drunk from the wine, and overwhelmed by the sexual delights this primitive city contained. It worried him a little, as sex with his friends in the gymnasium at Athens would seem so tame and boring after this. And would any of them believe him?

He forced himself to concentrate. The Spartans were regaling each other with tales of combat. They were exciting stories, but, since his own people were depicted throughout as the idiotic and cowardly enemy, he struggled not to interject. He wanted to point out that it could not be simply money that had allowed Athens to hold off their victory for so long, and if the Athenians were so cowardly it was a miracle they ever fought battles at all. But he kept quiet.

Eventually, a word appeared in the middle of the conversation that caught his attention: 'Plan.' Lyador had said it, and the other colonels were nodding in evident agreement. Orestes looked between them.

'You've found some way, I take it, to finish the Athenians off.'

Endrocles looked at him suspiciously. 'We believe so.'

Orestes nodded, pretending to be only mildly interested. 'Are you sure it will work?'

'It will work,' said Aganos. He leant forward. 'The Athenians are not stupid. Or not all of them. They know when they can't win.'

Orestes frowned. 'What do you mean?'

Aganos grinned, staring at him with his piercing one eye. 'You'll see. The whole world will see.'

Six

G atha stood on his bunk and addressed the rest of the barracks. He was naked, a slight growth of a beard on his chin. Gatha was the shortest in their company, but with the broadest chest, and every part of his body – his treetrunk legs, his solid, discus-throwing arms – was pure muscle. He stood with his legs slightly apart, perhaps because the thigh muscles were too developed for him to stand otherwise. It made his cock dangle like a delightful toy.

'Tonight, my friends, I think we should try something different,' Gatha said. His nine companions, including Hector, watched him attentively. Hector cast a glance at Epharon, who was staring with particular diligence at Gatha, trying to ignore Hector altogether. 'I think,' Gatha went on, 'we need a little competition.'

The company laughed, curious and excited. Gatha explained. 'I think we need to know which of us does things *best*.'

Severon slapped Gatha's leg, laughing. All around, hoplites were eagerly awaiting the rules of this new sport.

'There are several categories in this contest,' Gatha went on. 'I've thought of a few. Maybe you can think of more.' From the back of the room, somebody whistled. Gatha quietened them down. 'We all know already who's got the best cock and the juiciest balls.' There was more laughter. Severon leant across and slapped Hector's shoulder. 'I'm not saying the *biggest* cock, mind you. Obviously, that's mine.' He gripped his dick, which was limp but starting to swell a little in his hand, and waved it in Severon's face. There were more whistles, and some shouts. 'But what I'm talking about here isn't just that sort of rubbish. The best javelin thrower isn't the man with the best javelin, after all. No.' They were all laughing softly, and watching him, intrigued. 'In the military arts, we measure also – and above all – skill.'

The company clapped, delighted. Gatha was still gripping his cock, which was fully erect now; and he was probably right: his cock *was* the biggest, a huge weapon out of all proportion to his short, stocky body.

'So: what skills? I propose the following contests. Who sucks the best? Who fucks the best (I'm talking stuffing his cock up a happy soldier's behind)? Who's got the moistest, tightest, most fuckable arse? And who's got the most imagination?'

Gatha was delighted with himself, and the company cheered and laughed. Hector noticed that most of them were hard already, eager to get the contest underway.

Gatha had it all organised. The last stage of the contest was to be the prize for who could shoot furthest, so it was important that any hoplite with ambitions in this field refrain from coming beforehand. Gatha handed out little pieces of parchment and charcoal for the soldiers to score their comrades out of ten. Many of them couldn't write, but they could at least count.

The first contest was to find the soldier with the finest sucking technique. They cleared the bunks to one side, and stood in a circle. Each soldier would suck the rest of them in turn; they had only a short time each to demonstrate their abilities, but it was up to each hoplite whether his aim was a slow, succulent blow job or a hard, aggressive one.

Hector stood in the circle of nine, as Gatha prepared himself in the middle. Their ten dicks were all gorgeously hard, and several young Spartans were so aroused by this game they were having some difficulty in not simply grabbing their cocks in their fists and wanking immediately to climax; but as the competition

76

continued they would learn to be patient. Everyone was laughing, enjoying the absurdity of the contest. Gatha, smiling happily, got down on his knees and got the game under way.

Hector watched as Gatha started on a soldier opposite him, a dark-skinned, slender youth with a broken nose, the veins in whose smallish cock were throbbing already in eager anticipation. Gatha was of the aggressive persuasion: he grabbed his comrade's dick in his hand and smothered it with his lips, gripping tightly on the soldier's balls as he bobbed his head up and down like a madman.

It was thrilling to watch. Hector's cock was almost vertically erect. He was glad of this silliness, glad it could take his mind off his worries.

The young hoplite was bending back his head, his chest puffed out, breathing out, through pursed, lascivious lips. The others watched, eyes hungry; some of them murmured, 'Go on, Gatha, suck it, suck it!' One of them suddenly grabbed Gatha's head, and thrust his own cock forward, bending his knees to stuff it into the discus thrower's mouth. The circle of soldiers, with rigid dicks in their hands, closed in tighter.

Hector watched his stocky friend move on to the next soldier, a tall youth who had to spread his thighs wide, and bend his shaking knees to thrust his pelvis forward so Gatha, still on his knees, could reach him. All eyes watched in greedy anticipation. Soldiers grunted and made their mouths into little circles, exhaling loudly in lust, their buttocks twitching as they each began to tremble with desire. 'Gatha, Gatha!' Hoplites fought to be next, hissing through clenched teeth, the muscles bulging in their chests.

Grinning, Gatha turned to Severon, and licked his finger, forcing it into the tall warrior's arse as he sank his mouth greedily over the dripping, thick cock. Gatha's dick was as hard as rock, swinging before his stomach as he went around the room dispensing rough, manly pleasure. Hector knew well the kind of suck Gatha gave. He liked it. He bit his lip now as he waited his turn.

All over the room, soldiers complained that they would never survive the whole round without coming, let alone still be able to compete in the final shooting contest. Gatha stopped work on his latest victim to warn them they had a long time to go yet. There were a couple of laughs, but by now they were all too consumed with wanton hunger to see this only as a game. Gatha went back to his prey – Timos, a tremendously muscular wrestler, whose neck was a solid wall of taut lust and whose face was flushed with passion.

Then Gatha reached Hector, and buried his face in Hector's groin, swallowing his cock to the base. Hector cried out, in part because Gatha hurt a little – but it was a delicious, hot pain. He staggered on his feet, almost losing his balance, as his cock rammed against the back of the discus thrower's throat.

It was then, as he opened his eyes, that Hector caught a glimpse of what he feared. Outside, watching them through the window, was Pausanius, his face a grimace of frustrated carnality.

Gatha had completed his round, dispensing pleasure to each of his nine comrades, and it was the turn of Timos, the wrestler. Despite his size and rough masculinity, Timos gave a slow, sensitive, exquisite suck, gently drawing back the foreskin and drooling spit over the cock before easing his warm lips down each voracious shaft. By the time he reached Hector, his eyes were glassy with delight and pleasure, and a long line of pre-come dripped from the tip of his thick dick to the floor. He gasped as Hector's cock pressed against his lips, kissed the tip, briefly buried his face in Hector's balls, before sliding his mouth over the shaft, sighing. Behind him, the others huddled close, their hard-ons in their hands, muttering, 'Suck Hector's cock, Timos . . . Faster . . . Suck it . . .'

Hector saw Pausanius through the window, his shoulders rocking as he wanked himself, jealously watching the strong-backed wrestler gorge himself on Hector's cock. 'Mine, Timos, mine . . .' Soldiers thrust their dicks forward, and with another sigh Timos chose Epharon, inhaling his rock-solid shaft. 'Uh!' Epharon moaned, gazing, glassy-eyed, at Hector, panting, grinning slightly, grabbing the wrestler's head to force him further down until he choked and whimpered. 'Suck it,' Gatha hissed, stroking himself. 'Suck Epharon's sweet young dick . . .'

It was Hector's turn. This, of course, would drive the captain crazy, as Hector went from one hard cock to another, tasting it, drawing it into his mouth and feeling its texture against his tongue. Each cock was so beautifully distinct: Gatha's was thick and fat, Severon's firm and rich with salty juices. Timos's was heavy, with a bulbous head, straining to burst and seeping pre-come. Hector was suddenly overwhelmed with lust in this garden of cocks. Oh, he thought, desperately, how he loved men's cocks: succulent, massive, sweaty cocks, filling his mouth or ravishing his arse. For a while he forgot everything except the gloriousness of this forest of wonderful hard-ons to suck, this frenzied, dreamy capitulation to his insatiable hunger for cocks.

But then, before his face, was Epharon. He hesitated, and looked up into Epharon's eyes, still full of love and hurt. The captain was watching. The captain was jealous. He had to make sure he spent no longer on Epharon than any of the others. Yet he wanted so much to take Epharon's pain away, if only for a few moments. And his cock was so lovely, so delicious.

He grabbed Epharon's dick and smothered it with his lips. The young hoplite almost buckled with excitement, and thrust himself deeper into Hector's mouth, grabbing his hair to propel Hector's face forward. There was anger in this gesture as well as pain. For a moment, Hector thought how luscious indeed Epharon's sweet dick was, how much he loved to suck it, how delightful it was to fuck Epharon's tender arse. But the captain was watching: he had to control himself.

Hector tore his mouth away, tenderly kissed the tip of Epharon's dick as if in farewell, and quickly moved on. All around him were grunts of raw carnality. Soldiers were exhorting him, in rasping whispers: 'Suck him, go on, Hector. Suck him hard!' He sank down on another cock, no longer knowing or caring whose it was.

Finally, it was Epharon's turn to do the sucking, and Hector's comrades were feverish with anticipation, knowing how good at it Epharon was. But it was clear from the beginning that he was racing through the others, anxious to get to Hector, and saving him for last.

Hector was alarmed. Pausanius was still watching through the window, no longer masturbating, simply waiting for Epharon to condemn himself. Hector knew how fantastically Epharon sucked. He knew that when Epharon's lips enclosed his shaft, sore now from the various mouths that had engulfed it, desperate to come, he would tremble with passion, sob with pleasure. He couldn't let that happen.

As Epharon knelt before him, licking his lips and gritting his teeth with lecherous eagerness, Hector grabbed his own dick firmly in his hand, wanked it a few times, and spurted spunk into Epharon's face. Epharon tried to seize Hector's cock, to drink down the rest of his come, but Hector wouldn't let him. He turned away, his knees bent and his buttocks quivering, and shot the rest of his load on to the floor.

Epharon looked up at him, hurt again.

Gatha protested, loudly: 'Hector! You're hopeless. I said no coming.' Other soldiers were also annoyed with him, as all of them had somehow managed to hold themselves back. But Hector glanced over at Pausanius's stern face at the window, and stepped away.

Lying in his bed in Ariadne's inn, Orestes tried to clear his head. He was drunk, and the unadulterated debauchery of the last few days was overwhelming him. This was not what he had expected. Cleomenes, the priest, then *six* Spartan colonels, hungry for his dick, had turned him into a walking erection. He couldn't think of anything but sex. Even now, lying here, only hours after three consecutive orgasms, his cock was hard and he wanted to masturbate himself into oblivion.

Worst of all, there was Ariadne's gorgeous, mysterious son. He thought of Hector, replenishing his manhood from his comrades' aching cocks, and he squirmed with jealousy. He knew this was absurd. Since meeting Hector he had himself indulged in the wildest sex; it was irrational to be jealous if Hector had done the same. And of course, he had to remind himself, he had absolutely no claim over the young Spartan: there had been nothing sexual in their encounter at all. But he knew what the Egyptian priest had meant. The whole time, his thoughts had been on Hector. With Lyador and his company of delicious erections, Hector had been constantly flashing into his mind. He kept wondering what Hector was doing at that moment, who was savouring Hector's luscious juices . . .

He needed to think. He needed to get his priorities in order. He was a spy. He was there for one reason: to find military secrets. He wasn't there to fuck Spartan officers or fall in love with beautiful Spartan soldiers.

There. The thought had formed itself in all its ridiculous intensity. After a few moments alone with a sullen, confused boy, he was falling in love.

But as he remembered that muscle in Hector's neck, that powerful sinew from his shoulder to his throat, Orestes' cock pulsed hard in his hand. He thought he could come, even now with his balls surely empty, just imagining Hector's neck. He rolled on to his stomach, as if that would help him sleep. But his cock just ground into the hard bed, and he imagined kissing Hector's long, wide, soft throat, and his hand was seeking out his hard-on to massage it. He pressed his thumb against his arsehole, imagining it was Hector.

This was terrible. He had come so many times today that his dick hurt. The muscle ached, and the tip was sore and red from so much rough, inconsiderate Spartan sucking. He pushed his finger into his arse, just a bit; his cock flexed against the mattress. He lifted his buttocks, so he could reach better, and pressed a little more, burying his finger up to the knuckle. His rectum clenched around it; his poor, exhausted cock was drooling a patch of pre-come on to the bed. And the tendon in Hector's neck was filling his thoughts. His finger was inside him now, as far as it would go. His other hand was between his hard cock and the hard bed, the wet patch of pre-come against it on one side, the hot, pulsing muscle pressing into his palm. He moved the finger back and forth, in and out, slowly caressing his prostate, imagining Hector's cock, Hector breathing into his neck, Hector's powerful legs gripping him from behind as he fucked him. He lifted his buttocks higher, reached down and gripped his balls and squeezed them. He pressed another finger against his arse, and slowly eased that in beside the other, fucking himself with two fingers, then three; his other hand grabbed his hard, aching cock in a fist, and suddenly began to pummel it. It was Hector fucking him, Hector's cock, Hector's rough warrior hands wanking him like this.

Orestes shot a dribble of spunk over the bed, what little he had left, and collapsed on its cold wetness, praying now he would be able to sleep. His rectum was clenched tight around the fantasy Spartan cock in his arse, and it was painful as he pulled the fingers out. Orestes wondered if he was going mad.

He tugged the coarse blanket around his shoulders, and dared to imagine Hector curled up in the bed beside him.

Gatha collected the scores and declared Timos the wrestler the winner of the first round. Strong wine was passed from mouth to mouth, the soldiers sharing the carafe, wiping their lips with their arms. But no erections relented, except Hector's: the hoplites were eager for the next stage in the contest.

'The next part's more complicated,' Gatha explained. 'We're going to take it in turns again, but this time you'll have to score each other. Marks for best fucker, and marks for best fuck. We may as well include marks for imagination while we're at it or everyone's going to go crazy.'

They lined up some bunks along one wall, and each soldier carefully lubricated his arsehole with oil, one or two forcing a few fingers in to loosen themselves a little in preparation. Then nine of them bent forward, arses in the air, in a row, as the first contestant got ready to fuck them. Timos, as winner of the first round, went first.

Hector was sixth in line. It seemed quite ridiculous, leaning forward on the hard bunk like this, his arse just waiting for Timos's cock. He looked along the line, and could see Gatha, grimacing with ecstasy as the wrestler plunged his dick inside him. Soldiers were wriggling eagerly, forcing their erections down on the bunks. 'Fuck me!' Gatha gasped. Hector twisted his neck to see Pausanius, still at the window, his eyes moist, his shoulder rocking as he wanked himself again. It was this that made Hector's dick surge to erection once more. However angry and afraid he was of Pausanius at this moment, he hungered for the captain's cock. He felt the thrill of knowing that Pausanius was staring at his exposed arse, and that each time a soldier fucked him the captain would tremble with jealous lust.

Timos reached him, testing Hector's arsehole with his fingers, then gently easing his cock inside. Hector cried out, shocked by the size of it. But then it filled him, his muscles clenched around it; his own cock rammed hard into the bed as the wrestler forced further in, withdrew a little, then buried himself up to the base of his dick. Hector cried out again, pressing back his hips to take the wrestler further inside. 'Fuck him!' hoplites were hissing. 'Fuck Hector's gorgeous arse!' Hector buried his face in the bed, thrilled to the core, shivering with excitement to think this was only the first of nine hard cocks about to fuck him.

It didn't last long, because Timos had three more arseholes to fill before taking his place at the end. But soon Severon's slenderer, longer dick was inside him, then another, then Gatha's. This was incredible. Cock after cock sank into Hector's flesh, and his whole body was stiff with pleasure, his hands were in fists, he ground his teeth, buried his head into the bunk and sobbed in ecstasy.

Suddenly, he realised it was Epharon sliding his cock into him, moaning his name as he kissed Hector's neck. Epharon caressed Hector's body, sought out his nipples to squeeze them tight, as he thrust his dick inside. Hector shivered as goosepimples travelled from his groin to the back of his neck. He couldn't help it: when Epharon lifted him higher, kneeling on the bunk to plunge ever deeper into Hector's arse – now a little sore, but throbbing and tensing and gripping his friend's cock so tight – Hector relented. Let Epharon fuck him, let him sink his sweet dick inside, if that was what he wanted – but then another hoplite urgently hissed behind them, 'My turn, Eph, give me a piece of that juicy arse . . .' Epharon was forced to move on.

Hector took his turn to fuck. He was in a haze, like a dream caused by some mysterious potion. He thrust his cock into one arse after another, unable to tell who was who, completely taken over by wanton delirium, possessed by the urgency of his cock, the simple, grunting passion of the soldiers who spread their legs for him. Almost nobody, now, was in the simple position of bending over the bed. They were adopting experimental angles, like Timos, on his back, his contorted, lustful face gazing up as Hector rammed into his arse. Timos's hard cock slapped against his stomach, as he lifted his legs to let Hector go deeper. Hector had forgotten where he was: it was a dream of arseholes and powerful hard-ons, and firm, yielding bodies, and grunts of carnal abandonment. There was no doubt this was the best orgy the company had ever had.

He came to his senses when he realised the mouth pressed against his, the arsehole gripping his cock so strongly, the arms squeezing his body, were Epharon's. They were kissing passionately, their tongues seeking out each other's throat. His cock was so, so hard inside Epharon's syrupy arsehole that he thought he would explode. But this was disastrous. He pulled away, leaving Epharon gazing at him miserably, and sought out the next warm hole. Around him were moans of orgasmic frenzy, as his comrades could bear it no longer and started to come, shooting warm spunk into one another's arse or on to their bodies; a few had gone back to sucking, and growled in debauched bliss as spurts of come covered their faces. Hector emptied his balls into the arse of a soldier with fairer hair and skin than the rest, flat on his back, whose body convulsed as he came himself, spunk drenching his chest.

When the sounds of sex had finally died, and the ten hoplites lay exhausted, each across another's body, Hector glanced over at the window. The captain had gone, but he didn't know how long ago. Gatha started instructing people to write down their scores so he could collect them and find the winners of each category; he was disappointed they weren't going to have the shooting contest, but maybe they could leave that for tomorrow.

Hector glanced over at Epharon, who was lying, already on

his bunk, his eyes closed. He went up to him, and sat, apprehensively on the bed beside him. Epharon opened his eyes.

'You all right, Eph?'

Epharon nodded, and smiled. Hector wanted to cry: Epharon had so little malice, he was so unable to sustain his anger.

'You know Pausanius was watching us.'

Epharon nodded again. 'I don't care what he does to me, Hector.'

Hector took his hand. 'You've got to care. Do you understand me?'

'Maybe. But the fact is I don't.'

Hector sighed, and took his hand away. 'I tried to protect you, Epharon.' He added, sorrowfully, 'You're a fool.'

Epharon just shrugged, and turned over as if to go to sleep.

Gatha's voice bellowed from across the barracks. 'We have the results!'

It seemed Timos was the overall winner, beaten only in the category of fucker, which Gatha won. Hector suspected he had fixed the figures. But what did it matter? The world was pressing in on him. He lusted after a captain it would be a disgrace to have. He was obsessed by a traveller from Syracuse it would be an even worse disgrace to have. And his dear little friend Epharon had embarked upon a course of self-destruction.

Seven

Orestes had to know about this plan the Spartans were hatching. Early in the morning, he prayed to Athena, pleading with her to help him. In his bag he carried a small wooden effigy of the goddess, which he nervously placed on his bed and knelt before, bowing his head, murmuring ritual phrases. He had to do it quickly, because it would be suspicious indeed if someone caught him praying to the goddess of Athens in a Spartan inn.

He found Ariadne watering her plants in the courtyard, the slave girl beside her. She smiled at him, and commented that he had slept very late. The sun was already high in the sky. There was something strange in her demeanour, and, when Orestes made to leave, she asked if he would like to stay and share a watermelon.

They sat in the shade of the courtyard. The sheep was still fattening for the Festival, gazing at them as it chewed its food. Orestes looked into Ariadne's face. She looked away, awkwardly.

'I wanted to ask you something,' she said eventually.

Orestes took watermelon pips from his mouth. The fruit was like ice on his tongue. 'Please. Whatever you want.'

Ariadne laughed, embarrassed. 'I want you to tell me – you've travelled to many places, haven't you? Tell me: how strange are we Spartans? Are we just like other people, or are we – are we mad?'

Orestes swallowed the melon, its cool, crushed flesh slipping down his throat. 'In what way?'

'In other cities, in other places. Do mothers hand over their sons to the state, and only see them once in a while, and then, when they see them, act like strangers?'

Orestes thought for a while. 'Not like they do here,' he said at last. 'Everywhere, young men have to fight. To train as soldiers. Mothers see their children go off to war. And sometimes they don't come back. But no. Sparta is . . . more extreme.'

Ariadne nodded sadly. 'And what do you think? From the experience of your travels. Forgive me for asking, Orestes. I meet many travellers. But none, really, like you. How old are you?'

'Twenty-four.'

'You seem wiser than that. I don't know why. It's what seeing the world does, of course. But I want to know what you think. When I handed over my son, Hector, to the army, was it a terrible thing to do?'

'It's what you had to do.'

'But I could have refused, perhaps. I could have stolen him away in secret, and gone to a city that is less cruel to its mothers. But I didn't. I gave him to them.'

Orestes thought of his own mother, worrying about him at their home in Athens, and he was nearly moved to tears. 'He loves you, Ariadne. Whatever the army's done to him, it hasn't taken that away.'

She smiled, gratefully. 'Did he tell you that?'

'Yes, actually. He said he missed you.' Orestes remembered Hector's beautiful face, his strong neck lit by the lamps. He wanted so badly to see him again. 'You have a very fine son.'

She nodded, pleased. But then her face grew serious. 'In your city, are the men like they are here?' He wasn't sure what she meant. 'I mean our soldiers. They don't have much time for women. They marry, of course, when they are older. And – obviously – they father children. But they often seem to see women as . . . It's each other they love. I wondered if it's the same all over the world.'

'No.' Orestes laughed, nervously. 'What about your husband. Surely he loved you. You're a beautiful woman.'

'Oh, he loved me. He was a passionate man, with many loves, I think. Not a few slave girls, I imagine. And yes, he loved me, and he made me happy. But his first love was the men he served with. I always knew that.'

Orestes nodded. 'I think, again, Sparta's a little more extreme than most of the world. In Syracuse, there are men who love men. And men who love women. And those who love both. What happened to your husband?'

'Katlekos was his name. A fine, handsome soldier, proud of his son. He died in battle. Most Spartans die in battle.'

She turned away again, hiding her moistening eyes. Orestes wondered if he should comfort her, somehow. But he didn't know how. 'In battle with Athens, you mean.'

'Yes.' She turned back to face him, and her expression was quite impossible to read.

'Do you hate the Athenians, Ariadne?'

She frowned, as if genuinely puzzled. 'Hate them? They mean nothing to me. I've never met an Athenian. They're just the people we're always fighting.'

She cut another slice of watermelon and offered it to Orestes. 'I'm only a woman, Orestes. I don't understand this business of war. But I find it hard to believe that whatever it is we're fighting for is worth so much death. I've lost my husband, and I'm afraid of losing my son. To be honest, if I hate anyone, it's the elders of Sparta, who take our children away, and keep sending them into war to satisfy their own pride.'

Orestes spoke with difficulty, the thought forming only as he said it. 'Every Greek city has pride. Maybe they all have too much.'

'Do you think so?' She looked carefully into his face. 'I think so. I think pride is a stupid thing. What use is it, or honour, or glory, or any of these things which men prate on about so endlessly, if all your sons are dead?'

Orestes looked down, and lifted the slice of melon to his lips.

'Do you love your mother, Orestes?'

'Of course.'

'Then why are you wandering the world like this? Isn't she worried about you? I hope you go home often, just to let her know you're alive, and haven't drowned on some voyage across the sea.'

Orestes looked at her, solemnly.

She shook her head. 'I'm sorry. I'm sure your mother is very proud of you.'

He didn't speak for a moment, then nodded. 'I hope so.' He glanced up at her and smiled. 'But not too much.'

She laughed, overacting a little. Orestes was about to stand and leave her, when she caught his hand. 'My son. Hector. Did you like him?'

He cleared his throat. 'Very much.'

'I have a silly mother's dream, Orestes. That a traveller, someone quite free of responsibility to any army, will meet Hector, and Hector will fall in love with him. And the traveller will spirit him away from all this bloodshed. Even if I never saw him again – if I knew he was away from all this – I think I would be happier.' Her voice was trembling slightly, and she was gazing seriously into his eyes. 'Of course, it's impossible. Nobody can escape the Spartan army, least of all her soldiers.'

Orestes squeezed her hand. 'Believe me, Ariadne. If it was in my power to spirit Hector away, I would.'

She laughed again, and pulled her hand from his. 'Maybe someone will, one day.'

In the middle of sword practice, Hector was ordered to report to Captain Pausanius in his quarters, with Epharon. They slipped on their tunics and went to the small wooden shack were the captain lived.

Pausanius was sitting behind a table, scratching his chin, when Hector and Epharon entered. They stood to attention. There were no other seats, and even in the shade it was hot. Hector felt slightly faint, and wished he did not have to stand.

'Hoplites,' said the captain gravely. 'You know why I have called you here.'

'I think so, sir,' said Hector.

'I was watching you last night.'

'I know, sir.' Hector looked into Pausanius's eyes.

'Who won the contest?' asked Pausanius casually.

'Timos, sir,' said Epharon.

Pausanius leant across the table, looking at Epharon, his eye blinking. 'Do you know why he won, Hoplite Epharon?'

Epharon looked at him, and then at Hector, and suppressed a giggle. 'He's a fantastic fuck, sir.' He glanced again at Hector, pleased with his answer.

But then Pausanius rammed his fist on to the table. Hector jumped. Epharon, beside him, grew pale and serious. Pausanius looked into Epharon's face with a deathly anger. 'Maybe he is, Epharon. But he shares himself equally, doesn't he? He gives the same to all his comrades.'

'Yes, sir.' Hector realised that Epharon was trembling. But the expression on the young soldier's face was not of fear.

Pausanius noticed this, too. He leant back. 'It's my opinion, Epharon, that you have grown much too fond of Hector, here.'

'Sir.' Hector took a small step forward. 'May I speak?' Pausanius regarded him coldly, but eventually nodded his permission. 'Sir, as you know, the lads always have favourites. For a day or two. Sometimes even a month. There are always . . . couples who pair off for a while. You must remember what it's like, sir. You develop crushes. There are times when there's a particular comrade you want to be with, sleep with at night.'

Pausanius nodded, and for a while seemed lost in his thoughts. 'I know. A particular cock which fascinates you, which burns into your dreams. One lad's lovely erect prick which you long for more than all the others. A lad whose eyes you want to gaze into all night, as you stroke each other's chest and balls. An arse you could fuck from dusk till dawn, or a special cock you want rammed, relentlessly, into your hole. Of course, soldier.' He stared into Hector's eyes, and Hector's heart beat slightly harder: the captain's lechery was barely disguised, and, despite his anxiety, it aroused him; he could feel the pressure in his loins as his cock started to stiffen. Pausanius turned to Epharon. 'And the army turns a blind eye to all that carrying on. We know that, in a group of ten of you, you will like some lads more than others. But is this the case with you, Epharon?'

'I don't know, sir.'

Hector glanced down to where his cock was slightly tenting his tunic. Pausanius noticed it, and for a moment stared inscrutably, before he looked back at Epharon. 'Tell me honestly, Epharon, what you feel for Hector.'

Epharon could not speak, but again Hector was not sure it was from fear. The tension of the moment at least caused his erection to subside.

'You understand, soldier,' the captain went on, his voice hard and remorseless, 'that there is love, and there is love. There is a love of a man for his comrades, all of them. Intense, passionate, physical love, the love that brings you in from a hard day's fighting still with the energy to fuck each other to sleep. But there is the love also of a lovesick fool, a man who has lost the will to be a soldier, who will do stupid things and risk his comrades' lives to save the one he adores most, who forgets who he is and what he has to do. That is the love which makes you weak, Epharon. Which can make a man cry.'

Epharon looked down at Pausanius, then at Hector. Hector was willing him to speak. All Epharon had to do was deny it, to insist on his innocence. But Epharon did not speak.

'Sir,' said Hector, 'there is nothing of that sort between myself and Epharon.'

'Isn't there? Tell me, Epharon. Tell me the truth. When you've got Hector's lovely cock in your mouth, when you're drooling over it, tasting every drop of its juices, gripping his balls in your hand and grunting, clasping his buttocks in your fists, begging him never to stop – you love him, don't you? Just him. You lie awake at night hoping he's watching you. When you're training at day you want Hector beside you. He fills your dreams. If you could, you would run away from Sparta, from the army, from your duty. Wouldn't you?' He rose to his feet and spoke in a terrible, thunderous voice. 'Tell me the truth.'

'Yes, sir.' Hector turned to him, horrified. 'Yes, sir. I love Hector more than anything or anyone in the world.' He took a deep breath, fighting his urge to look at Hector as he spoke. 'I adore him. There's nothing else I can say.'

'He doesn't know what he's saying,' said Hector, panicking. 'You know Epharon, sir. He's passionate about everything. He's a bit crazy –'

'Enough.' Pausanius glared at them both. Hector shut his eyes, and said a silent prayer to whichever god might be listening. 'Epharon,' said Pausanius in a voice like death. 'You have disgraced yourself and your company. You have been weak, and you are a risk to your comrades. An infection. A corrupting influence. You are expelled from the army. Go. Collect whatever things you have, and get out of my sight.'

Hector looked, horrified, between Epharon and the captain. Epharon simply turned and left the hut, strode out proudly into the sun. Hector was about to follow him, when Pausanius called him back.

'You are not dismissed, hoplite.'

Hector returned to attention. But he wanted only to run after his friend and comfort him. There was a long, awful silence: Pausanius knew what Hector wanted, and was determined to deny it to him. If he could, Hector knew, Pausanius would keep him there until Epharon had left the camp.

'I'm not convinced, Hector, that you don't share your silly friend's infatuation. You are a better soldier than he is, so for now I will overlook it. But be warned.'

Hector forced himself to give the right response: 'Thank you, sir. Thank you, Captain Pausanius.'

Pausanius seemed suddenly to soften. He looked into Hector's eyes, and his face twitched, his eye blinked. 'Go on. You can go. Be sure to return to your practice,' he added. Hector nodded, but raced from the hut to find his friend.

Epharon was sitting on his bunk, putting his few possessions in his bag when Hector ran through the door. He looked up, sadly, and packed away his sword. Hector sat beside him, and took his hand.

'Do you have anywhere to go, Eph?'

Epharon fought back tears – but failed to stop them: they brimmed from his clear, hurt eyes. He shook his head. Hector knew Epharon's parents were both dead. He had nobody in the world except his nine dear comrades, and now he might never see them again. Hector wanted to weep himself. He put an arm around Epharon, and his young friend sobbed on to his shoulder. Hector could see Epharon's cock harden under his clothes, his desire even stronger than his pain and loss.

'Listen,' said Hector gently. 'Go to my mother's house. Tell her you're my friend. She'll take care of you.'

He stood, took Epharon's hand and lifted him to his feet. Then he put his arms around him, and held him tightly for a moment, before leading him to the door.

Epharon looked back at him, drying his eyes.

'It'll be all right, Eph. I'll come and visit you.'

'When?'

'Soon. Tonight, after dark, if I can. Don't worry. Everything will be all right.'

Hector stood in the doorway and watched Epharon walk away, down the hill towards the city in the distance. Epharon did not stop to wave. Desolate, he turned his back on the only life he had ever known.

Orestes' afternoon had been utterly frustrating. He had called on Cleomenes and Lyador, but neither of them was in. He worried that the entire Spartan officer class were in some terrible discussion which might seal the fate of the war, and he still didn't know the details of their plans.

When he arrived back at Ariadne's, he found a young Spartan sitting in the shade speaking to her. He was barely twenty, if not younger, and, by the raw puffiness around his eyes, it looked as if he had spent the last hour crying. Orestes hesitated, as this was some private matter, and he began to go to his room. But Ariadne called out to him.

He crossed, embarrassed by the young Spartan's tearful face, and sat with them in the shade. Ariadne introduced them.

'Epharon is a friend of my son's,' she said. 'A casualty of war.' She smiled, grimly.

'What happened?' Orestes asked. Epharon glanced at Ariadne and shook his head.

'Perhaps he will tell you when he is ready.' She looked hard into Epharon's eyes. 'Let me only say: I wish with all my heart that a dishonour like this would befall Hector.'

Epharon stared at her, as if she were some strange animal. Yet his gratitude was palpable, and he kissed her hand.

Ariadne looked at Orestes. 'Our friend needs to know about the places you have seen,' she said. 'He needs to know that certain things that are crimes here are not crimes in other places. That not everyone sees the world as cruelly as Spartans do.'

Epharon smiled awkwardly at Orestes. 'You're from Syracuse.' Orestes nodded. 'Maybe that's what I should do now. Travel. See the world. Forget Sparta. Like Sparta has forgotten me.'

Orestes stared at him. Epharon had a bright, boyish beauty, his body slender and gently contoured, his face, even swollen with tears, full of energy and youth. 'So you're a friend of Hector's.'

Epharon managed to grin, with a kind of determined pride. 'I like to think I'm his best friend.'

Ariadne showed Epharon to his room, and Orestes helped her straighten the woollen mattress. It was probably the smallest in the inn, but it was fine for his purposes, and she insisted that, as Hector's friend, he had no need to pay.

Orestes wondered if it would be useful to talk further with Epharon. He had been able to glean that the Spartan had been dishonourably discharged in some way, and thought perhaps this would make him a potential ally. Although it was not yet evening, he invited Epharon back to his quarters for some Corinthian wine, which he promised was far superior to Spartan, and they sat on the bed together, drinking it from Ariadne's clay cups as the shadows drew in.

'Have you ever been in love?' Epharon asked him suddenly.

Orestes thought for a while. 'I don't know. Infatuated, certainly. In love, perhaps. There was a young man, long ago, in Syracuse. Maybe I was in love with him.'

'There's nothing wrong with it, is there? Being in love, I mean. It just happens. You can't help it. One minute you're playing around like you normally do, laughing and carrying on. And then you realise: by the gods, I love this man. It's as simple as that.'

Orestes frowned. He didn't understand these Spartan obsessions. 'You're in love with Hector. Am I right?'

'And I don't care. I care because they've expelled me from the army, and now I can't be with him. But I don't care about all this shit they tell you. Weakness. Disgrace. It's just shit.'

'I thought they *wanted* you to be lovers in the Spartan army.'

Epharon looked at him. There was a drool of wine at the corner of his mouth. 'Well yes. I suppose it's complicated. I never thought of it as complicated before. But it is, isn't it? Lovers, but not in love. It used to seem so straightforward. Now it just seems like shit.'

Orestes laughed. 'You've . . .' He hesitated, realising that the words were quickening his pulse. 'You've made love to Hector, then.'

'Oh yes, of course.' Epharon seemed to find the question almost absurd. 'Rarely just with him, but occasionally. Once, we stumbled on each other by the river, and he fucked me – oh, he fucked me so well that night.' He shook his head as if he didn't want to remember. 'It's true, what they accused me of. I wasn't interested in anyone else any more. I just wanted Hector.' He sighed, a little dreamily. 'He's so . . . beautiful. He has the softest lips in the world. Like cherries.' He laughed, sheepishly. 'I love his voice. That's when I knew something was . . . wrong. It's one thing to love someone's lips; it's another to melt when you hear their voice. And his laugh. The best thing, the thing that makes me happiest, is when I make Hector laugh.' He stopped, stared for a moment into his wine, then gulped it down, handing the cup to Orestes to refill it.

Orestes spoke carefully. He couldn't help these twinges of jealousy in his gut, couldn't control them. 'How does Hector feel?'

Epharon sighed. 'He told me he doesn't love me. Not like I want him to, he said. I don't know. Do you think he was just trying to protect me? I wondered if that was it. He does love me, but he wanted to keep us out of trouble.' He looked at Orestes hopefully. Orestes shrugged. 'Probably not. He's very . . . Spartan, Hector. The perfect Spartan. He believes this stuff about honour and duty in a way I never did.'

He paused, thoughtfully, as if noticing, as Orestes had, how already he was speaking of his time in the army as finished.

'No,' Epharon went on after a while. 'Hector sees me as . . . his sweet little friend. His childish friend with a nice tight arse and notorious skill as a cocksucker, but not someone he could ever really love.'

Orestes stared at him in the gathering darkness, unable to banish the image of Hector and this adorable boy copulating by the river. He felt awkward, callous, because he hoped Epharon was right: Hector didn't want someone like Epharon. He would want someone like himself, experienced, wise, as Ariadne had said.

Epharon shook his head again. 'It came at a terrible time, this.' He looked up. 'We'd just been told we were chosen for this special mission. Something to end the war, apparently.'

Orestes shifted on the bed where he was sitting. 'A mission?'

Epharon shrugged. 'Don't know what. Something glorious, which would mean we would have to be brave and therefore probably all die.'

'But they didn't tell you what the mission was.' Orestes tried to restrain his eagerness.

'No.' Epharon swung his legs around and lay on his back. Orestes looked down at him, and thought with some wonder that this was a body Hector had made love to so many times. He thought, Hector has sucked his cock; his mouth has tasted Hector's spunk. His arse has squirmed as Hector has entered him.

The thought of going where Hector had been began to fill his head. His cock twitched and grew, and he reached out a hand to touch Epharon on the face.

Epharon looked up at him, sleepily, and smiled. Orestes bent down to kiss him.

Epharon's mouth tasted of the Corinthian wine. Lazily, he pushed his tongue into the sweet mouth, and his hands pressed, trembling slightly, against Epharon's strong, lean chest. As they kissed, he stroked Epharon's hair, and gradually Epharon stroked him back, tickling the back of his neck, tenderly. The boy's touch was gentle, sensitive. Orestes' heart was pounding, as he thought of Hector's tongue in this very mouth, these fingers which had touched Hector. He groped, clumsily, for Epharon's groin, and found his cock, hard, beneath the cloth. Orestes tore at Epharon's tunic, pulling it aside so he could grasp the prize in his hand, the erection Hector had explored so often.

Shaking with desire, he sank his lips over Epharon's smooth cock, loving the strength in the boy's hips as he pushed up, allowing Orestes the pleasure of every vein, every atom of the warm, solid flesh. He swallowed it to the hilt, gasping, moaning, plunging his fingers between the crack of Epharon's buttocks, seeking out the arsehole Hector had fucked. There was little gentleness to Orestes' lust: he was frantic, desperate for perhaps a taste of Hector's sperm still dry on the young Spartan's skin.

He buried his head under Epharon's balls, felt their furry weight against his forehead, forcing his tongue down into the sweaty heat of his arse. He pushed Epharon's legs apart, hard, lifting him so he could find what he wanted, and plunged his tongue into the small, puckering arse ring. Maybe he could indeed taste Hector there, as he pressed his mouth closer. Epharon whimpered, slowly wanking himself as Orestes pushed harder with his tongue, licking deep into the arse, smelling so strongly of dirty sweat. He bit at the hairs around the arsehole, slobbering spit over them, gripping the lean thighs in his hands.

He returned to Epharon's satiny balls, massaging the muscle from his arse to his cock with his flat, rough tongue. The balls brushed against Orestes' face as Epharon wanked himself. Orestes took them both in his mouth at once, filling himself with these balls that Hector had sucked before him.

He pulled himself up, and looking down at Epharon's dreamy, sad face, his cock in his pummelling hand, his dark, sweet nipples, his neck muscles rigid with pleasure, Orestes pushed his cock against the delicate arse, and sank it into him. Epharon moaned, lifting his body, spreading his legs so Orestes could go in further. His eyes were closed tight: he was obviously thinking of Hector. And it was Hector Orestes thought of, too – Hector's cock, which had filled this tight, eager arse; Hector, who had looked down from this very position at this beautiful, yielding boy. He gripped Epharon's cock as he fucked him. And Epharon flailed his head from side to side, murmuring as if in a dream.

The young Spartan's cock hardened to its maximum in Orestes' hand, and disgorged its torrent of come. In spasms, Orestes came into his arse, his hips out of control, thrusting faster and faster. He felt for a moment as if he *were* Hector, fucking his comrade in the barracks, worshipping his comrade's oozing cock.

Orestes fell forward, and kissed Epharon again, his tongue he knew tasting of the boy's arse, a gift from a place Hector had been and might never go again. As they kissed, and their bodies ground together, Epharon's spunk sticky between them, they were both, quietly, crying.

He kissed Epharon's face. 'Are you all right?'

Epharon nodded. 'Oh, yes. Just broken another law, that's all. But what does it matter now?'

Eight

Hector rode down the hill, the moonlight on the road ahead, the lamps of the city in the distance. His cloak billowed about him as the horse sped at full gallop.

He wanted to make sure Epharon was all right. He wanted to be sure he wouldn't do anything stupid in the face of his dishonour. But it wasn't only that: Hector hated to admit it, and hated himself for his selfishness, but he thought perhaps the intriguing traveller from Syracuse would still be at his mother's house. He longed to see Orestes again.

He slowed to a canter as he approached the inn. The lamps were burning, and he could hear talking in the courtyard. He tethered his horse and went through the gate.

They were all three there, drinking in the cool evening, as well as the burly sailor, Nekos from Pylos, of whom his mother had spoken briefly. They all looked up when he entered, and greeted him one by one. His mother kissed him, Orestes shook his hand, and Epharon crushed him in a powerful embrace. The sailor merely grunted in acknowledgement.

Hector sat beside Epharon, taking his hand. 'You're all right, then.'

'I'm fine. Your mother's been taking care of me.'

Hector was glad. He smiled at Ariadne, who was plainly delighted he had come.

'But you'll get into trouble, Hector,' said Epharon. 'Slipping away from the barracks at night. What if the captain checks up on you?'

'He won't. And Gatha will cover for me. I had to know you were all right.' He glanced at Orestes, who was watching him closely.

Ariadne brought another carafe of Spartan wine, and poured them each a full cup.

'Orestes has been to Athens, you know,' said Epharon suddenly. Hector turned to look at the dark, mysterious traveller who was dominating so many of his thoughts.

'And so have I, you know,' said Nekos bluntly. 'Don't like the place, personally. But, then, I don't like many places.'

'What's Athens like?' Hector asked. He sensed Orestes' discomfort, and was anxious to reassure him. 'Don't worry. They're our enemy, not yours. You can speak freely.'

'I do like Athens.' Orestes was still hesitant.

'Tell us how they celebrate the Feast of Dionysus,' said Ariadne. Hector watched, intrigued, as Orestes looked at his mother.

'It's an extraordinary occasion in Athens.'

Hector leant forward. 'Go on.'

'A holiday, like everywhere. The Athenians hold a special festival. Of plays. The city's finest poets compete for a prize – in tragedy, comedy and satire. I've seen some wonderful plays.'

'Isn't it just a lot of men prancing around dressed as women?' Hector asked. He could see there was some passion in Orestes' face as he spoke, and in the strange, expressive gestures of his hands. It intrigued him even more.

'Oh, no,' said Orestes with heat. 'They're – these poets are the Homer and Hesiod of the modern world. Their dramas are about fundamental human truths. In the plays of Sophocles, for example – he takes a story we all know, the story of Oedipus, and he transforms it into a study of destiny and the fundamental tragedy of humankind.'

'Which is what?' asked Hector.

'That we don't control our fate. The gods do.'

Hector glanced at Epharon, wondering which gods had decided such a cruel fate for him. 'Do you believe that?' He stared into Orestes' eyes. 'That nothing we do can change the gods' intentions?'

Orestes took a breath, and smiled at Hector. His smile was gentle and thoughtful, like everything about him. 'I think we're all on some path. We have to do what we can to make it our *own* path. But I believe in the gods. Don't you?'

'Of course.' Hector looked down. 'I think they're cruel and hurtful, and laughing at us.'

Orestes nodded, still smiling. 'Maybe you're right.'

'Tell us something else about Athens,' said Epharon. 'Is it true that the whole city makes all its decisions?'

'Almost,' said Orestes. Hector's pulse quickened again, as he noticed how long it took the visitor to tear his eyes from him and look at Epharon. 'There's an Assembly of all citizens which votes on everything of importance.'

'Isn't that a bit unwieldy?' Hector asked, pleased when Orestes turned back to him.

Orestes shook his head. 'I don't think it is, no. I think the reason the Athenians have done so many extraordinary things – their poetry, their architecture, their sculpture – is because of it.'

'And these things.' Hector leant closer. 'They're important, are they? Songs and buildings and bits of carved stone. They make the Athenians great?'

'And philosophy.'

'What's that?'

'What we're doing now. Thinking.'

Hector grinned. 'So I'm a philosopher. What do you say to that, Eph?' He glanced over at Epharon, who was visibly relieved to be included in this conversation, and laughed. 'But thinking doesn't protect a city from its enemies. The Athenians didn't *think* the Persian fleet into the sea, all those years ago. They rammed them with ships.'

Orestes held Hector's gaze, and it thrilled him, sent shivers of excitement through him. 'But surely, the point of sinking the Persian fleet was so Greece could be free.'

Hector raised his eyebrows. 'So the three hundred Spartans who sacrificed themselves at Thermopylae, giving the Athenians the time to prepare their fleet – what did they die for?'

The question seemed to throw Orestes, or perhaps he was only worried he had gone too far, and Hector was offended.

'I'm sure,' said Hector, 'that they didn't die so the Athenians would be able to think.' Epharon laughed. Hector grinned at him, seeing in his friend's bright eyes that urgent need to please him which was always there.

'No,' said Orestes eventually. 'But they died for some idea of freedom. Didn't they?' Hector shrugged. 'So it's a question of deciding what freedom means to you. I think . . .' He hesitated again, checking Hector's face for a reaction. 'I think the plays and endless arguments and all the stuff you Spartans seem to hate about Athens – they are part of it. The world would be . . . diminished without them.'

'He wants you to lose the war – that's what that means,' Nekos pointed out. Hector had forgotten he was there, and looked over at him, slightly shocked. He turned back to Orestes.

'Is that what you mean?'

Orestes sat back. 'That's none of my business.'

'But is it what you meant?'

The traveller blinked at Hector, silently. Hector suddenly understood that there seemed to be some strange battle taking place behind those soft, dark eyes. It was as if he didn't know the answer to the question, and had only just realised this himself.

Orestes took a deep breath. 'I don't want to see Athens razed to the ground, and everything she has ever given the world burnt from the face of history. No.'

'But if it's the other way.' Hector looked at Orestes' face. In the light of the lamps there was something almost transparent about him, something ghostly. He glanced down with a thrill at the lean thighs which disappeared under his tunic, and for a moment lost his train of thought, imagining the destination of those thighs with their dark hair. 'If it's the other way, and the

Athenians win, they'll destroy us, raze this city to the ground. And we don't have much the world would miss. Am I right? No poets. No beautiful buildings. No strange and complex thoughts. We're just a bunch of soldiers.'

Hector hadn't intended to sound so hard. He wanted to cross to Orestes and brush back his hair, to tell him it didn't matter what he thought, that he was beautiful and mysterious and fascinating, and, even if he wanted Sparta destroyed for ever, he would forgive him. He swallowed, silently, not sure what to say next.

'Why do you think the Athenians want to do that?' said Orestes cautiously. 'Maybe they just want to know they can sleep safely in their beds.'

'Of course they want to destroy Sparta,' grunted Nekos. 'I know a bit about Athens myself.' Hector looked over at him. 'Been there a few times. Met a lot of Athenian merchants. And I'll tell you two things about Athenians. They can argue you to death, and they think the rest of the world are scum.'

'That's not true,' Orestes protested.

'Oh yes it is,' said Nekos. 'Athenians will talk to you for one reason: if they think they can sell you something. It's all very well, this philosophy stuff, but if you're not from Athens and there are a few clever ideas in your head they won't even listen to you.'

Hector could see this was making Orestes angry. He wondered why it mattered to him so much, a traveller from Syracuse, at the other end of the sea. Orestes was shaking his head vigorously. 'There are plenty of great philosophers from outside Athens, even as far away as Thrace, whose ideas are taken seriously in Attica.'

'Yes, well. I wouldn't trust an Athenian with his mother's life. Seems that the Spartans are quite right to be afraid of them.'

'We're not afraid of them,' said Hector and Epharon in unison.

'Of course you're afraid of them,' retorted Nekos. 'You make a big deal out of how weak and effeminate Athenians are, but know perfectly well it isn't true, or you would have beaten them years ago. Fact is, they're every bit as warlike and dangerous as

Spartans, It's just that more of them can read. Take my advice. Don't listen to a word of this rubbish about how much Athenians love the freedom to think and all that. They might be pretty protective about their own freedoms. But they see you as a permanent, awful threat. And, if they can wipe out every last Spartan hoplite, believe me they will. It's dog eat dog, this war, and the only way it will end is when one city or the other is just ashes and a few memories.' The sailor stood, and clapped his hands together. 'I'm off to bed.' He turned and walked away.

Ariadne poured more wine. 'A rather disagreeable man, isn't he?'

'And he's wrong,' insisted Orestes, still agitated by the discussion.

Hector smiled at him. 'Why does it matter to you?'

Orestes shrugged, looking away.

Hector tore his eyes from Orestes and turned to Epharon. 'I hope Eph's not being too much trouble,' he said to his mother.

She smiled at Epharon maternally. 'Any friend of yours, Hector . . .'

'What are you going to do, Eph?'

Epharon looked at him, as if a little startled. 'I thought maybe I could travel the world, like Orestes.' He grinned, trying to be brave.

Ariadne leant over and tapped Epharon's knee. 'He's going to rest here for a while.'

Hector took his friend's hands tightly in his. 'The lads all sent their good wishes. I'm going to talk to Pausanius. There might be a way to change his mind.'

Epharon scoffed. 'I don't think so, Hector.'

'Just be brave. It'll be all right.' Hector glanced back at Orestes. The foreigner's eyes were burning into him. He didn't want to go. He wanted to stay, sink into Orestes' arms and fall into his bed. But it was late, he was in deep enough water already; and to do that with an outsider was a far worse disgrace than what Epharon had done. He offered his hand, and Orestes stood to shake it.

They squeezed each other's hand, tightly.

'Thank you for an interesting discussion,' said Hector.

'Thank you.'

Hector didn't want to let go. As their eyes remained firmly fixed on each other's, his cock swelled eagerly, and he had to take a sudden breath. He laughed to cover his excitement, and glanced down at Epharon.

Epharon knew what was happening: he had seen the look in Hector's eyes. He seemed so utterly sad, and there was nothing Hector could do about it. Epharon smiled, forgivingly, as Hector removed his hand from Orestes'.

'I'll see you all soon.' He kissed his mother, and walked from the courtyard to untether his horse.

On the way back, Hector had to stop. He climbed from his horse, thinking of Orestes' sultry, mysterious eyes. The memory of his voice alone was a deep erotic charge, which thrilled him to the pit of his stomach. He gripped his aching hard-on and briskly stroked it, imagined kissing those moist, forbidden lips; in the throes of his fantasy he heard Orestes whispering sweet, tender words into his ear – and he shot come into the air, a fountain of milky fluid glinting in the moonlight, decorating the earth at his feet. He fell to his knees for a moment, panting, his head spinning.

Then he leapt back on his horse and quickly rode on, worried by the late hour.

There was something he could do for Epharon. It was a terrible risk, and if it went badly would make everything worse. But the sadness in his friend's generous face when he recognised Hector's desire for Orestes had made him determined to try.

Nine

The following morning, Orestes was woken by Cleomenes. He stirred in his sleep as rough lips smothered his cock, and awoke to find the Spartan sucking him eagerly. For a while, Orestes lay in half-sleep, enjoying the hard pressure of Cleomenes' mouth. He thought of reaching out and grabbing Cleomenes' cock, but decided just to lie there and let the Spartan officer bring him to orgasm, thirstily drink his sperm. Then Orestes watched Cleomenes stand by the side of the bed, his face a grimace of lechery, until he rained down globules of spunk on Orestes' body.

'Hoo! Needed that!' exclaimed Cleomenes, tugging Orestes off the bed. 'Come on. Got a treat for you.'

They mounted their horses in the street, and rode from the city up to the hills. It was close, the sun hazy in a white sky. Even riding, Orestes was sweating. Hot sticky moisture clung to his legs and the flanks of his horse.

'Thought you'd like to see some soldiers training,' Cleomenes explained suddenly, galloping beside him, as if he had intended this to be a surprise but was bad at keeping secrets.

Orestes glanced over, unsure why Cleomenes would want to show him their army preparing for combat. He galloped after him to the top of a hill, where Cleomenes had stopped, and was looking down at the valley beyond, his face bright with pride.

When he saw the ranks of young warriors engaged in their various pursuits, he understood why Cleomenes was eager to impress him. It was, indeed, a remarkable sight. In this camp – and Orestes was sure there were others in the neighbouring valleys – there were perhaps a couple of thousand Spartan hoplites, most of them naked, testing their skills and strength. It took Orestes' breath away.

On one side of the plain, naked athletes tossed javelins and discuses. Nearby, pairs of soldiers practised their swordplay, their polished shields dazzling in the sun. To the left, young Spartans wrestled with each other, their bodies shining with oil, and groups of barefoot hoplites raced in a relay around a circle marked out by wooden posts. It was like the Games in Olympia, but with a different atmosphere entirely: the Games were a kind of holiday, competitive but full of the sound of cheers and laughter. This place had a grim, businesslike air: there was no applause, no exhortations to success, only the grunting effort of men who knew they might die. And it was so unlike his own gymnasium in Athens, where, between the athletics, pockets of men discussed politics or ethics. Orestes sat on his horse beside Cleomenes and stared in wonder.

Cleomenes rode down the hill a little, and Orestes trotted after him. As they drew closer, he could see the concentration on soldiers' faces, the hard, determined grimaces as they wrestled and fought and perfected their martial skills. He could see their lean, powerful bodies in detail. For a moment, he watched two sturdy hoplites wrestle, the thick, muscular arms of one seize his opponent – a shorter youth, with a neck like a pillar – under the groin, and lift him into the air. Their oiled bodies slipped against each other; Orestes' eyes were drawn to the moist, dewy prick of the shorter one, sliding against the arm of his comrade, as he was deposited into the dust. He climbed to his feet, earth sticking to the ointments on his limbs, and hurled himself forward, grasping the other around the waist.

'Aren't we magnificent?' said Cleomenes, with no trace of humour.

'Absolutely,' Orestes agreed.

Cleomenes stood in his stirrups, and called over to a man who seemed to be an officer, unlike the hoplites clothed in light, polished armour. He stepped forward and saluted, standing to attention.

'At ease, Captain.' Cleomenes turned to Orestes. 'Captain Pausanius, this is Orestes, a visitor from Syracuse. I thought we should show him how great a military force we Spartans are.'

The captain nodded, but he looked at Orestes suspiciously. Orestes recognised his name. This, of course, was Hector's captain, the one he so clearly lusted after. He could see why: Pausanius was a strong, charismatic man, with the aura of a ferocious warrior. But shivers of jealousy passed through Orestes as he gazed down at the man he saw as his rival and his enemy.

Cleomenes got down from his horse, and beckoned for Orestes to follow. They walked with Pausanius across the field, past more wrestlers, and a group of soldiers in full armour, fighting each other with swords and shields. The noise was fearsome – the clash of iron on iron, the battle wails of the practising soldiers.

'Do people ever get killed?' he asked Cleomenes.

'Sometimes. Wounded, more often. It's part of the training to be able not to kill. When men first join the army, of course, their swords are wooden. These here are experienced fighters: they know how to use their weapons. This practice is to keep them in shape.'

Orestes nodded, noticing the further suspicious glance Pausanius shot him. 'Perhaps,' said the captain, 'our guest has a particular preference. Some aspect of our routine he would especially like to see.'

The comment was shot through with insinuation, and Orestes thought, of course, of the sexual athletics that would come later; his eyes rested on two beautiful young Spartans parrying each other's sword, and swinging their muscular weight into each other's shield, and his pulse quickened a little.

108

They passed the sword fighters, and reached the circle of runners. A race was just being prepared: about twenty soldiers grouped together across the field, waiting for the sign to begin.

To his delight, Orestes saw Hector among them.

Hector was naked, now, too far away to observe closely, but even from this distance his body was everything Orestes had dreamt about. He was rubbing chalk into his bare feet, bending down so the sun caught the oil, shining on his wide, smooth back. His chest had little speckles of hair around the nipples, and his stomach was flat and ribbed with muscles. The tiniest curls of flesh made wrinkles as he bent forward, then vanished as he straightened his body and focused on the race ahead. He hadn't seen Orestes: he was absorbed in his task, concentrating hard on limbering his body. Orestes watched, captivated, as he shook his arms and legs to loosen them, and the dark shape of his cock wriggled between his thighs.

Abruptly, as if at a command, although Orestes heard none, the racers were off. They charged at great speed around the circle, passing the wooden markers. Hector was indeed very fast: he was soon outstripping his rivals, hurtling towards the home stretch within sight of easy victory.

Then he was running face on to Orestes, and saw him. The surprise, the lapse in his concentration, was instantly clear: he slowed, perceptibly, amazed to see Orestes there. And it gave another runner the chance to overtake him. Hector quickly recovered his composure and pressed on, but the ground he had lost cost him the race.

There was no applause at the end. The athletes merely moved on to their next activity. Orestes turned, and saw the hostility and doubt in Pausanius's face.

'That soldier seemed to know you,' he said to Orestes, narrowing his eyes.

Orestes knew that Hector's visits to his mother's inn were not permitted, and he was afraid of causing Hector any trouble. 'No, Captain. I don't think so.'

Pausanius continued to stare at him.

Cleomenes clapped Orestes firmly on the back. 'Probably

thought he'd seen some vision and for a moment forgot he was racing,' he chortled. Then he turned to Pausanius, more sternly. 'Warn your young sprinter to keep his mind off beautiful strangers when he's running,' he said.

'Yes, sir.'

Cleomenes clearly found the whole thing amusing, however, and they walked on. Orestes followed Hector with his eyes as he prepared to wrestle a short, stocky man with a beard. Hector glanced back at him, secretively, then threw himself at his opponent. He was trying to impress Orestes, obviously, especially after losing the race. And Orestes couldn't help staring at Hector's clenched, naked buttocks as he strained to topple his sturdy partner. They walked quite close, and Orestes for the first time got a clear view of Hector's long, flaccid but thick cock, his balls hanging loose in the heat.

Cleomenes took him by the arm. 'Don't get too excited, Orestes,' he whispered, seriously. 'It is quite forbidden for hoplites to screw around with outsiders. That's one Spartan dick you'll never taste.'

Orestes gave him a look, feigning incomprehension, and Cleomenes laughed, and thumped him on the back.

'Although I must say,' the Spartan added, 'it looked delicious.'

Later, returning to the horses, Orestes had a lot of questions. 'So the prohibition is against rank-and-file soldiers and outsiders. Officers seem to have the opposite requirement.'

'Yes,' said Cleomenes simply, evidently seeing no contradiction.

'It doesn't strengthen the manhood of a hoplite to swallow a foreigner's sperm, then.'

'No.' Cleomenes swung on to his horse. Orestes hesitated for a moment, then climbed up on to his own. 'It's a matter of blood,' Cleomenes explained. 'Hoplites are of the common stock.'

They rode up the hill together.

'And what would happen to a hoplite who broke this rule?' Orestes asked.

Cleomenes shrugged. 'Banishment.'

Orestes was silent for a while as the rode back towards the city. Eventually, he risked the question he wanted to ask. 'I'm a stranger, Cleomenes. I don't mean to be rude, or critical. But it seems very . . . It's difficult to understand why there's one rule for the ordinary soldiers, and the exact opposite for their commanders.'

Their horses trotted slowly down the dusty road.

'Not all commanders.' Cleomenes turned to him. 'For commoners, the magic of foreign sperm would be too powerful. It might corrupt them, rot away at their manliness from within. Their own blood does not have the potency to resist. But for us, old, powerful families with strong, ancient blood, there is no danger of contamination. Instead, we absorb its magic. Incorporate it. Conquer and devour it.'

'I see.'

Cleomenes laughed. 'You don't see.' He kicked his horse's flanks and rode ahead. After a moment, Orestes raced after him.

Hector stood in the doorway of Pausanius's hut, and looked into the shade. The captain was sitting at his table, a flagon of wine beside him, in darkness, cloths pulled over the windows to keep out the sunlight.

'You wanted to see me, sir.'

Pausanius looked at him with undisguised longing, and Hector walked in. He pulled the wooden door behind him. It was the middle of the afternoon, and the air was thick with moisture.

He stood facing the captain, who gazed at him, drinking his wine. He was plainly quite drunk; his eyes were red, the blinking more exaggerated than usual.

'Today, Cleomenes brought a visitor to the practice. You seemed to know him.'

'No, sir.'

'When you saw him, you faltered and lost the race.'

Hector stared at him, thoughtfully. 'No, sir. I felt something sharp against my foot. And my comrade was very fast today.'

Pausanius regarded him carefully.

'Anyway, sir. How would I have known him?'

'I don't know.'

Hector took a deep breath. 'Actually, sir, I wanted to talk to you, anyway.' Pausanius scowled at him, unhappily. 'It's about Epharon, sir.'

'That matter is closed.'

Hector braced himself; he tightened his hands into fists. 'What you did wasn't fair, Captain.'

'No? And who are you to judge my decisions?'

Hector hesitated. He was very nervous. He had been in battle many times, won prizes for bravery. But this was the most dangerous thing he had ever done. 'What would it take, sir, to make you reverse your decision?'

Pausanius blinked at him cautiously. 'What are you suggesting, Hector?'

He looked into Pausanius's eyes. Pausanius knew what he was suggesting, and his face was flushing slightly – with lust, not embarrassment. Hector took a deep breath, and spoke with the clearest confidence. 'I am suggesting, sir, a terrible sin.'

The room was hot and silent, as Pausanius stared at him. He licked his lips, and glugged another mouthful of the wine.

Hector took another breath. 'I'll give you what you want, sir,' he said, softly. 'We don't have to tell anyone. But, in return, you recall Epharon to service.'

Pausanius looked at him from under heavy eyelids, his face burning with lechery. Hector could see that the captain was trembling slightly. 'You love your little comrade that much, then?'

'As a comrade.'

'To sell your soul to the Fates.'

'I think the Fates already own it. Sir.'

'I see. And you think I'm prepared to do the same. To risk the most terrible ignominy for the sake of one hour of your arse.'

Hector stared at him, and decided he had to act immediately. He pulled his tunic over his head and revealed his nakedness to Pausanius. He had no erection; in fact his cock was shrivelled with fear, his balls were tight as if in the coldest winter's night. But Pausanius gazed at him with the most unbridled, heartbroken lust, as Hector knew he would.

The captain slowly stood from his table and stepped around it. He came close to Hector, and bent into his face. His breath smelt strongly of rough wine. His eyes were shining with a layer of tears.

Hector stood quite still as Pausanius walked around him. He listened to the soft tread of his sandals on the earth floor. He could hear the captain's breathing. He stared ahead, feeling eyes burn hungrily into his back.

Then Pausanius faced him again. He swallowed loudly, his desire taking control of him.

After a moment, the captain looked hard into Hector's eyes, with a faint glimmer of hatred. But his eyes wandered down Hector's body, and Hector trembled. He was afraid. But he stayed perfectly still, and waited for Pausanius to speak. The captain was struggling with desire, and Hector was ashamed. He hated this. But he had no choice.

'You realise, Hector . . .' Pausanius's voice was shaking and little more than a whisper. 'You realise that it will not be enough if you simply . . . give yourself. Like a prize of war. Like a conquered woman, lying there, silently, waiting for the torture to stop. That won't be enough.'

Hector looked into his eyes. His heart was racing, but there was no stirring in his loins. Pausanius's mouth twitched with agonised desire.

He pressed a hand against Hector's naked, trembling chest, and ran it down to his stomach, stopping just short of his dick. The captain's lust was like heat in his rough touch. Pausanius bent slowly forward, and put his lips to Hector's neck. Hector closed his eyes, as the captain's tongue grazed against his throat, as the hand moved down from his stomach and caressed his pubic hair, brushed almost imperceptibly against his cock.

Pausanius lifted his face, and slowly kissed Hector's lips. Hector responded, opening his mouth, allowing the captain's tongue to slip inside. He tasted the wine on his breath. Pausanius pressed his mouth against Hector's ear, and whispered, hotly.

'You have to beg me, Hector. Beg for my cock. Beg for it in your mouth, wail with pleasure when I thrust it into your arse, plead with me not to stop.' In a voice full of pain, Pausanius ploughed on, the lust like treacle on his tongue: 'To treat my cock like it's the most glorious prize, to worship it, adore it, suck it like a Thracian whore. I want you to squirm for me, spread your legs as wide as they will go and scream with the basest lust when I fuck your tight little arse.'

It was working: Hector was forgetting his fear, and remembering how much he did indeed want his captain. The sheer helplessness of Pausanius's surrender to depravity was sending tremors of excitement through him. His cock was rising, hardening in tingling anticipation. His heart was pounding, as Pausanius bent forward to bite his stiff, sensitive nipple. Hector swallowed, hard.

Pausanius's voice was a lascivious murmur. 'How badly do you want to feast on my cock, Hector?'

'I want your cock, sir,' Hector whispered. 'I want your thick, warrior's cock.'

'What do you want to do with it, soldier?'

Hector was overcome with urgent excitement. He clenched his fists. 'I want to worship it,' Hector gasped, shivering. 'Suck it, hard, feel it in my mouth . . .'

Pausanius looked down at Hector's hard-on, and inhaled, shaking. He snarled, and ripped off his tunic. And there was his naked body, broad chest with a layer of hair over the defined, powerful flesh. Rising from the thick, dark mane of his groin was his cock. Hector gasped with amazement. It was a huge, fat, solid shaft of throbbing muscle and bulging veins, dripping with the juices of desire, so heavy it was incredible it could stand as erect as this; his balls were big and round, curls of black hair covering them like fur. His wide, solid thighs were trembling, his knees were shaking. The enormous cock, like a ferocious weapon of war, flexed, stretching yet harder. Hector gazed at it, transfixed, his own dick swelling in craving. The disgrace of this moment, even the purpose of it, seemed nothing. He was here, with Pausanius, gazing at the splendour of the war hero's incredible club of a cock, and suddenly everything else was forgotten. He gasped again, and gazed hungrily into Pausanius's face, twisted with wanton yearning.

'Suck it,' Pausanius hissed into Hector's ear. 'Suck it now.'

Hector slowly dropped to his knees. The captain towered above him. His cock loomed over Hector's face like a greedy, lunging hydra. Aggressively, his legs apart, the captain grabbed Hector's head. 'Suck it now.'

Hector seized Pausanius's weapon in one hand, tightening his fingers under the swollen, purple head. It was like a wonderful beast which oozed pre-come over Hector's fist. He let go, and it sprang against his face. He touched the shaft with the tip of his tongue, licking slowly up towards the tip, eased back the foreskin, and slowly wiped his lips over the head. By all the gods, he wanted this cock with feverish lust. Pausanius gasped; his knees shook uncontrollably.

This wasn't just for Epharon. This was because he had dreamt of this moment for a long time, the moment when he would sink his lips over his captain's cock, forget honour, forget disgrace, forget everything. Just gorge his soul on this marvellous hunk of throbbing muscle. It was more than he had dreamt of, bigger and fatter and more wonderful than he could ever have hoped.

Through gritted teeth, the captain demanded, 'How much do you want my cock, Hector?'

Hector moaned, mesmerised by the glorious thing before his face. 'Oh, I want your cock,' he whispered. 'I want to suck it, suck . . .' He bent forward, pulling the captain's hard, moist shaft down to meet his lips, and opened his mouth. He was panting with desire, his mouth stretching to encompass the monster he was about to taste.

Then he sank his lips down over it. It filled his mouth. As he forced his way down the warm, heavy shaft, it beat hard against the back of his throat, and he gagged, but kept on sucking. He reached up with one hand and seized Pausanius's heavy, rocking balls. His own cock was flexing and straining with urgent passion; he could feel his arsehole puckering in terrified anticipation of receiving the monster that now engorged his mouth. He gasped, moaned, twisted his head around Pausanius's dick. The captain gripped him by the neck, ferociously guiding him up and down the shaft, around the huge bulging head. Pausanius could hardly stand from shaking with excitement.

'Worship my cock!' he whispered. Hector's chest was heaving with lust. Dribbles of pre-come were oozing from his own, stiff, throbbing dick.

Grasping both hands around Pausanius's fat shaft, Hector buried his head under the huge, hairy balls. The monster cock rose above him, hot and wet in his trembling hands, as he slobbered deliriously over the tight, tough scrotum. Then he rammed the cock back, deep into his throat, grunting.

'Do you want me to fuck you, soldier?'

Hector withdrew his mouth and stared, breathing hard at the beast that would penetrate him. 'Fuck me, Captain,' he murmured. 'Fuck me into oblivion . . .'

Effortlessly, Pausanius lifted him on to the table, throwing him down on to his back. Hardly able to contain his urgent passion, he forced Hector's legs aside, and pressed the head of his cock against the hoplite's arsehole. A thrill of tremulous excitement coursed through Hector's body; every muscle in his chest tightened in lustful preparation, as Pausanius smeared fistfuls of spit against his tender, twitching arsehole, and then, slowly eased his cock inside.

Hector shouted with ecstatic pain as the monster slipped against his prostate, and briefly Pausanius covered his mouth to quieten him. Hector lifted his legs apart, and pushed hard against the weapon that was impaling him. It filled him, as if it would pass through his arse into his stomach and out through his mouth, and he moaned with unrepressed carnal pleasure.

'Fuck me,' he whispered as the captain bent close to kiss his face. 'Do it. Fuck me hard.' He felt the monster flex inside him, and then start to pump. It was agony, exquisite, delicious agony. His own cock was rigid like a piece of thick, hard leather, slapping against his stomach as the captain ravished his arse. Pausanius seized Hector's dick in his hand, squeezing it, yanking down the foreskin, wanking it dementedly as he sank deeper and faster into him, biting his neck, kissing his ear. His voice was guttural and frantic.

'Feel my hard cock inside you, Hector. Beg me not to stop.'

Hector's balls bashed painfully against the captain's stomach as Pausanius wanked him, mercilessly, impaling him like a trapped animal with his enormous cock. He felt the weapon swell to its hardest, firmest size, and then hot spunk emptied into his rectum, as the captain groaned and bit into his neck.

Sobbing with desire, Pausanius pulled his dick from Hector's arse and fell, desperately, on his cock, taking it deep into his mouth. The tables were suddenly turned, and it was Hector who was master: he wrapped his legs around the captain's back, as Pausanius helplessly slavered over Hector's stiff, taut dick, until the young soldier began to spasm: he emptied his balls into Pausanius's throat, spurt after uncontrollable spurt, as the captain squeezed the base of his cock with his lips and drank every drop he had to give. Even when Hector was spent, Pausanius kept his mouth glued to the raw, slippery dick, as if he would never let go.

Eventually, Pausanius stood, and stepped back. Hector lay with his eyes closed, waiting for his heartbeat to slow and his breathing to return to normal. His arse was horribly sore, his insides stretched, the entrance stinging; he wondered if he had been made to bleed.

When he looked up, Pausanius was staring at his sweat-drenched body with an expression of painful sadness.

'What have you done to me, Hector?'

Hector sat up, and looked into Pausanius's eyes. He was nervous again now, but this was what he had come here to do. 'You have to recall Epharon to the army, or I will tell everyone.'

'You're a monster,' said Pausanius, the horror of what they had done only now, it seemed, fully dawning on him.

'I'm Epharon's friend.'

Pausanius choked back a sob.

Hector wished with all his heart this moment was not as it was. He was ashamed. He had told himself his motives were pure, for Epharon's sake alone. But he had satiated himself on Pausanius; every moment of that incredible, brutal fuck had been the purest lascivious pleasure for himself. Even the pain in his arse was part of the exquisite torture. But there was no tuning back now, and the matter of Epharon remained to be resolved. 'The disgrace would be for me, also,' Hector reminded his captain. 'But I'm prepared to take my chances with the gods.'

Pausanius looked at him, desperately, and spoke in a breathless monotone. 'You won't breathe a word, if I just recall Epharon to service.'

'That's right.'

In haste, and anger, Pausanius thrust his arms into his tunic, pulling it over his head. 'Where is he?'

'He's at my mother's.'

Pausanius crossed the room and sat in his chair. He poured himself a cup of wine with trembling fingers. 'And you won't say anything.'

Hector lifted his tunic off the floor. 'Of course not. But understand this, Captain. If you don't do as I say, I will sacrifice myself.'

Slowly, Pausanius nodded. He gazed at Hector's still naked body wistfully. 'Go, then. You have leave to go to your mother's house and tell Epharon the good news.' There was no humour in his face, just pain and the first twinges of renewed lust. He stared longingly at Hector's cock, which was still quite hard, still slick from the captain's spit, a drip of spunk still leaking from the bloated head.

'Thank you, Captain.'

Hector slipped his tunic over his shoulders and walked out into the afternoon heat. As he left, he could hear Pausanius softly weeping.

Ten

———

Orestes was alone in Cleomenes' house. The Spartan had told him to make himself at home, and he would be back shortly. Later they were saying prayers for the Festival of Dionysus, which began the following evening, and he had invited Orestes to join him in the temple. Now, Orestes found himself alone, as even the slaves were outside in the courtyard preparing the decorations for the Feast.

Or not quite alone. Orestes noticed, across the room, an elderly man in a plain robe, arranging papers in boxes. He wandered across and watched him.

The man looked up. 'Can I help you, sir?'

By his appearance, and the cheapness of his clothing, it was clear the man was a slave. He was about fifty, with a greying beard. Orestes imagined he must have been in the family's service all his life. But this was plainly no manual slave, given the task of drawing water from the well, or sweeping the floor. The man had an intelligent face, and his hands were not roughened from labour.

'We haven't met before,' said Orestes.

'No, I don't think we have.'

Orestes laughed. 'Who are you?'

'I am Theddalus, slave to the family of this house.'

Orestes looked pointedly at the boxes, intrigued. 'What are you doing?'

Theddalus stood, putting a box on the floor. 'I'm arranging documents for my master.'

'Oh, you're a scribe.'

'Indeed.'

The was a certain arrogance to the man's tone which, while quite unbefitting a slave, Orestes found oddly charming. He wanted to know more about him. 'Where were you born, Theddalus? How did you end up here, a slave in Sparta?'

Theddalus looked searchingly at Orestes, as if slightly irritated. It was hard to imagine such a slave getting on well with a man like Cleomenes.

'I was born in Messenia. And where are you from, if I may ask?'

'Syracuse. You're a Messenian?'

'As I said.'

Orestes was intrigued. 'Your people have been enslaved by the Spartans for generations.'

Theddalus turned his face slightly, once more apparently irritated. 'That is correct. Long ago the Spartans reduced my people to the status, as they say, of helots. Slaves, if you prefer.'

'It must be a terrible thing,' observed Orestes.

'I'm sure you have slaves in Syracuse. Have you ever asked them how they feel?'

Orestes laughed. 'I imagined most helots were out planting crops in the fields or . . . were not scribes, anyway.'

'Nevertheless, I am appreciated for my skill at writing.' Theddalus picked up a couple of boxes and made as if to leave. Orestes glanced behind him, but stayed where he was. 'Will there be anything more, sir?'

'Yes,' said Orestes. 'I'd like to know what you think about the war with Athens.'

Theddalus looked at him with a pained expression. 'It is nothing to do with me.'

'Oh come, now. Surely it would benefit you and the rest of your people considerably if Sparta were to lose.' He looked carefully into Theddalus's eyes. Slaves were unpredictable. Some of them could be fiercely loyal to their masters against all common sense; others would seize any opportunity to murder them in their beds. He wondered which category this proud man fell into.

'Perhaps,' said Theddalus cautiously. 'But, then, perhaps the Athenians would enslave us instead.'

Orestes took Theddalus by the arm, as if leading him into a quieter place. The slave bristled slightly, perhaps not liking to be touched. 'Imagine –' Orestes frowned, trying to phrase his question as carefully as he could. 'Imagine you knew, from your work for your master, about something important.'

Theddalus looked at him, puzzled.

'Just imagine. And suppose in return for what you knew the Athenians were to offer you . . . something. Suppose they offered you your freedom. Or . . . guarantees that your people would not be enslaved again. Should Sparta fall. Should her power in the region be . . . eliminated. What would you say?'

The slave looked down at the boxes in his hand, then firmly into Orestes' eyes. 'I would first, I think, want guarantees that I was not being tricked into saying something foolish.'

Orestes let go of his arm. 'Of course. And likewise, I suppose, anyone making such an offer would want to be sure they could trust you.'

'Yes, I suppose they would.'

Orestes nodded. He wasn't sure he could go any further with this man. 'Thank you for your time, Theddalus. I should let you get back to your work.'

He was about to turn away. But Theddalus stopped him, with a tone in his voice of some urgency. 'I would certainly think about it, however.'

Orestes looked back at him. He had to be very careful. If Theddalus was loyal to Cleomenes, he could betray him as a spy if he gave any more away. But he was here to find information, and maybe this was the perfect opportunity, a slave who might hate his masters, but who might be privy to their plans, a scribe innocently recording secret discussions. It was possible.

'In the first place,' Theddalus went on, 'I would suggest to any Athenian interested in what I might know that I was doubtful as to their . . . promises. I would advise him to look under his own nose for whatever dangers his city and his people might face.'

'What do you mean?'

'If I was an Athenian, rather than a Messenian slave, I would take care that my own people all felt as certainly as I did that Sparta was the enemy.'

'I don't understand.' Orestes was looking at him, eagerly, unable to contain his interest.

But Theddalus was still highly suspicious. 'It's not so hard to understand, sir. And I am speaking hypothetically, of course. But an Athenian might, as you have done, assume that he has potential allies in Sparta. I mean people who, you might think, have an interest in the . . . fall of the oligarchs. People with a grudge. Slaves, say. But then I would wonder. I would ask myself, if I was this Athenian: perhaps the Spartans have allies they can count on in Athens. Citizens of Attica who look to Sparta and its ways with more . . . admiration than the rest of their countrymen.'

Orestes stared at him. 'And suppose – just suppose – this was less hypothetical on your part. Might you be in a position to provide details?'

'Of course it is purely hypothetical, sir. But were I in a position to provide details – should I know any details, perhaps as a result of intimate knowledge of my master's affairs – that of course would depend on these guarantees of which have already spoken. I would need to know, in this amusing and imaginary situation, that whoever was offering me some reward for my intelligence had the authority to give it.'

'Yes, of course. Thank you. This has been most interesting.'

Theddalus nodded, but he was clearly waiting for Orestes to go on.

'Perhaps we could continue this diverting discussion another time,' Orestes suggested. .

'That might be most rewarding, sir, for both of us, I hope.

Good day to you.' He walked away, clasping the boxes to his chest.

Orestes crossed the room and sat down on an uncomfortable Spartan chair. He was excited, but not sure how to proceed. Of course, he did not have the authority to offer freedom to an entire people of slaves in the event of a quick Athenian victory. He probably could guarantee this particular slave's freedom, if only by buying Theddalus himself and then setting him free, which he could do immediately if Cleomenes would agree a price. But he still didn't know how trustworthy Theddalus was. He couldn't spend a fortune buying him, only to find he knew nothing of any importance. It was unlikely, in any case, that Cleomenes would be prepared to sell so educated a slave, and one no doubt so hard to replace, especially if he possessed secret and valuable information. Yet he couldn't push further with his questions, or make a definite proposal, without giving himself away completely and running the risk of betrayal. It was deeply frustrating, perhaps to be so close to something yet so limited in courses of action.

Soon afterwards, Cleomenes arrived back at the house. He greeted Orestes with his familiar firm handshake, and announced he had arranged a visit with a friend of his whom he was sure Orestes would find fascinating.

They walked a short distance to the house of a man called Eumaneus. He was plump, in his forties, with the manner and clothing of a wealthy merchant, a rare breed, it seemed, in this austere city. He welcomed Orestes with a fleshy squeeze of his hand, and took them into his living chamber. It was quite unlike anywhere Orestes had previously visited in Sparta: relatively lavish in its design, with comfortable cushions to sit on, and shady little palm trees around the room; sunlight beamed in through an open ceiling.

Orestes soon realised that his host wasn't Spartan. He was Etruscan in origin, from Italy, although he spoke perfect Greek. He had chosen many years ago to live in this city, but he had houses elsewhere, including one, he announced proudly, in

Syracuse. Orestes was relieved to find that he apparently spent little time there, however, and none of his questions was too probing. It had been some years since Orestes himself had lived in Syracuse, and anyone familiar with the city might soon have doubted his honesty. But Eumaneus seemed pleased to talk only about places they had visited; he was anxious, indeed, to impress him, although Orestes wasn't sure why. Perhaps it was just a natural part of his character, an eagerness to be taken seriously.

Nevertheless, it intrigued Orestes why a wealthy Etruscan would set up home in Sparta. And it surprised him that this soft, overfed foreigner would be a friend of Cleomenes.

'I hope you will forgive me,' he said in a break in the conversation. He glanced over at Cleomenes, who seemed quite at ease in this comfortable house. 'But you seem – well, a little out of place in Sparta.'

Eumaneus laughed, wheezily, his body wobbling slightly as he did. 'Indeed I am, my friend. But you know what they say: the crocodile needs the little bird that picks the flies from its teeth.'

Cleomenes smiled, although Orestes doubted he knew what a crocodile was.

Eumaneus looked fondly at the severe Spartan commander. 'The Spartans are a practical people, fundamentally. They know what they're good at: and they're good at two things. Killing people, and fucking them senseless.'

Orestes laughed, taken aback by Eumaneus's candidness. Eumaneus grinned at him; the fat around his neck formed a second chin.

'They are certain things they're no good at at all, and one of them is trade. So there is a place for people like me, who can get absurdly rich helping the Spartans out.'

Cleomenes' eyes were shining, and he grinned wickedly at Orestes. 'But that's not all, as you'll see,' he said, jovially.

Eumaneus grinned again. 'Also, as you may have noticed, the Spartans have extraordinary sexual appetites. This is what attracted me to the place to begin with.' He lifted a chubby hand sadly to his eye. 'I was a young man, then, of course. The Spartan aristocracy was all over me, as a foreigner to assist in

124

recharging their virility. Believe it or not, I was very much in demand.' He glanced wickedly at Cleomenes. 'Your father, the ephor, for example, used to . . . well, I'm sure you can imagine what he used to do.'

Orestes stared in amazement at Eumaneus, finding it hard indeed to imagine him as a strapping youth in demand from men like Cleomenes.

Eumaneus understood the meaning of his look. 'You don't have to look so surprised,' he chortled. 'Anyway, I developed quite a taste in Spartan men. But as I grew older, and my charms, shall we say, dissipated a little, I found another way to provide them with a service. The Spartan elite has remarkable rules about whom their underlings can bugger, but have a rather relaxed attitude to themselves.'

Cleomenes laughed, seeing no irony in this.

'So —' Orestes was not following his point '— what do you do?'

'When Spartan notables are bored with each other, and unable to find some agreeable helot to drop his loincloth and touch his toes, they come to me.'

Cleomenes laughed again, but there was a certain impatience now in his attitude. 'Let's just show him, eh?'

Eumaneus inclined his head politely at the Spartan, and rose to his feet, beckoning Orestes and Cleomenes to follow him. He led them out into an adjoining room, a shaded, cool chamber, covered in cushions, with a portal to one side.

'It is my honour to reveal to you my latest collection.' Eumaneus clapped his hands, and through the portal appeared a row of beautiful, naked young men.

They were all foreign. Orestes could quickly place, at least roughly, where each came from. The first was Persian, or perhaps from Babylon — somewhere east — with dark skin and slightly aquiline features, his hair to his shoulders tied in knots. Behind him was a tall, muscled Nubian from Africa. Then came a northerner, broad-shouldered with shaggy yellow hair and blue eyes. And a tough, hardy-looking youth with a round face and thick, unkempt black hair, who looked like a Macedonian shepherd. They stood in a line, facing Orestes and Cleomenes, grinning. For a moment Orestes assumed them to be slaves, but there was a relaxed provocativeness to their attitude which suggested not: their sleek penises were each surging to erection, as though they approved of Eumaneus's guests – except for the thickset Macedonian, who seemed struck with terror.

Cleomenes clapped the Etruscan on the back. 'Excellent! You have been working most hard, my friend.' He swiftly removed his tunic and swaggered towards the row of men, his cock climbing proudly as he walked.

Eumaneus looked at Orestes, waiting for him to follow. 'See what a wonderful man I am? I go around the world, offering the most gorgeous boys I find a job. They are handsomely paid, I am rich, and everyone is happy. Sparta is a particularly favourite destination for my lads, as Spartans are so fabulously virile. But come on, my friend, take off your clothes – enjoy yourself!'

Cleomenes was starting to indulge his lusts with the blond northerner, who was sinking to his knees, preparing to take the Spartan's erection in his mouth.

Nervously, Orestes crossed the room to join them. The Nubian and Persian took his hands, welcomingly, and lifted his tunic over his head. Cleomenes, already thrusting his hard-on lustfully into the blond northerner's mouth, reached out and grabbed Orestes' cock, which was starting to swell. Gentle hands caressed Orestes' back, smoothed over his buttocks. Orestes' dick reached full erection in the Spartan's hand. He looked around him at the four foreigners: the northerner excitedly sucking at Cleomenes' cock; the Nubian, his long, thick rod with a fat, red head, pulsing in his fist; the easterner, broad, hairy body and thick cock; and the shepherd, the one who most excited Orestes, his stocky body trembling nervously, his cock lifting slowly to erection. 'You like Philipus,' Eumaneus observed, standing just behind them. 'Be gentle with him, Orestes. It's his first time.'

Philipus, the shepherd, swallowed nervously. His eyes were feasting on Orestes' erection, which was still in Cleomenes' fist. Orestes reached out and cupped his hand under the Macedonian's balls: Philipus's eyes burnt with lust, and his mouth twitched into a slight, amazed grin. The easterner stroked Orestes' chest with a delicate touch, while the Nubian squeezed his buttocks. Cleomenes was grunting beside them. Philipus seemed overcome for a moment: his mouth was open, his eyes wide. Cleomenes, the northerner glued to his dick, leant forward and touched the Macedonian on the shoulder. 'Go on, lad: suck it . . .'

Philipus's knees seemed to give way, as he stared feverishly at Orestes' cock, and then, as though base, demonic lust had suddenly seized control of him utterly, he smothered it with his mouth. He gagged but didn't stop, his bright eyes gazing up at Orestes' body. Orestes watched, tremendously excited, as the young Macedonian, his mouth hard and inexpert, but ferociously greedy, inhaled his dick.

The Nubian and the Persian dropped their heads to lick gently at Orestes' nipples. Orestes moaned as the hungry shepherd's mouth fed on him. The Persian carefully bit his nipple; the Nubian caressed his back and slipped his long, thick fingers down the crack of Orestes' arse, pressing into his ring. He glanced down at the northerner, his shaggy fair hair flailing the Spartan's hips as he rejoiced in Cleomenes' cock; Orestes reached out to grasp Cleomenes' arse in his hand. Philipus was moaning obscenely, taking Orestes' cock as deep into his throat as he could bear it.

The Nubian dropped his head to probe Orestes' arse with his hot, rough tongue. The Persian, pumping his dick, thrust his head under Orestes' groin to balance his balls in his moist lips. Orestes squeezed hard at Cleomenes' arse, savouring the hardness of the muscles, digging in with his nails. His mind was completely empty of thoughts except for the carnal pleasure of this moment: free of worries, free of his dreams of Hector. There was just the abject indulgence of the young shepherd gorging himself on his bulging dick, the probing Nubian tongue, the softness of the mouth against his balls.

He glanced briefly to one side, where Eumaneus was watching, voyeuristically wanking under his robe. Even that seemed a perverse pleasure: the delight of being watched.

Cleomenes pushed the northerner to the ground, lifted his pale legs over his shoulders, and rammed his cock inside him.

The northerner wailed in pain, gripping his dick in his fist. Orestes gripped Philipus's head in his hands, and lifted his face away from his groin. He sighed as the Macedonian's thick, rigid dick loomed into view, the veins throbbing, slithers of pre-come drooling from its tip. He bent down and buried it in his mouth, as the Persian swallowed Orestes' cock, and the Nubian's tongue pushed further and further into his arsehole. Philipus gasped in delight as Orestes devoured his young dick.

Cleomenes was fucking the northerner with total abandonment beside them; Orestes glanced aside as he sucked, thrilled by the utter rigidness of the northerner's cock as the Spartan speared him. Philipus's stocky, powerful legs were shaking with lust. His cock was salty and rich in Orestes' mouth. The Nubian, his body rocking as he wanked himself, was moaning, his tongue deep in Orestes' arse, slick now with his spit. The Persian was sliding his lips up and down Orestes' throbbing shaft, murmuring occasionally in his foreign language, adoring this Greek prize.

Philipus bent his knees, thrusting his full, succulent dick between Orestes' lips; the Athenian seized his swinging balls in his hand, sliding the other hand up into the sweaty, tender arse, slowly slipping his thumb up Philipus's crack. The Macedonian trembled, as if he was going to come, and snatched his cock away: the head was engorged and red, shining with Orestes' spit. He turned, and thrust his arse into Orestes' face. Orestes grabbed his arsecheeks, pulling them apart to submerge his tongue into the pink, puckering hole. The Nubian's tongue was plunged into Orestes' rectum; the Persian was gobbling, choking on Orestes' rock-hard dick. He had to have the Macedonian's arse: the firm, sturdy body, yielding to his probing tongue, was exciting him unbearably.

He stood, pulling his aching rod from the Persian's mouth, and – seizing Philipus by the shoulders – pressed his wet shaft against the moist arsehole. Philipus pushed his arse back, pleadingly, his chest heaving with lust. Orestes pushed with the head of his cock, sliding it into the Macedonian's arse: Philipus gasped, pressing back, demanding to be taken. His arse enclosed Orestes' cock in a single, slow glide of tight, eager muscle.

As he started to pump, he could feel the Nubian lathering his own arse with spit, and then the delicious pressure of the long, leathery cock, squeezing inside. It filled him, sliding into his gladly accepting hole. The Persian was beneath them, slobbering his mouth from the Nubian's heavy balls to those of Orestes and then Philipus, rapturously savouring the hard, heavy muscles between their legs. Beside him, the northerner was gripping Cleomenes to him with his thick thighs, his fists clenched, beating on the floor.

Orestes grasped the Macedonian's cock in his hand and pumped it, crying out in pleasure, the Nubian's dick driving into him, and his own plunging into Philipus. The Macedonian's stocky, farmer's frame knotted in ecstasy, and spunk hurtled from his cock. On the floor, the northerner shot come over his shoulder, sobbing in orgasm; Cleomenes fell forward to drink his sperm. Orestes' arse tightened around the Nubian's dick as he unleashed his load into Philipus, and the Nubian emptied his balls inside him. Cleomenes, pulling out his dick, his powerful chest a wall of solid, tight muscle, spurted his load over the northerner's face. Burying his face in Orestes' groin, the Persian, wanking beneath him, whimpered as he hit climax and fell backward, a huge burst of hot come slapping against Orestes' thighs and sliding down his leg.

The Nubian eased his cock out of Orestes, but Philipus clung to him, holding him inside, his dick still hard in Orestes' hand. Orestes sank down, kissing the Macedonian's thick neck, savouring the rectal muscles tightly clenching around his aching shaft. Cleomenes reached out and fondled Orestes' buttocks. To one side, Eumaneus was coming into his hand, hidden by his robes, his podgy face dreamy with happiness.

Eventually, Orestes extracted his dick from the Macedonian, who turned and clasped his lips to Orestes', flinging his arms round his chest and pressing his slippery, raw erection into Orestes' groin.

They collapsed together on to cushions, Orestes at Cleomenes' side, while the four foreigners gently washed them and towelled them dry. Adoringly, Philipus rubbed sweet-smelling ointments into Orestes' chest; the Athenian lay back, closing his eyes.

In a thick Macedonian accent, Philipus whispered into Orestes' ear, 'You've got a gorgeous, gorgeous cock.' Orestes smiled, and kissed him.

For what seemed an age, he lay on the cushions, half sleeping, as Philipus, then the Persian, then the Nubian, then the northerner, caressed his body, licked his dick, hard again – until he couldn't tell who was who. He seemed to entwine briefly with Cleomenes, felt his hard Spartan flesh against him, sighed as a warm mouth enclosed his dick again, and gradually drifted into sleep.

When he awoke, Philipus was serving him a drink of squeezed lemons and ice with honey. The Macedonian was still naked, his cock puffy as if it could surge to erection at any moment. Cleomenes was lying on his chest, the Nubian massaging his back.

Eumaneus was curled up like a cat on a cushion, sipping wine from a glass. 'I trust you have enjoyed yourself, my friend,' he said.

Orestes nodded. He glanced at Philipus, who had settled down beside him, and suddenly, for the first time since his arrival at Eumaneus's house, thought of Hector. He felt, immediately, guilty. He shook his head to discard the thought, but it wouldn't go. There was no logic to it: but he knew, however delicious Philipus was, it was Hector he longed for; and it seemed almost wrong that he had given his body to these other men.

'Can I get you anything else?' asked Philipus in his rural dialect.

Orestes shook his head. He looked over at Cleomenes, luxuriating in the Nubian's massage. The Persian was picking the seeds from a pomegranate.

'You're from Macedonia,' Orestes observed. Philipus grinned. 'When did you leave to come here?'

'Mr Eumaneus met me about two weeks ago, and asked if I would like a new life in Sparta. I'd never heard of Sparta. But he promised me I'd make a good living and enjoy myself. So I said goodbye to my family and got on the boat.'

'You were his first,' Eumaneus reminded Orestes.

Philipus grinned again. 'Didn't know what to expect, to be honest. Thought I might not like it.' His penis swelled against his thigh. 'But if everyone I get to do it with is like you, this job's going to be fun.'

Orestes smiled. Hector was still preying on his mind, and he felt a twinge of lust in his loins. Philipus was fully hard again.

'When they said you got to suck a few cocks, I thought: don't know if I can do that. But, well, seems I like it.' He licked his lips. 'When you were fucking me, it was incredible. My dick's never been so hard. Thought it was going to burst.' Across the room, the Nubian, his dark cock climbing to erection, was sliding his oiled fingers into Cleomenes' arse: the Spartan was starting to writhe in pleasure. The Persian, pomegranate at his lips, was watching, getting hard. Philipus's cock jerked, stretching to its limit. 'I'd love to suck your cock again,' he whispered to Orestes.

Orestes could feel his dick starting to swell: the Macedonian was so sweet, so desirable. But he felt guilty still. 'I'm tired,' he said. 'I think maybe I should go.'

Philipus's face fell in disappointment. But Orestes stood, looking around for his clothes. Eumaneus smiled, and rose to accompany Orestes from the room. Philipus shook his hand, nervously, to say goodbye, then seemed to forget about him, and crossed the room to join the Nubian with Cleomenes.

Eumaneus went with Orestes to the door of the house.

'Do I owe you money?' asked Orestes.

'No, no. Cleomenes has taken care of that.'

Orestes hesitated. 'You know, I'm surprised by the Spartans' attitude to you,' he said suddenly. 'You seem – I mean no offence – to be everything they disapprove of.'

'I know,' the Etruscan laughed. 'But they're horny little boys, at heart.'

'You like them, don't you?'

'I adore them, my friend. I always have.' He inclined his head, and added, without any insinuation as far as Orestes could tell, 'If the Athenians knew how adorable they were, they'd be far less anxious to wipe them off the landscape.'

Orestes smiled. 'Less adorable on the battlefield, I imagine.'

Eumaneus scoffed. 'Oh, not really. If you wanted to defeat the Spartans in a war, all you'd have to do is drop your shields and wave your dicks in their faces.'

Orestes laughed, and shook his hand in farewell. 'Say goodbye to Cleomenes for me.'

Eumaneus waved to him as he walked away down the street.

Hector arrived at Ariadne's house, swung his legs off his horse and called out excitedly for Epharon. His friend came running to meet him in the courtyard, and embraced him.

'It's all right, Eph. I promised you it would be. Pausanius has agreed to take you back.'

'What!' Epharon threw his arms around Hector again, over-whelmed with joy. 'That's incredible, Hector! How on earth did you persuade him?'

'He's a reasonable man.'

Ariadne walked from the house, and Hector kissed her on the cheek in greeting. 'I can't believe how much I'm seeing of you, Hector.'

He grinned. Epharon was still reeling with Hector's news. 'Hector's persuaded them to take me back!' he exclaimed, laughing.

Ariadne smiled, but she looked at Hector quizzically. He turned away, suddenly unable to look at her, as the shame welled up in his chest.

Epharon ran off to get his things, anxious to return to his comrades as soon as possible, leaving Hector alone with his mother.

'Is Orestes still here?' he asked nervously.

'Not at the moment. He has apparently struck up quite a friendship with Cleomenes.'

'The ephor's son.'

Ariadne nodded. Hector looked away. Cleomenes was an extremely powerful man, and a handsome one, he thought

132

grimly. There was a knot in his stomach at the idea of them together. Immediately, he could not help thinking that the prohibition on sex with outsiders did not apply to a man like Cleomenes, and the knot grew tighter. For a moment the thought flashed in his mind that after today he was already lost, already had disgraced his honour, so it would hardly matter if he abandoned it completely. But then he looked at his mother's worried face, and thought what a calamity it would be for her if even today's shameful episode became known, and strengthened his resolve. If Orestes was fucking a man like Cleomenes, it was all for the better.

Ariadne took his hand. 'How did you persuade your captain?'

He couldn't look at her. 'Like I told Eph, he's not such a monster.'

But she seemed very doubtful, and he took his hand away. Epharon came running from the house, with his small bag of belongings. He took Ariadne in his arms, tightly, and kissed her forehead. 'Thank you. I can't thank you enough.'

She smiled, and wished them both well as they left her.

The sun was burning deep amber, low in the sky, inflaming the horizon, as Hector rode with Epharon squeezing on to the saddle behind, making their way back to the camp. By Hector's side, attached to the saddle, was his sword, and as he had to sit forward, the sheath scraped his leg uncomfortably. Epharon gripped his arms around Hector's chest to hold on, and Hector could feel the heat of his friend's desire as the horse trotted up the hill. He felt Epharon's cock rubbing against the small of his back, the tightening in Epharon's embrace. The friction of the jogging horse, rubbing Epharon's hard-on against his back, was exciting the younger hoplite, making his erection sticky. But Hector was happy his friend was so happy, confident he had done the right thing whatever the cost and whatever the shameful truth of his motivation.

'Don't you ever learn, Eph?' he protested playfully.

'Sorry,' whispered Epharon. 'Blame the horse.'

Hector did not have an erection. He was too troubled by the

distress of his captain when he left him. Indeed, it did irritate him that Epharon was always and permanently so aroused by him, so unable to control his passions. If Epharon had more self-control, he thought with sudden bitterness, none of this would have happened.

But he knew that wasn't true. This was nothing to do with Epharon. Pausanius, however ashamed Hector was of what he had done, was at fault. Pausanius had been jealous of Epharon, and had vindictively persecuted him out of his lust for Hector. The hero was not so heroic. He had agreed to Hector's terms. He had slobbered, like a dog, over Hector's cock. Hector had to remember that.

But then he did remember it, the desperate abandonment of the captain's lust, and it began, despite his every effort, to arouse him. He hoped Epharon wouldn't notice his suddenly hardening dick, in case his friend thought he was responsible for it. Epharon's erection was still rubbing against his back.

'Look, Eph,' said Hector. 'We can't arrive in the camp with your prick like the mast of a ship. Not under the circumstances. Can't you just control yourself and then have a quick fuck with Gatha?'

'Sorry,' said Epharon again.

'I think we should get down and walk.' He reined in the horse, and waited for Epharon to dismount, which he did with transparent disappointment. Then Hector swung out of the saddle, on the other side of the horse to hide his erection from his friend, although it was starting to abate now.

They walked along, the horse between them. 'I've still got a hard-on,' said Epharon.

'Just keep walking. Nobody can walk for long with a hard-on.'

'Well, talk to me about something. Tell me what you said to Pausanius.'

'I told you. I just reasoned with him.'

'But tell me what you said.'

'I said that . . . you know. He was wrong, he'd got the wrong end of the stick, and you're not in love with me.'

They were silent for a moment.

'But I am in love with you, Hector.'

Hector grunted, frustrated and annoyed. 'You'll have to stop being in love with me, then, won't you?'

'How am I going to do that?' said Epharon, sadly.

'Just give it time. You'll get sick of me. I'm boring.'

Epharon laughed. 'But that's not what I meant. The captain was right. If he was wrong, I could see –' Hector saw Epharon glance over the horse's back, and tried to avoid his eyes.

Suddenly Epharon stopped. Hector held back the horse, and looked at him. 'What is it now?'

'You threatened him, didn't you? You accused him of dishonourable jealousy.'

'Eph, you have an amazing imagination.'

'Didn't you?'

'Oh, of course not.'

'But it wouldn't be enough, would it?' Epharon was staring at him in horror. 'You'd need to have . . . he fucked you, didn't he? And you promised not to tell.' His voice was a soft, appalled whisper.

'No.'

'You did. It's the only thing that makes sense.'

Hector let go of the horse and stepped towards his friend. There was no way he could lie now. Epharon had understood the truth, and his eyes were full of it. 'It's nothing, Eph. Nothing.' Hector gasped, imploringly. 'It's – it's a stupid rule, anyway.'

'But Hector – the disgrace!'

'Eph, no one will ever know.'

Epharon stepped back, wiping his face. 'Hector, how many times have you told me that the honour is in your heart, not what people know.'

'It had to be done, Eph. I couldn't let you pay for the captain's lust.'

'Oh, Hector.' Epharon was distraught. 'You did that for me? But this is terrible!'

'It's not. It's nothing. It's *done*.'

Epharon was nearly in tears. 'This is terrible!'

Hector rushed to take his hand, to somehow console him. But Epharon backed away. 'So what happened? You offered yourself to him and he fucked you. Oh, Hector.'

Hector was seething with frustration. As if the bitterest truth might be all that would soothe Epharon's pain, he yelled, 'Yes, he fucked me. All right? He fucked me with his huge fat cock and I loved it, Epharon. I loved it!'

Epharon turned and ran. Hector gasped with fury and impatience.

'Eph! Epharon!'

But Epharon kept on running. Hector turned back and jumped on his horse and galloped after him, his face red with rage. He caught up with him, and tried to reach out, to grab Epharon by the arm, but Epharon pulled away. He was in floods of tears, running in circles like a madman. Again, Hector tried to grab him.

Then he jumped from his horse and raced after Epharon on foot. Catching him, he seized his shoulders and pulled him to the ground. For a moment they lay on the dusty soil, panting. The sun was a hemisphere of blazing colour sinking beneath the skyline ahead of them.

'I can't go back, Hector.'

'Of course you can go back. I just got fucked by a captain so you could go back.'

Epharon looked at him, still with tears pouring down his cheeks. 'But how can I face anybody, knowing what you've done for me? How can I show my face, knowing that because –' He sobbed, unable to speak. 'Because I am a stupid little fool, you have dishonoured yourself and your comrades in this terrible way. It's all my fault!'

Hector wanted to hit him. He tried to pull him to his feet, but Epharon curled into a ball, still sobbing.

'Why is it terrible? Who says it's so terrible?' hissed Hector.

Epharon stared at him, wiping the snot from his nose. His eyes were burning, filled with terror. Suddenly, he bounded to his feet and raced across the field towards Hector's horse. The horse flinched slightly, and backed away, but Epharon pursued it, catching hold of its reins.

Hector watched him run away, shaking his head with fury, too exhausted and drained of will to chase him.

Then, with a pang of terror, he realised what his friend intended to do. 'Eph! Oh, for the love of Zeus!'

He charged as fast as his powerful legs would move towards Epharon, desperately, crying out Epharon's name. But before he reached him he saw Epharon lift the sword that was sheathed beside the saddle, saw it flare in the light of the terrible sun, saw the despair in Epharon's contorted, anguished face.

'Eph, don't!'

Hector started to sob. He could run faster than anyone in Sparta, fast enough to win prizes in Olympia, but not fast enough to reach Epharon in time.

He heard Epharon cry out. 'There's only one way to erase your disgrace, Hector. Hector, my love.'

Epharon gripped the sword in both hands and plunged it into his stomach. He screamed in agony and toppled forward.

Hector fell to the earth beside him, weeping helplessly, turning Epharon round to see his face. The sword was deep in Epharon's belly; blood was seeping out of him on to the dirt.

Hector wailed in despair. Gently, he seized the sword and eased it from his friend's limp body; Epharon barely felt the pain. His eyes were glazed already.

Hector sobbed, clasping Epharon to his chest, stroking his hair. 'Please,' he whispered. 'Whichever god can hear me – Zeus, Diana, Aphrodite . . . Athena!' Suddenly he cried out to the god of his enemies. 'Athena, I beg you, save his life, don't let him die . . .'

Feebly, Epharon lifted a hand to Hector's tear-stained face. Blood oozed from his mouth, but he tried to smile. 'It's all right now, Hector. You don't have to worry any more.'

His hand dropped, and his eyes became empty stones, as his body slumped in Hector's arms. Hector clutched him, sobbing, sobbing, until the sun set over the hills and the sky grew black, and a cold wind swept against his skin.

Eleven

Orestes joined Cleomenes, Lyador and other Spartan aristocrats in the temple of Dionysus. This was the beginning of
the Feast, the offering of prayers and libations to the God of
Wine and Song. The next day would be long preparations for
the frenzy of merriment of the night ahead. Now, the city was
still. A priest sang incantations at the front of the temple, like all
buildings in Sparta a simple, stone affair with little ornament.
Cleomenes knelt beside him, his hands clasped to his head.

It struck Orestes as incongruous: he could imagine Cleomenes
in prayer to the God of War, but this seemed strange. He
seemed, almost, smaller. There was the strong scent of incense
from nearby. Outside, the wind was gathering for a possible
storm. In here, Orestes felt safe and protected. His thoughts
wandered, nevertheless, to his own city, to the preparations for
the festival there. He wondered sadly what wonderful plays he
was missing, and might never see. For he was close now to his
target, he felt sure. The closer he came, the greater the danger
he was in.

After the service, Cleomenes wanted him to join their company for dinner. But Orestes had promised to spend the evening
with Ariadne; and frankly he couldn't face a night of whatever
debauchery Cleomenes might have had in mind. For the first

time since his arrival in this extraordinary place, it seemed to him his mind was clear of lust, able to think about something other than straining Spartan dicks and rough, passionate sex with these hardened soldiers. He wanted to keep his mind clear.

Although, he had admit, there was still Hector. He doubted Hector would be at Ariadne's tonight, but there was always the possibility and, even if he remained forbidden fruit, what delicious fruit he was.

The wind was strong, and carried flecks of rain, so Ariadne had abandoned her intention to eat in the courtyard, and laid out a table inside the house. The sheep was for tomorrow: for now she had a feast of roasted chickens and vegetables, piles of freshly baked bread, flagons of wine and bowls of oranges.

Orestes was surprised to find Epharon gone, and couldn't pretend to understand the complexities of the Spartan code of honour. So just he, Nekos and Ariadne sat around the table. But it was a pleasant evening. He enjoyed Nekos's absurd proclamations about whichever nation entered the discussion, and had grown fond of his brazen, boisterous humour. Ariadne he thought a wonderful woman, beautiful and elegant and wise, and sad. He and Nekos exchanged half-invented anecdotes about their travels, and Ariadne laughed and listened, while in the night outside the wind began to howl.

Then abruptly, as Ariadne was opening another carafe of wine, the door burst open, and Hector stood there. He looked terrible, drenched with rain, covered in wet earth, his face ashen and red with weeping. Ariadne ran to him, and took him in her arms, pleading with him to come out of the storm and explain what the matter was.

Hector sank on to a wooden seat beside Orestes, rested his head on his hands, and started to sob. He couldn't speak, such was his distress, and Ariadne was helpless to comfort him. Orestes watched, helpless himself, not sure which of them he should try to comfort; Nekos gazed on in quiet amazement. But it was perfectly clear that something utterly dreadful had occurred, and even the burly sailor knew sensitivity was required.

Eventually, Hector looked up, his eyes shining with tears, but the sobs that had come from the depths of his soul had passed. He looked empty, nearly dead with grief. Ariadne finally managed to take his wet cloak from him, and rushed from the room to find some clean, dry clothes.

Hector looked at Orestes, as if he had noticed him there for the first time. He reached out and took Orestes' hand and squeezed it, as if he just needed someone's hand to hold. Orestes gripped Hector's hand tightly, wishing there was something he could do to take away whatever terrible pain he was in.

Ariadne came back with a linen tunic. She helped Hector out of his wet clothes, and dried him with a woollen towel, and then put the clean clothes on his back. Hector was in a trance, barely moving, being dressed by his mother like a helpless child. Orestes watched, angry with himself for the desire he felt while briefly Hector was naked.

Then Ariadne brought her son back to the table and poured him a very large cup of wine.

'Sorry,' said Hector eventually. 'I'm sorry to ruin your evening like this.'

Orestes touched his hand again, not sure if he should.

Hector faced his mother. 'Epharon's dead,' he said.

Ariadne lifted her hand to her mouth in horror.

'What happened?' asked Orestes in alarm.

'He killed himself,' Hector whispered, shaking his head in sorrow, or anger – or hate. Orestes couldn't tell at all what was going on in the young Spartan's mind.

'I thought . . .' said Ariadne, her eyes wide in shock, 'I thought you'd resolved everything.'

'No, Mother. I thought I had. But I was wrong. And now he's dead.'

Orestes wanted to know what had happened, but, if Hector was going to tell, he would do so in his own time. He asked if there was anything he could do, and Hector smiled at him, distantly, and shook his head.

'I shouldn't be here,' said Hector. 'They'll be wondering where I am. But I suppose . . .' He seemed to be talking to himself. 'When they find what happened, it won't matter. And nothing matters now.'

The pain in Hector's face was enough for Orestes to die from. He wanted to take the beautiful young Spartan in his arms and console him, stroke his hair, and somehow relieve that awful pain. But he felt stupid, and treacherous. Because here was he, a spy in this man's city, who on a battlefield would have willingly killed his friend, or even him. He had lied to Hector from the moment he had first met him. So what right did he have even to be here in this room witnessing his misery, let alone attempting some part in comforting him? He hated the fact that, as he was feeling the heat of Hector's despair, it stirred his loins, made him want him even more. Orestes shook his head in dismay at his own shallowness.

'You need some sleep,' said Ariadne to Hector. He nodded, and stood. He was unsteady on his feet, and swayed slightly, as he bid them goodnight and followed his mother out of the room.

Orestes and Nekos were silent when they had gone. The sailor cracked his fingers and looked at Orestes solemnly. 'What do you think went on?'

Orestes shrugged, and exhaled. 'I don't know.'

'They're strange, these Spartans. Mad, every one of them.'

Orestes lay in his bed staring at the ceiling, listening to the wind and the rain outside. The storm was passing. Perhaps tomorrow the weather would be fine in time for the festivities. He thought of sweet, boyish Epharon, who had lain with him in this bed, only a couple of days ago.

He looked up when he heard the pad of footsteps in the corridor outside. Hector stood in his doorway, his tunic draped around him, with no belt at the waist. He looked ghostly.

'Are you all right?'

'I can't sleep. I don't want to wake my mother.'

Orestes climbed out of bed, wrapped a blanket around himself, and lit a candle, offering Hector his bed to sit on. He sat beside him, not too close, afraid of what he would do if he was too close. Hector's skin was the colour of ochre in the candlelight, which flickered in the breeze, making patterns of shadow on his unhappy face.

'Can you tell me why he killed himself?' Orestes asked gently.

Hector looked into his eyes. 'To save my honour.' He sighed. 'But I have no honour.'

Orestes didn't know what to do or say. He just stared at him in the feeble light.

'Epharon was the . . . *nicest* member of my company. He was sweet, loving. He didn't care if he won things, or beat you in wrestling matches or races, or anything. He just wanted everyone around him to be happy.'

'Was he in love with you?'

'Yes. And, you know, he wasn't ashamed of it. That was the extraordinary thing.'

'Why should he have been?' asked Orestes. Hector's beauty in the candlelight was astonishing.

'I don't know, any more. The army considers it weak. It's stupid, isn't it? You encourage a group of men to regularly, daily, dote on each other, take every imaginable pleasure in each other's body, and then condemn them if they go that one step further and call it real love. That's what women do: love.' He shook his head, as if the whole universe had become a mystery to him. 'I don't understand any more. It used to seem so simple, these rules and traditions, and whatever it is they are. But it's . . . madness.'

'I don't pretend to understand,' said Orestes.

'I envy you,' said Hector. 'Not being Spartan.' He shivered a little in the cold. 'I thought I'd put everything right. But all I did was break another one of these . . . rules. A much worse one. If anyone finds out I'll suffer more than Eph did. It seemed – I thought it was so obvious. The rule was as stupid and pointless as the one Eph broke. So what did it matter? But he couldn't see that. He thought I'd done something terrible for his sake, and had to die to save me.' He shook his head in confusion and despair.

'Will it? Save you. His death.'

Hector shrugged. 'Only if the gods are appeased.' He laughed, bitterly, his self-hatred palpable. 'And the terrible thing – *another* terrible thing – is that I never would have betrayed Pausanius anyway.' He snorted, enraged with himself. Orestes could piece together what had happened, and felt a chill of jealous loathing for the suspicious captain, imagining him having his way with Hector. 'I'm a fraud, Orestes. Epharon killed himself for a stupid, self-loving fool.'

Orestes touched his hand, and as soon as he did so Hector gripped it. For a while they were silent, clasping their hands together. Orestes wanted to throw his arms around him.

Hector looked up, and took his hand away. 'I hear you've been the guest of Cleomenes.'

'Yes.'

'I imagine he's been entertaining you well.'

Orestes wasn't sure what he meant. He nodded. 'He's shown me some very intriguing aspects of your society.'

Hector laughed, softly. 'Is it true what they say? That the oligarchs believe they gain strength by seducing foreigners?'

Orestes shifted awkwardly on the bed, but didn't answer.

'So you've been fucking your way through the entire Spartan aristocracy, have you?'

Orestes laughed. 'Some of them.'

'What about Cleomenes? He's a very handsome officer. I've often thought, when I've seen him, strutting around: I bet he just adores getting fucked up his arse.' He grunted, cynically.

'He seems to enjoy it.' They smiled at each other. Orestes was nervous, and spoke carefully. 'It seems another strange rule, that one. That it's positively valuable for an aristocrat to savour the pleasures of an outsider's – But if any of you did it –'

'I know,' said Hector, interrupting him. He shivered again. 'One rule for the rich. But you can't imagine how seriously they take it. If a hoplite is caught with a foreigner, it's the most terrible disgrace of all.'

Orestes nodded. Now, looking at Hector's face in the soft glow of the candle, and talking about these things, he felt his desire surfacing. His cock was hardening under the blanket. It seemed the cruellest fate that he should be alone with Hector under such circumstances, and discussing the very reason why they could not make love.

Hector smiled at him, and spoke with heavy, awkward sincerity, as though this were something he was compelled to admit. 'If I was an aristocrat, Orestes, I would want to drain every drop of whatever it is foreign sperm could do for me out of you.'

Orestes' dick was completely rigid now, pressing against the rough cloth of his blanket. He tried to laugh, but his voice cracked. Hector's lips were dark and slightly puffy; Orestes stared at them, at the white teeth just visible inside his mouth, at the gauze of stubble on his chin.

'I've been –' Orestes began. 'I've been captivated by you since the night we met.' Hector nodded, smiling sadly. 'Your mother asked me to steal you away and save you from the army.'

Hector laughed, finally a laugh free of bitterness. 'Did she?'

'I don't suppose you'd consider it.'

'No.' Hector laughed again. 'I'm tempted to break the last rule, though, I have to admit. It would be nice to spend the night in someone's arms. I'm so . . . lonely.' His voice wavered, as tears welled up in his eyes again.

Orestes moved closer, and put an arm round Hector's shoulder. Hector wiped his hand against his nose.

'You're a beautiful man, traveller from Syracuse. I envy those aristocrats with all my heart.'

Orestes' gripped Hector's shoulder, wanting so badly to kiss him. His cock was throbbing against the blanket, and he glanced down to Hector's groin. There, to his quickening pulse, was the firm shaft of his hard-on, lifting the cloth of his tunic. It would be so easy to lower his head, caressing Hector's beautiful chest, and sink his mouth over that pressing, needy cock. But he had to fight his desire. There was a vein in Hector's neck, pulsing furiously.

'I wish I understood your prohibitions,' he whispered, allowing his hand to rest against Hector's cheek.

'It's not for my sake. I don't care about any of that any more.

144

It's for my mother. The disgrace would destroy her. She'd lose her inn, be banished with me. You see, I have to find the strength, for once, not to be selfish.'

Orestes nodded, his breathing heavy, his heart pounding in his chest. He stroked Hector's cheek, and the Spartan leant, tenderly, into his hand.

'No one would know,' said Orestes, his throat dry.

'The gods would know,' said Hector. 'And they hate me.'

Orestes stared at him, his chest swelling. 'Can I just kiss you?' he whispered.

Hector turned his face, and looked at him. Closing his eyes, unable to resist, he offered his lips. Their mouths met, and Orestes moaned with pleasure as they bit gently into each other's lips, their tongues touched. Hector's mouth was moist and warm. He put up a hand to caress Orestes' face, and Orestes twisted his body to put a hand on the Spartan's chest. The blanket slipped from his shoulder, and he felt the cold air against his hard, pulsing erection. Hector was shivering, as he moved his hand down Orestes' naked chest, and lightly touched his cock with his fingertips. Orestes pressed his hand into Hector's groin, feeling the solid, erect muscle.

Hector took his hand away, and stood. 'I can't do this, Orestes. I want to – I want to do it more than anything in the world. But I can't. I – I'm afraid.' His erection was an exhilarating bulge in his clothes. He glanced down, swallowing hard, to look at Orestes' cock, standing straight from the curls of the fallen blanket. 'Can we just talk?' said Hector in a breathless voice. 'I ought to leave. But maybe we can just talk.'

Orestes couldn't speak. He wanted to pull him back, sink his tongue again into that warm, soft mouth, worship Hector's cock as if it were the incarnation of a god. But he understood. He had to be strong. He pulled the blanket up around his shoulders, and sat back. Hector perched coyly on the end of the bed.

'Let's talk about your travels,' Hector suggested.

So they did. Orestes told him about Egypt, the pyramids, the merchants of Phoenicia, and Hector listened, wide-eyed, keeping his distance. Once, there was a moment's silence, and Orestes couldn't help himself: he leant forward, and their mouths met briefly again, and he touched once more Hector's wonderful, yearning erection, but again Hector managed to pull away, and Orestes apologised.

Slowly, as Orestes talked, Hector leant back on the bed, his head against the wall, and closed his eyes. Orestes watched him gently relax, his eyelids start to flutter in the light, as lulled by Orestes' voice, the Spartan finally slipped into sleep.

Orestes stared at him, head on one side, a tiny drop of spittle at his lips as he slept. He hoped Hector's dreams were happy. He didn't know what to do. His desire for Hector was filling his heart till it might burst. There he was, snoring gently on Orestes' bed, body stretched out. His loose tunic was curled up his thighs; the shape of his soft, tantalising cock was clearly visible under the cloth. His chest, so muscular and wide, rose and fell with his breathing. The blood pulsed through his body, beating gently in the vein at his neck. Perhaps Orestes could touch him, kiss his sleeping body, without waking him. Perhaps he could caress that luscious bulge at his groin, coax it to hardness, without waking him, delicately take the gorgeous organ in his mouth, feel its warmth against his tongue, and Hector would only stir in his dreams, never know.

Gazing at the Spartan's dormant beauty, Orestes quivered with longing. Perhaps he could at least touch the dark smear of Hector's nipples with his fingers, or kiss his thick, inviting neck. Clasping his own insistent erection in one hand, he reached out with the other to touch Hector's thigh. Barely making contact, grazing his palm against the dark hairs that covered Hector's legs, he inched his hand towards the groin he yearned to kiss. He was trembling, in anguish.

Hector stirred in his sleep, shifting his body, licking his lips. But he continued to snore, quietly, his face an angelic picture of peacefulness. Orestes dared to brush his hand over the mound of his cock. And his heart almost stopped as the mound moved, the cock flexed, slowly coming to life. Orestes froze, with his hand barely touching the object of his most intense craving, but it grew and gently forced its head against his hand, like a kitten searching for something to suckle. Orestes held his breath, his cock rigid and pulsing. He stroked its tip, which was moist and tender, while his other hand remained suspended over Hector's sleeping hard-on. Maybe he could, just for a moment, kiss it through the cloth. He bent forward, his breathing hard, his body rocking with the pounding of his heart, the cock before him alive, stretching, begging to be caressed. He closed his eyes and inhaled the smell, the slightly acrid scent of Hector's cock, its long, thick shape forming a ridge of muscle, lifting the cloth of his tunic from his stomach. The cock lifted its head and kissed Orestes' lips, a tiny patch of moisture forming on the linen. With one hand squeezing his own erection, Orestes edged his other hand under the cloth; his fingers brushed against the hair of Hector's scrotum. He ached to take each of Hector's balls carefully in his mouth and roll it against his tongue. Perhaps he could lift the tunic from his thighs, bare Hector's cock to the cool air, and warm it with his breath.

In his sleep, Hector moaned. Orestes' cock throbbed in his hand. He glided his fingers up and down his own aching shaft, and shuddered. Hector's cock lifted again to press against his lips, and he briefly traced its length with his tongue; his other hand hovered under the tunic, gently tickling the swell of the Spartan's balls.

Orestes prayed to Aphrodite for strength. He knew, with unshakable certainty, that what he felt at this moment was love. It was not only this frightening, compelling desire. It was love. And, if he loved Hector, he had to respect his wishes. It would be a terrible thing to take Hector now, while he slept, whether he woke or not. It would be unforgivable.

He willed himself to sit back, take his mouth away, withdraw his hand. He thanked the Goddess with a silent wordless prayer, and sat, still grasping his own cock, gazing down in adoration at Hector's beautiful, sleeping body.

He covered Hector in the blanket, snatched his cloak from where it had been tossed on the table, and crossed the corridor to Hector's room. Pulling the curtain that covered the door behind him, he threw himself on the bed. His erection had not abated whatever, and it took only a few swift movements of his hand to bring torrents of the thickest spunk shooting over his chest.

Orestes lay in the dark, his heart still pounding as the sperm dried to flakes on his body, the image of Hector's face fixed vividly in his mind. He longed to sleep, to forget this torment. But he felt as if he would never be able to sleep again.

Twelve

Orestes slipped out early to buy hot cakes for breakfast. It was the day of the Festival of Dionysus, and Sparta was bright with excitement. The storm had passed; the streets, washed clean by the rain, were steamy and glinting in the sunlight. Everywhere, garlands hung out over the streets, coloured candles burnt in windows, children played games wearing little masks. It was an extraordinary sight, and impossible to believe that this was the middle of a long, bitter war.

But Hector was already about to leave when he got back. He was kissing his mother, dressed in his hoplite's tunic, still slightly damp but drying in the heat of the day. He smiled when he saw Orestes and gripped his hand in farewell. Orestes followed him to the stable where his horse was tethered.

Hector paused to feed the poor animal, which had been drenched in the rain. He looked at Orestes gratefully. Orestes stood, helplessly, anxious to hold him there for seconds longer, but unable to think of a word to say. Hector climbed on to his horse, and leant down to grip Orestes' hand. 'Thank you,' he said.

Orestes clung to Hector's hand, peering into his eyes. 'Will I see you again?' he whispered.

Hector pulled his hand away. With effort, he asked, 'How long will you be staying in Sparta?'

Orestes looked away, lost for a reply. It was agony to think how far he had deceived this beautiful man, agony that Hector was in fact his enemy. 'I don't know,' he said eventually. 'Maybe not much longer.'

Hector nodded. 'I'll never forget you.'

Without further words, which were, it was clear to both of them, impossible, Hector clicked his heels and his horse rode off. Orestes watched him disappear up the street.

Hector stopped at the grave where he had buried Epharon, and rearranged it. The storm had caused havoc. He found some olive branches and made a little wreath to lay on the earth, and said a prayer to Hades, Lord of the Underworld, wishing his friend safe passage. He had placed coins in Epharon's eyes the night before, when he had buried him in the driving rain in the military style.

Then he stood back and saluted him, and rode on to the camp.

His comrades greeted him anxiously, very concerned by his disappearance the night before. He told them Epharon was dead, and they stared at him in shocked silence, before each in turn began to weep. It was the great holiday of Dionysus today, and there was no training: instead of preparing for the festivities, Gatha, Severon, Timos and the rest went inside their barracks and said prayers for their dead comrade, holding each other in consolation.

Hector went to find Pausanius. The captain was standing by the side of a small wood at the side of the field, wearing only his tunic, looking up at the sky. He heard Hector approach, and turned to him, giving him an angry, embittered stare.

'You didn't come back last night, Hector. I could punish you severely for that.'

'Epharon is dead, Captain.' Pausanius blinked at him, as if for a moment not understanding what he had said. 'He killed himself.'

The captain took a step towards Hector, tense. 'You told him the truth?' Hector looked down, ashamed. Pausanius wiped his face. 'What will you do now?'

Hector lifted his head, and looked at the captain with sudden hatred. Epharon was dead, and only because of Pausanius's dishonourable lusts, his jealousy; and all Pausanius could think of was his own skin. All he wanted to know was that Hector would still keep his promise not to betray him. For a moment he thought that he would. In anger he would run into the middle of the camp and scream loud enough for the gods to hear that Pausanius had fucked him. The disgrace would be his also, but at least it would be sweet revenge for Epharon. But he couldn't do this. His friend had died to save Hector's honour, and he owed it to Epharon to keep silent, continue in the army, hide his shame.

'Don't worry,' he said bitterly. 'No one will know why Epharon died. They'll think it was because he was dismissed from the army.'

Pausanius nodded, gratefully. 'Very good. You may go, hoplite.'

Hector walked away. In the fields ahead, soldiers were preparing for the Festival of Dionysus, laying out tables with simple food and huge pots of wine. The air was filled with their excitement.

Only his own company, mourning Epharon, did not share the feverish mood. In the barracks, Gatha had already opened a flagon of wine to drown his grief, and Hector sat beside him. Around them, the others were softly crying still, muttering their prayers. Gatha looked at Hector tearfully.

'I could kill Pausanius,' he said through gritted teeth.

'What good would that do?' said Hector. He wanted to say, It's *me* you should kill. It's *me* who in the mask of self-sacrifice fell to my knees and gorged my lusts on Pausanius's cock. When I was there on my back, that monstrous beast impaling me and I was sobbing in ecstatic pain, was I thinking of Epharon?

He turned away from Gatha, suddenly unable to bear the righteous indignation in his eyes.

Orestes forced himself to think of the task at hand. So he was in love with Hector. People fell in love all the time. There was nothing special about it. Their cities were at war, and he was on a mission to secure Hector's defeat. Perhaps, if that defeat was absolute enough, Hector would die. Bringing the war to an end and saving Athens from the uncultured hordes was more important than his own petty emotions.

He had wasted too much time already.

But as he walked through the streets of Sparta, its people preparing for the feast, it was so hard to maintain his hate. There was no play contest; these people would never appreciate Sophocles or Euripides, or waste their time discussing the tragedy of the human condition. But there was a great deal in their excitement that was so similar to what would be happening now in Athens. He wished there was a god he could pray to who would help him; but it seemed as if none of the gods were listening. Or Hector was right, and they listened and laughed. He felt abandoned, alone in a foreign city without a hand to guide him.

He stopped at a tavern in a quiet street and bought a cold drink of sweetened lemon. Theddalus, the slave, had worried him. Clearly, he seemed to be saying that there was some danger at home, in Athens, that the Spartans had allies there. But was it conceivable? If there were traitors, who would they be?

A fat woman stood behind the counter of the tavern, cleaning earthenware cups. She grinned at Orestes, revealing several missing teeth. 'Ready for the feast tonight, are you?'

Orestes smiled back. 'I don't really know what to expect. I've never observed the feast in Sparta before.'

'Thought you wasn't from round here. Oh, you'll have a good time, sir. Promise you that.' She cackled, rather lecherously, and Orestes wondered what she could mean.

When he went back out into the sun, Orestes made a decision. He didn't know what to do. He needed to speak to Theddalus again, but he didn't know what to offer him in exchange for whatever he knew. But today was a great religious festival. All of Greece would be celebrating it. At home, in Athens, they would be preparing to stage the first of the tragedies; he wondered what marvellous, subtle games Euripides would have played this year with their favourite myths.

Decisions could wait. He should observe the feast. Today was not a day for troubles.

By the end of the afternoon, the hoplites were starting to drink, and singing songs. Gatha had been asleep for hours after consuming his flagon of wine, and the rest of Hector's company, also drunk, were finally trying to lift their spirits by talking about battles they had fought and recounting the adventures of the great heroes of the past. In a corner of the barracks, Timos and Severon, playing at being Achilles and Patroklos, were slowly sucking each other's dick. Soon the rest of them would join in, the first stage of a long night of fucking for Dionysus.

Hector didn't want to be there. He gazed over at Timos, his eyes closed as he drew Severon's long cock into his mouth, and felt nothing. Hector climbed from his bunk and went out.

The field was full of little parties of hoplites. Some of them were starting to play, fondling each other, pouring wine into one another's mouth. Nearby a powerful young soldier, known as a great swordsman, was standing on a table offering his impressive cock to each of his comrades in turn.

Hector turned away. Without knowing where he was going, he walked from the camp. The sky was growing dark. He could see, far away, the festival fires lit on the outskirts of the city, where children would be playing. He turned away from the city and headed up the hill.

Between two valleys, in each of which was a camp of hoplites, was a thick woodland, which Hector knew well. He pushed his way through the undergrowth, the burning orange of the setting sun already partly hidden by the dense leaves. Later, groups of soldiers would be fighting their way into the wood for the one night of the year when warriors could have the bodies of those of different companies, when it was permitted to fuck strangers – as long, of course, as the strangers were still other hoplites. But now it was deserted, and he was alone with his thoughts. He had brought with him a clay carafe of sweet wine, and he found a little clearing and sat by himself, guzzling from the bottle, listening to the sounds of the woods around him as the darkness drew closer.

Suddenly, Hector heard movement in the bushes behind him, and he turned to see who was there. A shadow stood between the trees, as far as he could see dressed in a long robe and wearing a hood over his face. 'Who are you?' Hector demanded.

The shadow stepped closer, passing into a beam of moonlight. Hector couldn't see the face beneath the cowl.

'Who are you?' Hector repeated.

The figure slowly pulled off the hood, and revealed a dark-skinned, youthful face with eyes of silver which caught the light of the stars. The face smiled, and the young man spoke in a faintly foreign accent. 'I am a messenger from Aphrodite,' he said.

Hector stared at him, slightly afraid. It did indeed seem possible that this was some supernatural apparition. But he wished he had brought his sword. He remained where he was, sitting on the forest floor, but prepared himself to fight or run if he had to. 'Why would Aphrodite send a messenger to me?' he whispered.

The young man stepped closer. 'Why do you think, Hector?'

'How do you know my name?'

'Tell me,' said the Egyptian, standing now over Hector, casting his shadow. 'Why does your city fight my mistress so fiercely?'

Hector crept back, trying to see the face in the shadow, pushing his back against a tree. 'I don't understand.'

Calmly, the Egyptian priest released the string that tied his robe, and let it fall to the wet floor of the forest. Rising from the darkness of his slender body was a firm erection. Hector could smell its soft, exotic scent. His own cock thrilled with excitement and lurched upward. It seemed that the cool breath of the apparition was caressing his body, touching his nipples with delicate invisible fingers. The priest moved over him, his sweetly odoured cock close to Hector's face.

Hector trembled, as the invisible fingers decorated his skin with chilling goosepimples. But he was afraid. His chest rising and falling quickly with the rapid beating of his heart, he lifted a finger and touched the stranger's cock. It flexed, and a droplet of pre-come flicked from its tip and landed on Hector's cheek.

His throat constricted with desire, Hector managed to speak. 'I can't do this. I mustn't surrender to this.'

The Egyptian pushed his cock forward and brushed it against Hector's lips. Hector gasped, his cock swelling impossibly hard as the invisible fingers danced over its surface. He put out his tongue and licked the pre-come from the divine dick.

'I mustn't do this,' he whispered. The hairs on his neck were erect. He could feel the fabric of his tunic against every part of his chest, a sensual pleasure almost too beautiful to bear. The invisible fingers continued to caress his straining cock and tickle deliciously at his balls.

The Egyptian's cock nuzzled against Hector's face, touching his lips, his nose, his eyes, smearing honey-flavoured juices on to his flesh. The balls brushed gently against his chin.

'Yes, Hector,' said the strange, accented voice. 'You must.' Hector was about to surrender. He kissed the balls, balanced them on his tongue and sighed in wonder at the silky hardness of the erection pressing at his face. 'But not with me.'

The apparition had gone. It had vanished, suddenly, into the night, and Hector was alone in the damp forest with an aching erection, breathless with painful desire.

Still trembling, a little afraid, he climbed to his feet. He looked around, as if he might see the messenger running away through the trees, but there was only the rustling of forest animals.

Hector broke abruptly into a run, and charged away into the woods.

As darkness fell, Orestes followed a procession up the city streets into the fields that surrounded it. The parade was of men and women and children, all brightly dressed in fancy festival costumes. They had slaughtered their sheep and had a huge meal of roasted lamb and boiled vegetables, and Orestes was a little drunk. Ariadne walked with him for a while, then told him he should go on alone, that the real delights of the festival lay ahead, and she would meet him later.

Children danced around fires, which glowed luminously in the darkness. Orestes watched, fascinated, as strangers gave him wine and bread and goat's cheese. As the night moved on, he noticed Spartans were disappearing into the surrounding olive groves, or running out into the fields, carrying torches. Intrigued, he started to follow them. There was a bright moon, and a thick sky of stars, as if the God himself had sent the storm the night before to clear the heavens. Everywhere there were shining torches, casting their crimson glimmers over the wet earth.

A young woman suddenly appeared before him, taking his hand and laughing. She pulled him with her and, bemused, he followed her to a small copse of trees, where she pressed his hand to her small, delicate breast. Smiling, she leant up and kissed him, caressing his chest. He could feel her heart beating solidly inside her, and for a moment returned her kiss. Then he pulled away, and apologised. She smiled, without malice or anger, and ran away, leaving Orestes to walk on alone.

Everywhere he looked their were couples starting their love-making, the old as well as the young, men and women, men and men, women and women. He saw one beautiful woman with long, dark hair, naked in torchlight between two sturdy lads who looked like peasants, each with a firm erection, kissing both of them. Orestes was amazed; his cock began to stiffen.

On the wet soil of a tilled field, two women were caressing each other's breasts, sliding their fingers into each other's cunt, and sighing as the mud clung to their bodies. Nearby, a large man with a hairy back was fucking a plump, huge-breasted woman, grunting with lust. A skinny youth was sucking in a frenzy at the engorged cock of a round-faced, bearded farmer.

He was stopped for a moment by a tanned, rough-faced boy of sixteen, a helot he thought, who fumbled at Orestes' groin and stuffed his mouth over his stiff cock. Orestes shut his eyes briefly, and allowed the boy his pleasure, then gently pulled him away. The helot's cock was fat and hard; as soon as Orestes had lifted his head, he turned and lunged for another passing stranger, urgently seeking another cock to suck.

Orestes' heart was thumping. He was amazed at the frenzied orgy developing around him, the carnival of the beautiful, the ugly, the young and old, giving vent to their earthiest passions. He took off his tunic, baring his skin to the cool air, his erection firm at his stomach. He wasn't sure what he wanted to do – whether he wanted to fuck some stranger by the side of a tree or not. But it was exhilarating, this wanton festivity. And he wondered if perhaps out here he might find some hard Spartan body to indulge his lusts that would stop him thinking about Hector.

He watched two handsome peasants by an olive tree, their bodies coated in moonlit sweat, one on his knees sucking the other. The one being sucked beckoned him closer, and dropped his head to smother Orestes' cock with his mouth. Orestes stayed there for a while, enjoying the hard energy of the peasant's eager mouth. But the night was young. He pulled himself away, and walked on, his cock slick with the peasant's warm spit, his skin prickly with excitement.

There were torches in a small wood of thick, dank leaves, and he made his way towards them, gripping his erection in antici-pation. A young woman was sobbing in orgasm as he passed her, flailing her head as some thickset man with a round, pert arse fucked her. Orestes looked down at the arse, rising and falling, and wondered if he was allowed to fuck it, if the man would just carry on while Orestes slipped his cock inside and fucked him while he fucked her. The idea excited him, sent thrills through him, but he decided to go on. He went into the trees, following the torches.

In the little wood, six youths were fucking each other in a line. Orestes gasped in astonishment, his cock surging to its fullest erection as he watched. They were all quite rough-skinned labouring types. Each of the four in the middle had his cock rammed into the arse of the boy in front as a dick pummelled forcefully into his own. The one at the front, a fair-haired, solidly built peasant of about nineteen, was wanking his cock furiously, looking back at the row of thick, young bodies which had somehow found the rhythm to do this. At the back, a slightly older youth was straining every aroused muscle to keep in time; Orestes gazed at his firm, hairy buttocks, and decided to join the chain.

The peasant gasped in delight as Orestes lathered spit on to his arsehole and sank his cock slowly into his arse. It was an incredible sight, these six sturdy bodies leaning over one another, grunting and moaning and gyrating their hips. Orestes' knees were trembling. The youths were like one long, hard, hard cock going from one body to the next; or it was as if they were skewered on a single pole of firm, wet muscle, each of them simply gliding his thighs along it. The lad he was fucking came: he felt the rectum tighten around his pumping cock, and for a moment the arse came to a halt. Others were coming further up the line, and Orestes withdrew. He wanted to wait. He was obsessed now with this crazed orgy of lust, and wanted to wait to find what further depraved pleasure might await him. He left the row of youths, wailing in excitement as they shot their spunk into one another's arse, and pushed on through the trees.

He found a little brook, where he stopped to wash his penis, splashing cool water over the reddened head. He threw water on to his face and chest, wiped away the sweat of his exertions, and closed his eyes.

When he opened them, he saw, to his amazement and joy, Hector's face reflected in the water.

Orestes and Hector stared at each other across the stream. The sounds of lovemaking were a little distant: they were alone here. Orestes stayed crouched by the side of the water for a moment, and Hector stood, naked and bathed in silver moonlight, staring at him, unable to speak. His cock was a dark shadow pointing at the stars, and he was trembling.

Hector suddenly ran forward, splashing across the brook; Orestes stood, and they threw their arms around each other. Their lips and tongues met, their yearning erections squashed together. Each of them moaned with insatiable desire, as their

158

tongues almost fought: Orestes forced his tongue in Hector's mouth, then Hector pushed it back with his. They stroked each other's face, and pulled passionately at each other's hair. They ground their hips into each other's body, forcing cock against stomach. Hector dropped his hands to grasp Orestes' buttocks, squeeze them in his fists, drive Orestes' cock hard into his groin. Orestes wrapped a leg around Hector's knee, pulling him into him, as if their bodies could meld. He slid his hand between Hector's buttocks and pressed his finger against his arsehole.

Panting, delirious with desire, Hector dropped his head, kissed Orestes' throat, bent forward to suck his nipples. He bit hard into Orestes' skin, sinking to his knees on the wet grass by the stream as he licked down Orestes' chest, his hands kneading Orestes' arse. Orestes stroked Hector's head as the Spartan descended towards his straining, ardent cock; he smoothed his hands over Hector's shoulders, bent forward to rub his strong, wide back. His knees shook, his arse trembled, his dick flexed in raging need.

Hector stared at Orestes' erection, savouring this moment. He edged his mouth towards it, his eyes wide open as if afraid to miss any second of the experience. He kissed the tip, licked his tongue around it, and Orestes moaned, squeezing Hector's shoulders in his hands. Hector's cock was utterly rigid, kicking at the air; his balls contracted. Every muscle in his hard young body was shivering with arousal, as he took Orestes' cock into his mouth, grunting with passion, lowered his lips down the thick, pulsing shaft, and buried it in his throat.

Orestes reached down to grasp Hector's cock, slivers of pre-come oozing from its swollen, throbbing head, as the Spartan feasted on him, sucking, harder and harder at the dick he had longed to possess. Hector wailed with frenzied lust, grabbing Orestes' balls hard in his fist. For a moment he took his mouth from the slick, slippery shaft, and covered the hairy sac with his tongue, coating it in spit, then seized the cock again between his lips. Orestes, bending forward, gripped Hector's hard-on tightly in his hand, massaging him, then squeezing his tight young scrotum.

Orestes pulled Hector up, and dropped to his knees to take his turn. Hector's cock plunged into his mouth, as the Spartan cried out in ecstasy, staggering backward. His whole body shook with pleasure as Orestes roughly forced his mouth down over the glorious, engorged dick, groaning, his heart pounding in his chest.

Hector lost his balance, and the two of them fell into the cold water of the stream. But Orestes lunged again for the Spartan's cock where it rose above the water, and swallowed its full weight, his head partly submerged so he could hardly breathe.

Hector pulled Orestes' head from his groin, and they kissed, madly swallowing each other's tongue as the brook rippled around them, each clasping his arms around the other's wet, cool body. They rolled again, until they were sitting, mouths still stuck to each other, beating one another's back with their hands, Hector's thighs resting on Orestes', their balls and erections crushed together.

The Spartan lifted himself from the water, and pressed his cock into Orestes' chest. Then he slowly lowered his arse over Orestes' solid shaft. Orestes scratched at Hector's back, grazing his fingernails down the hard, wet skin, as Hector's arsehole pressed against the head of his cock.

Orestes thrust upward, slowly, and his cock squeezed gently into the twitching arsehole of the man he loved. Hector pushed down, harder, taking the head of Orestes' full, taut dick inside him. There was nothing to lubricate him but the water of the stream, but Hector seemed not to care: his arse was opening to welcome Orestes inside. Thrills shot through both of them, and each sobbed with lust and pleasure. Orestes lifted his hips, pushing further and further inside, until Hector had taken the whole shaft. They rested like that, tongues exploring one another's mouth, Hector's cock flat against Orestes' stomach, the pulsing length of Orestes' dick filling him, while the stream bubbled gently around them, tickling their legs and buttocks.

Hector pushed down hard, bit suddenly into Orestes' lips, balanced himself on the Athenian's shoulders, and started to rock. He lifted his body up and down, the muscles of his powerful legs straining to hold him, tightening his rectum around the rod of desire buried inside him.

Orestes rocked with him. 'Hector, I love you,' he murmured, as the muscles gripped his cock.

Hector kissed him, groaning; he held fast to Orestes' shoulders, and cried out, 'Fuck me, Orestes, fuck me!' Then, with a sob of helpless devotion, 'I love you, oh I love you.'

Hector rolled back into the stream, pulling Orestes with him, raising his thighs so Orestes could continue to fuck him. He lifted his ankles on to Orestes' shoulders, and gazed desperately into his eyes. Their bodies were glistening with water. Little waves cascaded from their rocking bodies; clouds of mud spread around them as they thrashed their hips. His feet struggling for purchase on the bed of the brook, Orestes plunged ever deeper inside the Spartan's tender, welcoming arse. Hector seized Orestes' buttocks, pinching them with his fingers, as his thick cock splashed against the surface of the water. Orestes gripped Hector's hard-on tightly as he fucked him, wanking him fiercely, his fist crashing in and out of the stream.

Hector gazed up at Orestes, and through clenched teeth whispered: 'Oh, your cock is fantastic . . . Fill me with it, fill with your incredible cock . . .' Orestes gasped, his hand tight around Hector's thrilling shaft, his dick like iron in the Spartan's tight, sweet arse. He fell forward, pushed his arm under Hector's neck and kissed him, as Hector's legs bound powerfully around his thighs, holding him inside, forcing him in deeper and deeper. Hector sobbed, 'This is incredible . . .'

'I love you,' Orestes repeated.

'I love you,' Hector moaned.

Orestes convulsed, his hips raging back and forth beyond his control now, as he came, shooting thick bursts of spunk into Hector's arse, and at the same moment the Spartan wailed, thrashing the water, his cock disgorging its load.

The feathery strands of Hector's come mingled with the water around them as they lay, the brook lapping against them, holding each other, kissing, murmuring tenderly. Orestes didn't pull out his dick: it stayed hard as Hector flexed his muscles around it lovingly. Hector looked up at him, his eyes misty. 'Fuck me again,' he whispered.

Orestes smiled and shook his head. Gently easing out his dick, he stood in the stream, and bent down to lift the Spartan from the water. As soon as they were back on dry land again, Hector fell to his knees and buried his face in Orestes' loins, worshipping his still-hard dick. Orestes pulled him away from the brook, and pushed him, quite hard, against a tree.

With a moan of passion, he seized Hector's cock, still wet from the stream, and still rigid as rock, and gripped it. Then he spat copiously on his hand, and smothered Hector's shaft in spit. 'Fuck me, now,' he whispered. 'Send me to heaven on your wonderful cock. Fuck me like a Spartan.' He put one hand against the tree, beside Hector's head, and kissed him. For a moment they gripped each other's charged erection. Then Hector turned Orestes around.

The Spartan sank to the ground, kissing Orestes' buttocks, which quivered with excitement, thrust his tongue into his arsehole, moistening it; then he stood, and forced his cock inside Orestes in a single, swift, painful thrust. Orestes wailed in an agony of pleasure, pushing his legs apart, taking the full length of Hector's strong, thick cock.

It was quicker this time. Hector ravished him from behind like a wild dog, biting his neck and grunting with effort and lust. Orestes scrambled to keep hold of the tree. Without touching his dick, he came, shooting come on the forest floor, overwhelmed by the exquisite power of the cock up his arse; and Hector kept on pumping, filling him with his rod of hard, hard flesh, until Orestes came again, a third time, spunk trickling from the slit of his dick as Hector emptied himself inside him, moaning in an ecstasy of satisfaction.

Exhausted, they sank side by side against the tree, and grinned at each other wickedly. Hector slid down to rest his head in Orestes' lap, nuzzling his prick, which was sore and swollen, but softening. Tenderly, Orestes cupped Hector's balls in his hands;

and they sat, quietly, for a while, each of them wishing time could stand still.

Eventually, Orestes spoke. 'Are you going to be all right?'

'I think so.'

Orestes smiled, and touched Hector's nipples with his fingertips.

'I thought that honour was a private matter,' said Hector. 'What you knew in your heart. But it isn't. You can commit whatever crimes you want as long as nobody finds out. That was suddenly clear to me tonight.'

'Was this a crime?'

Hector looked up at Orestes with shining, adoring eyes. 'Of course not. I love you. I hardly know you, but I love you. Maybe we're old souls, as they say.'

'Maybe we are.'

'I feel as if everything I ever believed was a lie. And all that matters is that we love each other, and I'm here with you.'

Orestes fondled Hector's softening cock. 'But just for tonight.'

Hector took his hand, and turned his head to kiss Orestes' balls. 'Yes. Just for tonight. Whatever I feel, whatever I want, I'm still a Spartan. And so is my mother.' Orestes nodded, sadly. 'So I have no choice. I have to return to the army, and pretend you never existed.' There were tears in his eyes.

Orestes took a deep breath. 'I'll be leaving Sparta soon, I think.'

'Will you? Where will you go?'

Orestes looked down at him, his face quite miserable. 'Oh, I don't know. I can go anywhere. Nowhere special.'

As Orestes and Hector lay in the darkness, Hector's head in the Athenian's lap, they didn't see the movement that shook the branches of the trees a short distance away. They didn't see the naked body that had been watching them all along.

Hatred and jealousy burnt into every corner of Pausanius's face as he stared at them.

Then he slipped away through the trees and made his way back to the army camp.

Thirteen

The streets of Sparta were thick with people clearing away
the detritus of the festivities. Orestes wound his way
through the potholed lanes to Ariadne's inn, to find her sitting
in the courtyard, sewing some cloth into a dress. She smiled,
happily, when she saw him.

'So was our Spartan festival the equal of others you have
attended?'

He nodded. 'It was extraordinary, Ariadne.'

'Well, I see you managed to stay out all night. Let me get you
some breakfast.' She stood.

'No, I'm not hungry.' He avoided her eyes. 'I'm going to
have a sleep, I think.'

She watched him with some concern as he walked towards
the house. 'Is everything all right, Orestes?'

He turned to look back at her. 'Of course.' He forced a smile.
'Of course.'

Hoplites were sleeping dreamily throughout the camp as Hector
arrived at his barracks. There was the soft noise of hundreds
of snores. Soldiers lay, each entwined in another's body, across
the practice field, smelling of overdrinking and in need of a
wash. As he reached the entrance to his barracks, he saw

Pausanius standing a short distance away. He looked over at him, anxiously.

'I've been waiting for you, Hector.'

'I'm tired, Captain.'

'I'm sure.'

Hector frowned, suspiciously. The captain walked towards him, and as he drew closer Hector could see the expression in his face: malicious, but somehow triumphant.

'Come with me, hoplite. We have to talk.'

Pausanius closed the door to his hut behind them. It was dark, the curtains across the windows tightly drawn. There were several carafes of wine on the table. Hector was deeply apprehensive. Pausanius looked at him, and smirked.

'I've been thinking, Hector.' He emptied a dribble of wine into his cup and swallowed it in one. 'You see, I was a great hero, once. And you admired me.'

'I still admire you, Captain.'

'No, you don't. You think I'm a lustful idiot. And you're right. But does it matter?' Hector looked into his eyes, puzzled. 'When I was fucking you, when you were drooling over my fat cock like the little whore you are, I thought, This is what matters. You loved it, didn't you, my thick hero's cock ramming into your tight little arse? Your prick so hard and needy, your soft balls bashing away at my stomach. Did you hear yourself, Hector, begging me to fuck you harder? By the gods, when you emptied your balls into my throat, you were my helpless slave, weren't you?'

Hector took a deep breath.

'It's all I want, now, Hector. No more glory or victories. All I want is you on your knees worshipping my dick, your little heart pattering away in your chest and your prick dripping with lust for me, or flat on your back with your legs in the air, begging for my cock in your arse.'

Hector cleared his throat. 'You know that can't happen, sir.'

'Why not?' snapped Pausanius. 'What makes you so special?'

'I did it for my friend, sir. And he died because of my dishonour. I owe it to him never to repeat it.'

Pausanius sneered. He pulled his cock from under his tunic. It was hard, the veins bulging on the shaft. Hector glanced down at it, and it had no effect. At this moment, his thoughts were filled with Orestes and the pain of their parting, and the captain's cock meant nothing to him.

'You did it because you wanted to, Hector.' Pausanius dropped his tunic back over his cock; its shape was still clear under the fabric, but Hector looked away, into the captain's eyes. 'But anyway, that doesn't matter, either. We're going to do it again, whether you want to or not. And again, and again, until you beg me for mercy, or beg to die.'

'I don't think so, sir,' said Hector adamantly. 'For the sake of my dead friend, I would report you, whatever the cost to myself. I can't live with the responsibility for his death any more than I do already.'

'Is that so? Prepared to sacrifice yourself, are you? How noble.' He stepped closer. 'What about for your mother's sake, Hector?'

Hector blinked, looking at the captain in alarm. 'I don't understand, sir.'

'I saw you last night, Hector. With that pretty foreigner stuffing his dick inside you. You seemed to like that even more than you liked mine. Unless my ears were playing tricks, I heard you say you loved each other. I was touched.'

Hector stared at him, horrified. There was an awful shiver in the pit of his stomach.

'So this is my offer. Give yourself to me, whenever I require it. Just as you did before, mind you – it wouldn't be the same without your little whines of lust. And I will say nothing about the crime I witnessed last night.'

'You can't prove anything,' Hector whispered.

'I don't have to prove anything, Hector. I am telling the truth, and I am a war hero. Feel free to shout to the world that I am fucking you, but just think what all this would do to your mother.'

He bent forward and kissed Hector's lips, alcohol strong on his breath. 'That will be all for now. It's too early in the morning to pump your arse full of spunk. Maybe later.'

Hector wanted to kill him. For a moment, he considered it. Murdering a captain would certainly lead to his expulsion from the army, and yet maybe he could protect his mother from this terrible scandal. But he needed time to think.

Without another word, he spun on his heel and strode out of the captain's hut.

Ariadne stood in the door to Orestes' room. 'I'm sorry. Did I wake you?'

'No, no.' He sat up. She hadn't woken him: he had been thinking about her son.

'There's a man here to see you. He seems rather agitated. A helot, by the look of him. He says his name is Theddalus.'

'Thank you, Ariadne. I'll be right there.'

He waited for her to leave, and climbed from the bed, slipping his cloak over his shoulders; his erection quickly subsided.

What did Theddalus want?

He met the scribe slave in the courtyard. Theddalus was looking around, very nervously; he faced Orestes with an urgent stare. 'Is there anywhere here we can speak privately?'

Orestes took his arm and led him out into the street. Nearby was the little stable where his horse was tethered. They stood there in the shadows. Theddalus was very anxious.

'Regarding the matter of which we spoke before, I have some information which might be of some value to you.'

'Go on,' insisted Orestes.

'I think the matter of payment needs to be discussed first.'

Orestes looked at him carefully. 'What do you want?'

'What can you give?'

Orestes decided he had no choice but honesty on every count. 'I don't know. I can offer your freedom, and a place to live in Attica,' he said. 'I can speak to the Assembly, proposing some arrangement with the people of Messenia if Sparta is defeated in the war.'

'You're an Athenian citizen, then? A member of the Assembly.'

'Yes.' Orestes looked at him, coldly. 'And, if you sell this information to your master, I will see to it that your villages are burnt to the ground.'

Theddalus smiled at him. 'How would you do that, I wonder? Still, don't worry. I hate Cleomenes more than you ever could.'

'Does this price satisfy you?' Orestes asked impatiently.

'What guarantee do I have you will honour it?'

Orestes thought for a moment. 'I'll give you thirty drachma. Enough to buy a horse and cart for you and your family. You can set off immediately, if you want, for Attica. I'll write you a letter, and when you arrive my family will see that your freedom, and a small piece of land, are provided.'

'I could be killed on the road,' said Theddalus uncertainly.

'It's the best I can do.'

Theddalus looked at him, worried; but there was no doubt he was going to accept. 'The money and the letter first,' he said.

Orestes shook his head. 'No. The information first. I'm not signing any letters until we're outside the city and you're packed and ready to go.'

Theddalus eventually nodded. 'Will you be coming with us, then?'

Orestes considered this. 'I don't think so. I can't leave yet.'

'Pity. We could use the protection. Still, as you wish. My master – my older master, I mean, not Cleomenes – received letters yesterday from a group of Athenian citizens with whom I know he has had dealings in the recent past. They are planning a rising within Attica to be coordinated with a Spartan invasion. These Athenian notables are due to arrive today in Sparta to discuss the details.'

'Do you know who these traitors are?'

'No. But, as I say, they are arriving today.'

'Where will I find them?'

'Later tonight, they will be dining at my master's house.'

Hector's company was called suddenly to attention as Pausanius entered the barracks. He glanced nonchalantly at Hector, and waited as they lined up in a row, standing to attention.

'The time's come, soldiers, to prepare for battle. This company has been chosen, as you know, to participate in a moment of glory which will echo down the years to come.' He stepped back, slightly, and a shadow fell across the door.

A man stepped in. He was perhaps thirty, with a soldier's bearing, dark hair of short, tight curls, and with a trimmed, elegant beard. He stepped into the room, and nodded, curtly, at Pausanius.

'This is Dionakles,' Pausanius explained. 'He's a general in the Athenian army.'

Hector, with his comrades, let out a sharp gasp of breath.

A short distance from the city, Orestes rode with Theddalus, who was driving a cart in which were his wife, son, daughter-in-law and baby granddaughter. He was nervous about being seen with them, but equally anxious that they be on their way before he gave them anything incriminating in writing.

They stopped and looked back at Sparta. Orestes put his hand into his cloak and pulled out a sealed document, which he passed down to Theddalus. 'Safe journey,' he said, softly. 'Tell my mother I will be home soon.'

'Good luck,' said Theddalus. He clipped the reins of the horse, and his cart trundled quickly away over the dusty earth. Orestes watched them go, his heart heavy. His mind wandered to Hector, and he wished with all his soul he could be with him. He turned his horse and rode back to Sparta.

Why wasn't he leaving now, escaping with Theddalus and his family? He needed to know exactly who the traitors were; but Orestes understood clearly that this wasn't it. He couldn't leave without saying goodbye to Hector, if indeed he could bring himself to leave at all. And more than that: he couldn't leave until Hector knew the truth.

'Some of us in Athens,' Dionakles began, looking each amazed hoplite in the eye, 'have the greatest of respect for the Spartan way of life. We have often wondered: why are we fighting these brave young men, with their clean, simple ethics and codes of honour? Shouldn't we be brothers again, we Greeks? But the factions which dominate our city are made up of talkers and fools and men who think themselves intellectuals. And we have had enough of them. We want peace. And we understand that the only way to achieve peace is to become allies with Sparta in the overthrow of the Athenian empire.'

Who would make an alliance with Sparta? Orestes wondered as he galloped back to the city. What could they possibly hope to gain? There were, of course, divisions and political battles in the Assembly; but he could not imagine that anyone was so disaffected that they would make a pact with the enemy to secure their own success. It was insane. Whoever it was, he had to be careful. He was quite well known in the Assembly, although by no means one of its leading figures. A traitor would be sure to recognise him. There was no question of going straight to the ephor's house to find out who the traitors were. But he had to know.

Dionakles continued. 'Your officers have chosen a few companies of your best soldiers, yourselves included, who will be closely involved in the defeat of Athenian so-called "democracy". It isn't for me to tell you what an honour that is for you. I can tell you what an honour it is for me to be here, addressing you directly.'

'Our soldiers understand what is at stake,' said Pausanius. Dionakles looked at him, and smiled politely.

'A full-scale invasion of Attica would not serve our purposes or yours,' he explained, returning his attention to Hector and his comrades. 'The Athenian army would be warned well in advance, and rally their allies for a pitched battle. If anyone could be sure this would bring about an end to the war, we would have done it already. This has been, as you are aware, a war of attrition, each side too equally balanced to defeat the other. What is needed is a surprise attack, linked to an uprising from within. You will be small in number so that the surprise will be effective. And your task will be to seize, and murder, if you will forgive my forthrightness, the most important politicians in

Athens. With them dead, we will declare an end to the democracy and form a new government – of ourselves, of course, allied to Sparta. Between us, we shall control the whole of Greece.'

Orestes arrived back at Ariadne's inn, and joined her in the house, where she was still sewing. He smiled at her, and sat down. 'I'm going to be leaving, soon.'

'I see. I'll miss you.'

He nodded, and took her hand. 'I need to see Hector before I go.' Ariadne squeezed his hand, her eyes shining with understanding. 'Tell me: what would happen if I rode into the camp and asked to speak to him?'

She sighed. 'They wouldn't let you. It's quite unheard of for strangers to visit military camps unattended.' She looked at Orestes' face, as if she could see the love there. 'But I could send for him. Say I was ill, or something.'

Orestes wanted to kiss her. 'Would that be possible?'

'Of course. I'll send Petuna at once.' She called out for her slave girl, as Orestes took a deep breath. He was burning inside to see Hector, as if his life depended on it.

Dionakles had gone, and Hector's company were madly talking about the extraordinary turn of events. But Pausanius waited by the door, and beckoned to Hector. 'Hoplite, I need to speak to you alone.'

Nervously, Hector followed him outside. It was cloudy overhead, and evening was approaching. 'This isn't wise, Captain. People will start to think something is up, if you keep summoning me to private audiences.'

'You can tell them you have been given further secret information,' the captain sneered. 'I'm giving you a special commission. Making you leader of the company.'

They walked towards his hut. Hector glanced back. He wanted to run, escape from all this, find Orestes and bury himself in his warm, loving arms.

'My dick is as hard as a freshly forged sword, Hector,' the captain rasped into his ear. 'I'm going to wound you with it.'

Hector prayed silently to Aphrodite to deliver him from this torment, as the captain shut the door behind them, and lunged for the hoplite's groin. Hector's cock didn't stir. Even when Pausanius fell to his knees, covered his head in Hector's tunic and slobbered like a pig over his balls, his dick remained limp.

Pausanius, his own massive hard-on gripped in his hand – indeed like a sword – looked up at Hector with greedy eyes. 'This won't do, hoplite. If your sweet prick isn't as hard as mine, I'll report your crime with the foreigner.'

The captain stood, grabbed Hector's shoulders, and forced him down towards his bulging, avaricious cock.

'Suck it,' he hissed. 'Suck it hard.'

He buried his cock in Hector's face, still clasping the hoplite's shoulders, rocking him forward and back. Hector gagged on it, but Pausanius wouldn't release him. His dick thudded against Hector's throat. Hector wanted to die.

And as he felt his own cock spring, against his will, to life, he wanted to die there and then. It was hopeless: there was nothing he could do. This was the most terrible humiliation of his life. He loved Orestes, and wanted only him. He was ashamed, disgraced and dishonoured. But the captain's cock was a miracle; and this was the hero Pausanius, whatever he had become, whatever rot had set into his soul. Dismayed by the weakness of his will, Hector found his hands reaching up to seize the huge balls, grasp the slick, heavy shaft. His own cock surged greedily to its fullest, hardest erection, and he gripped it in his fist, horrified by the torrent of lust that rushed through him.

In despair, he grasped the captain's buttocks and pulled them to him, sinking the enormous cock into his mouth to the base. Pausanius grunted with debauched gratification.

Then Hector snatched his head away, and leapt to his feet. 'You want me?' he hissed, angrily. 'You're going to get me.'

Abruptly he pushed the captain backward; Pausanius toppled awkwardly, and Hector landed on top of him. They wrestled, their cocks sliding together, on the floor. Pausanius was strong, but Hector was consumed with rage and shame, and he pinned his captain down, slamming his back against the hard earth.

Triumphantly, he lifted Pausanius's legs, leant forward, and sank his cock into the hero's arse.

The monstrous cock strained with satisfaction, slapping hard against the warrior's stomach, as Hector pressed down, fucking him hard. Pausanius uttered a muffled moan of ecstasy, tightening the muscles of his arse around Hector's dick. Gripping his cock in both hands, Pausanius wanked it, rapidly, his teeth clenched and his neck bulging with effort. 'Oh, yes . . .' he whispered. 'Ram your wonderful prick inside me, oh yes . . .'

Pausanius came, shooting spurts of spunk across his chest, hitting himself in the face, writhing his arse in delight, as Hector convulsed in orgasm, amazed but horribly excited by the captain's utter, helpless surrender.

Hector pulled away immediately, disgusted with both Pausanius and himself. The captain lay on his back, drenched in come, his huge dick still solid in his hands, his eyes tight shut. Hector shook his own prick, splashing droplets of spunk on to Pausanius's face, and left the hut.

When he arrived back at the barracks he found Petuna, his mother's slave girl, saying he must go with her at once, because Ariadne was ill.

Fourteen

Ariadne left Orestes and Hector alone together in the courtyard. It was dark already but the stars that filled the sky
were brilliant and strong. Hector sat facing Orestes, his features
troubled and pale.

'I'm sorry if you were worried,' said Orestes. He ached to
touch Hector, just on his face.

'I was. I shouldn't be here.'

'This won't take long.'

Hector looked at him, miserably. Orestes didn't know what
was going on inside his beautiful head, but he wanted somehow
to soothe it.

That was impossible. After tonight, Hector might even hate
him.

'I want you to know, Hector –' he began; he paused, frightened suddenly of what he was going to say '– that I love you
like I never thought possible.'

Hector nodded, uncomfortably, shifting in his chair. 'I know.
But life is cruel.' He stared hard at Orestes, his expression stern
and unyielding. 'But you surely didn't bring me here just to tell
me that.'

'No. I haven't been honest with you.'

'It doesn't matter.' Hector wiped his hand over his face.

'Look –' He stood, very agitated. 'Orestes, you don't understand. We were seen in the woods.'

Orestes stared at him. 'Who by?'

'That doesn't matter, either. But I'm surviving on my wits at the moment. It's a nightmare.'

Orestes wanted to take him in his arms and protect him, banish his fears.

'I know you don't understand,' Hector went on. 'You try, but you think it's a foolish, stupid thing. And you're right. You're right to wonder why you can have Cleomenes' arse willingly, but mine is forbidden. But I am a Spartan, and Spartans have a strict sense of –' He struggled for the word.

'Hierarchy.'

'Yes. There are different orders, and I am of a low order. It's as simple as that. Certain things are forbidden to me. And therefore to you.'

'I do understand that.'

'Then why have you put my mother in this position? I've tried to explain to you: if we are exposed for what – for what I've done, my mother will be banished with me. It'll kill her. I can't stay.'

Orestes stood, and Hector faced him angrily.

'I might have been followed!' he said sharply.

Instinctively, Orestes looked behind him. The street beyond the courtyard was quite empty. He was torn now. The truth he had to tell might only make Hector's pain more unbearable. Who knew what disgrace these people might attach to sex with their bitterest enemy?

'But there's something you must know before we say good-bye,' he whispered. 'I can't leave without telling you the truth.'

Impatiently, Hector sat down again. 'Go on, then. Get on with it.'

Orestes hesitated. It was possible that, once he knew, Hector would run to his commanding officer and tell him everything. Orestes would be imprisoned, tortured and killed. But he had to tell him. 'I'm not from Syracuse,' he said eventually.

Hector looked through the dark at Orestes' face. 'What do you mean?'

'I'm not just a disinterested traveller, learning about Spartan customs, or whatever you think I am.'

'What are you then?' Hector's eyes burnt into him, as if he could not believe that his troubles had suddenly magnified.

'I'm an Athenian citizen, Hector. My father is one of the most prominent figures in the Assembly. And I'm in Sparta as a spy.'

Hector sat facing him in bewildered silence. Then he coughed in disbelief. 'A spy? For Athens?'

'Yes.'

'Well –' He laughed, a gasp of incredulous laughter. 'What have you learnt, then? Or can't you be honest about that?'

Orestes sighed, desolately. Hector was staring at him in out-rage. 'I've learnt there's an alliance between Sparta and some Athenian traitors.'

Hector stared at him for a moment, and blinked. Then he sat back, cracking his fingers. 'And what? You think I might know something, and you can wheedle some further intelligence out of me – is that it? Maybe you thought that in the throes of passion, while you were singing the praises of my tight Spartan arse, I might accidentally tell you our greatest military secrets. Sorry to disappoint you.'

'Hector, of course not.'

Hector glared at him. 'Why have you told me now?'

'Because I wanted you to know who I really am. If you hate me, it's the price I pay for loving you too much to lie any more.'

Hector shook his head, his eyes welling with tears. 'The helplessness of men before Fate, or something, you said. When you were telling me about your Athenian tragedies. I should have realised you were an Athenian then, you got so upset about it. Is there no end to my stupidity?'

He stood, abruptly.

'I must go. Tell my mother I'll see her as soon as I can.' He walked towards the gate. 'My advice to you . . .' He lowered his voice, and glanced at him, sadly. 'My beloved enemy, my advice is to get out of Sparta as soon as you can.'

'You'll inform on me.'

'Who do you think I am? I'm a Spartan soldier. In the last few days I have committed every possible dishonour, but treason will not be one of them.'

He strode to the gate and out into the street. Orestes watched him go, his throat tightening. He fought down a sob, and almost ran after him.

Then he realised Ariadne was standing in the door to the house.

'You argued, didn't you?' she said, softly.

He nodded. 'Did you hear what we said?'

'No. Of course not. I don't care what you said. I know my son loves you, whatever you or he have to say to each other. I don't care about anything else.'

The sob lurched out of his lungs, and Ariadne stepped up, putting her arms around him. Orestes tried to hold his pain back, but the sobs stuttered out, and he wept into her breast.

Hector galloped back over the fields in a state of utter panic. The wind blew the tears from his eyes as he raced towards the camp. What was he going to do? Now the nightmare was complete: Orestes a spy for Athens. And a spy who knew something about the mission he was himself involved in.

His duty was clear. Spartan victory might depend upon him. If Orestes' intelligence reached the Athenian command, they would be alerted to the plot, defeat it, and perhaps capture and murder the Spartans involved in it. His comrades. Himself. He had to tell someone there was a spy in their midst. Orestes must be caught and put to death.

But how could he do that? How could he play a part in the murder of the man he loved?

And, anyway, was it so clear? Dionakles and the other Athenians they were to be working with: they were traitors, weren't they? How could Sparta be making deals with traitors? How could they trust them? Even your enemies have the right to some honour. To ally with traitors was . . .

It seemed to Hector simply wrong. Of course, he didn't

know. He wasn't a general or a strategist, or a politician, just a low-ranking soldier with an insatiable hunger for cock. Important people had decided this was right. Who was he to contradict them?

But if there were people in Athens like Orestes . . . Orestes' family lived there. He had mentioned his mother. They were strange people, obviously, with peculiar customs. But could he play a part in seeing them murdered in their sleep? If Orestes' father was an important man, maybe he was one of the Athenians he would be told to murder. It was unthinkable.

Why did Dionakles want an alliance with Sparta? What had driven him to betray his own people like this? To betray Orestes.

With an awful jolt in his chest, he realised that Dionakles might well know Orestes, and recognise him. What danger would Orestes be in if that happened? Surely the visiting generals didn't know Orestes was here, or they would have reported him already . . . Unless they were part of some complex plan . . . But no, Orestes had said they were traitors.

Hector's head was spinning. He slowed his horse, needing more time to think.

Then he realised he was right by Epharon's grave.

He climbed from the horse, and slowly approached the mound of earth where he had buried his friend. The garland of olive twigs was still there. He knelt beside the grave, and put a hand on the soft, fresh soil.

'My dear Eph,' he whispered. 'What shall I do?'

Only the wind answered him, blowing gently against his face. He lifted a handful of earth to his cheek, and felt it, cold against his skin, as though it would bring him closer to his dead comrade.

There was a soft rustling sound behind him, and he spun around. He could see nothing. 'Who's there?'

Again just the wind whistled solemnly through the nearby trees.

'Who's there?' Tears spilt from Hector's eyes.

There was a shape, moving towards him through the night, a

shadow under the stars, gliding as if by magic across the dirt. It was a hooded figure, and he knew who it was.

'Messenger of Aphrodite,' he sobbed. 'Tell me what to do.'

The Egyptian glided up to him, lifting the cowl from his boyish face. 'Look into your heart, Hector,' he murmured in his strange, slight accent.

'My heart's useless,' said Hector angrily. 'My heart is breaking.'

'Who do you trust?' said the Egyptian. 'That's what matters.'

'I don't trust anyone.' Hector looked down at Epharon's grave. 'I trusted him. I don't trust anyone else.'

'You know that's not true.' Hector looked up pleadingly at the apparition's face. 'You trust the Athenian. You love him, and you trust him. You know you do.'

'Who are you?' Hector screamed. 'How do you know everything about me?'

'I am the messenger of Aphrodite,' said the Egyptian. 'And you trust me, too.'

Hector was alone by Epharon's grave, the wind stirring the topsoil, his horse snorting a short distance away. He climbed to his feet.

'I don't understand,' he wailed. 'I don't understand!'

Orestes found a place to sit and watch Cleomenes' house where he would not be seen. He hadn't seen Cleomenes since the night before the Feast, no doubt because the Spartan was busy with affairs of state. He hoped Theddalus was safely away from Sparta by now. He hoped Hector would forgive him.

Orestes sat in the shadows and waited.

Hector trotted into the camp, took his horse to the stables, and crossed the gravel towards his barracks. As he drew near, he heard the sound of a voice which he recognised as that of Pausanius.

Hector felt suddenly that something altogether strange was taking place. He didn't know why he thought this; but it was another premonition, of sorts. He held his breath, afraid of what he would see, and decided not to go straight in. He crept around the side of the barracks, and knelt down by a window to peer inside.

What he saw he could hardly believe. His eight surviving comrades were there; but so too was Pausanius, and Dionakles, and another, a swarthy, stocky man he didn't recognise, whom he knew at once to be another Athenian officer. All of them were naked. The Athenians were standing with one hand on their hip, the other gripping a thick, pulsing hard-on. Pausanius was speaking; and his huge cock was lurching to erection. The hoplites were standing in a row, some of them with cocks swelling greedily as the captain spoke, although all of them had perplexed, unhappy faces, as if their minds and their groins were at cross-purposes.

'We made offerings to Aries, God of War,' Pausanius said, his voice firm and authoritative. 'And Aries spoke to us, giving this union his blessing. So be assured, hoplites. What you are now about to do is no dishonour or disgrace. You are doing it for Sparta, to seal our alliance with these generals of Athens.'

The swarthy Athenian general seemed impatient, and swaggered forward, his pendulous cock lurching from side to side. The hoplites glanced anxiously at each other, but the insistent stiffness of their dicks was dispelling their doubts.

But for a moment, nobody moved. Hector watched through the window, afraid, appalled – but his heart was beating faster: he was captivated by the ghastly scene. The Athenian gripped his cock, holding it out to be adored. The hoplites' eyes nervously feasted on this forbidden, delicious offering. Timos stepped up to the Athenian, his impressive rod pulsing with intrigued lust.

Hector stared through the window, unseen, horrified but helplessly fascinated. His dick hardened; against all decency, he wanted to watch Timos be a slave to the Athenian's will. He thrilled at the prospect of his comrade's surrender.

Timos the wrestler sank to his knees, gazing up into the swarthy general's eyes, and slowly, sensuously, eased his lips over the voracious purple head. The general grunted in satisfaction.

The Spartan soldiers watched in amazement, slowly starting to wank themselves.

Hector shivered with awful, shameful excitement. His erection swelled further, the head easing itself from his moistening foreskin.

Dionakles, his cock thick but slightly flat, like a slab of meat, seized Severon by the shoulders and forced him down; the Spartan dropped willingly to his knees and started to suck. Pausanius was watching, his eyes aflame, his enormous weapon gripped tightly in both hands.

Hector was repelled yet forced to watch. He understood what was happening to his comrades: they were afraid, unsure of Pausanius's reassurances, but eager for a taste of new fruit. More than that: Hector shared the perverse thrill of being conquered by their enemies, of yielding, recklessly, to their power, suffering the humiliation and revelling in it. It thrilled him: his cock twitched as he stared at Timos, powerful Timos, gorging his mouth on the general's cock, his own straining to burst, bobbing at his stomach. Breathlessly, Hector gripped his erection and watched.

Gatha, drooling with lust, crouched down beside Timos to share the alien delights. They ran their tongues down each side of the dark length of the swarthy general's dick; then Gatha buried his mouth under the outsider's balls as his comrade seized the shaft and sank his lips back over it. 'Suck it, Spartan,' the general whispered, his buttocks trembling with pleasure.

Severon was joined by other young soldiers to worship at Dionakles' temple. An olive-skinned youth forced his tongue into Dionakles' arsehole, another ducked under Severon to suck the Athenian's balls. Hesitantly, but with eyes glassy with desire, a smooth, muscular hoplite approached his captain, gazing mesmerised at Pausanius's enormous cock, and greedily dropped to feast on it.

Hector wanked himself fiercely, wishing he could avert his eyes, but transfixed by perverse excitement.

The hoplites were losing their inhibitions, and began to surrender utterly to their basest, most obscene thirst. Timos's head was consuming the swarthy general's dick; beside him, Gatha was blubbering with uncontrolled lust, as the Athenian's balls collided with his face. Dionakles was leaning back, adoring hoplites attached to his nipples, his arsehole, his cock, his balls. Hector trembled as he gazed at the rigid, flexing cocks of his comrades, the sheer helplessness of their desire. Pausanius was thrusting his swollen shaft into a hungry face, grunting: despite everything, Hector longed to leap through the window and taste that cock again himself. He beat his erection, hot and hard in his hand.

The swarthy general pushed Timos abruptly away from him, and forced him to the bed. Knocking him down, face on the bunk and buttocks in the air, he pressed his cock against Timos's eager arse. Gatha, his erection beading pre-come in his fist, lay on his back to suck feverishly at the Athenian's balls as his shaft plunged into Timos's arse. Timos wailed in delicious pain, grinding his cock into the bed, reaching behind to grip the general's buttocks, pull him in deeper.

Dionakles pushed three hoplites to another bed, and lined them up, their cocks squirming into the bunk, as he sank his fat dick into first one arse then the next. Pausanius was fucking Severon, long and lean on his back, his taut cock mashing against the captain's stomach.

One by one, the hoplites began to exclaim in breathy, ecstatic gasps, 'Fuck me! Fuck me!' until they were almost crying out in unison, relishing their surrender. It was agony for Hector to watch; but he wanted to join this debauched, reckless Saturnalia, to offer his soft, pliant arse to one of these men. It shamed him to see his comrades so utterly discard their dignity, their pride, and capitulate so completely; but he longed to be part of the luscious ignominy. Gatha was slobbering like a deranged animal at the swarthy general's heavy, swinging balls, which crashed against Timos's arse as he fucked him. Gatha's entire stocky body was a knot of tense, lustful muscle: his cock was red and bruised from the violence of his wanking fist. Timos was yelling, wriggling his arse to accept the Athenian's thrusts. Every hoplite was a quivering, helpless slave to the cock he was serving, each erection like a pole of greased wood; their faces were contorted with the carnal voracity that had overwhelmed them. It was the same secret desire that had made Hector a helpless slavering idiot with Pausanius, a desire to be possessed which would erupt as soon as it had the chance.

His comrades were competing with each other now, begging Pausanius or Dionakles or the swarthy one to impale them; it scarcely mattered which. None of them made the slightest attempt to reverse the priority of power: they were consumed with the need to be fucked by forbidden cocks; their own dicks, shining with pre-come, and the wails from their throats were testimony to the thoroughness of their subjugation. Hector gazed at his comrades' stiff cocks, frenzied with excitement at the sight, staggering slightly as he pummelled his erection, reached under his balls to force a finger into his arsehole.

Gatha came, his hot spunk shooting high into the air, as he sobbed into the general's groin. Soon, others were coming, delighting in the dicks that ravished their welcoming flesh. At the window, Hector stifled his sob of orgasm, and collapsed on to his face on the earth, disgorging his load on to the gravel, his forefinger rammed inside his arse, the gasps of his comrades ringing in his ears.

As he gradually calmed down, Hector rolled on to his back. In the barracks, the orgy continued. He could hear Athenian voices demanding further favours, and Pausanius telling a gasping Gatha to devour his huge cock.

Hector had to get away: this was a monstrous thing he had seen. But not because of the carnal pleasure of his comrades, which was as innocent as it was overwhelming – but because he knew Pausanius was lying to them.

There had been no blessing from Aries. This was clearly a terrible, private arrangement between Pausanius and the Athenian generals. Pausanius had sunk into depravity: he no longer cared what became of him, or the hoplites in his charge. He merely wanted to fuck them, and enjoy watching the Athenians fuck them. Probably, when the orgy had been agreed, Pausanius had expected Hector to be there, and had planned to savour watching Hector, like the others, at the helpless mercy of those lunging Athenian dicks, and then to taunt him afterwards.

It convinced him of one thing: no good could come of this alliance with these Athenian traitors. And he no longer knew or cared what was right, or good, for Sparta. He had to find Orestes and save him.

Fifteen

Orestes was hidden across the street from the ephor's house, where lamps were burning, wrapped in his cloak, covered in shadow. He was uncomfortable in the dark, and starting to wonder if he had come to the right place. Perhaps the traitors were being entertained elsewhere.

But, just as he thought perhaps he should leave, he heard the sound of hooves on the rough street, and a group of horsemen drew near. Cleomenes was leading them, and he recognised Lyador. There were three other men with their faces hidden under hoods. He could not see who they were, but he knew he had found what he was looking for.

The horsemen dismounted and went into the house, before Orestes could catch sight of their faces. Deeply frustrated, he thought quickly about what to do. He had to know who these traitors were.

He crept out of the shadows, and across the road. There were windows in the side of the house, overlooking the street, and the shadows of men moved inside. Orestes hid behind the horses and tried to catch a glimpse of them. He could hear the murmur of voices, but see nothing: he would have to get closer. A horse whinnied softly as he pushed between them, edging towards the side of the house. The murmur of voices grew louder.

Orestes slunk quietly to the wall. He was visible here from the street, so he carefully sidled around the house. From there he could reach another window, more secretive than the one at the front, and peer inside. Cloaked in shadow, Orestes made his way around the corner.

The window looked into the main hall of the ephor's house, where guests would be entertained. He squatted at the wall, and lifted his head, tentatively, to look in.

He could see Cleomenes, sitting stiffly on a bench, uncomfortable, perhaps, with having the enemy in his house, and an older man, a stern, proud gentleman in the robes of a leading notable, whom he presumed to be Cleomenes' father. To one side was Lyador. But the three strangers had their backs to him. He could just hear their voices, speaking softly, as conspirators do; one of them he thought he recognised but could not place. Briefly, Orestes wondered how long it would be before the Spartan warlords were draining the Athenians of their sperm, and for a moment it seemed almost funny. But he strained his ears to hear what was being said.

Only snatches of conversation came to him. '. . . Matter of the greatest importance . . .' 'You must appreciate the sensitivity of our position . . .' 'Need to act ruthlessly and fast . . .'

Orestes shivered with anger. What were these people doing? What monstrous act were they proposing? He shifted on his feet, his calves hurting a little from the effort of crouching, and tried to get a better view, hoping to see their faces.

Then he heard the sound of more horses. He ducked further into the shadows and turned to see who this new arrival might be. Two men on horseback charged closer, then pulled in their horses and leapt from the backs, as though they were in a hurry, or late. And, as they quickly tethered the horses, Orestes could see who they were.

Dionakles and Kreon. Now everything made sense.

For a moment, Orestes was too shocked to move. He waited as the two Athenian generals disappeared from view, approaching the front door. He heard Cleomenes welcome them, and the murmur of introductions inside.

It was suddenly clear who the other traitors would be. This was a faction of old Athenian aristocrats, their families owners of large tracts of land in Attica, and with roots back into the distant past, from long before Athens was a democracy. Ever suspicious of the popular will, Dionakles and his group had at times openly advocated tyranny – the election of a king – as a way to best manage the war with Sparta. In their ranks they had some important intellectuals, harsh critics of the 'mob rule' they claimed had hold of the city, among them the peculiar philosopher Socrates, whose reputation had spread far across Greece.

Orestes couldn't believe that all of these people would be prepared to ally with Sparta: but clearly, there was a significant faction among them that had decided to think the unthinkable. It would come as no surprise if Dionakles and his coterie were secretly admirers of the Spartan system; but treason was incomprehensible. Orestes forced himself to concentrate. For certain, their motive here was not to allow the Spartans to march victorious through the streets of Athens. They had some trap prepared, no doubt, some plan to use the Spartans and then betray them. But that it was insane was perfectly clear: these fools were playing with fire, and the very survival of Athens.

He knew enough. Orestes crept back along the wall towards the street. He would have to leave Sparta tonight.

But in his haste he lost his footing and slipped, his foot scraping noisily against the grit on the ground.

There was sudden silence in the house. Orestes bolted for the street, then froze as he saw Cleomenes standing at the door.

'Orestes? Is that you?'

Orestes thought quickly. 'Sorry, Cleomenes, I see you have guests.' He indicated the horses. 'I'll come back tomorrow.'

'What were you doing?' Cleomenes peered at him through the darkness.

'Nothing. I thought I'd visit. It's all right.'

But, before Orestes could turn to go, Dionakles drew up beside Cleomenes, black against the light of the lamps inside. 'What is it, Cleomenes? Who's there?'

Orestes tried to shrink into his cloak, as the Athenian general's eyes searched the darkness to see him.

'Just a traveller from Syracuse,' said Cleomenes. But he had lost none of his suspicion. 'Why don't you come inside for a while, Orestes?'

'Orestes?' The name seemed to register in the general's mind, and he stepped out into the street. Orestes stepped back. 'From Syracuse?' He strode forward, and Orestes knew he must run. He turned and fled into the darkness of the Spartan streets. Behind him, he heard Dionakles shout with rage, 'He's not from Syracuse, you idiot!' And then he heard the scramble of feet, the snorts from the flayed nostrils of the horses.

Orestes turned, panicking, into an alleyway, scrambled over a wall, and hurtled, bent double, past low stone cottages. Chickens suddenly scattered at his feet, and he cursed the noise they made. He vaulted another wall, stamped through the mud of a pigsty, then raced down broken cobbles towards the deepest shadows he could find.

Not far off were the cries of Cleomenes, Dionakles and the rest, the stamp of the horses' hooves on the Spartan streets. People were appearing from their homes in the nearby alleys to see what the excitement was.

Orestes kept running. There was no sanctuary here. Nobody would protect him. He was completely surrounded by Spartans, each one of whom would seize him if they found him, and hand him over to their leaders. His horse was back at Ariadne's inn – but that was the first place they would look. His heart stopped suddenly, afraid that they would believe she knew all along who he was, and punish her. But what could he do?

He needed a horse.

He raced down a narrow street, the rattle of hooves further behind him now. But he was hopelessly lost. He stopped, looked around, afraid that whichever way he went he would only run straight into the people chasing him. He chose another street, and ran towards a little square he thought he recognised: perhaps he could gain his bearings from there.

There was the sound of galloping behind him. Orestes spun

around, tearing his sword from its sheath. A single horse with a hooded rider charged towards him, then suddenly slowed. The horse, a powerful stallion, reared up, then came to a halt, snorting and pounding the street with its hoof.

Orestes gripped the handle of sword, his body tensed to fight.

But the horseman lifted the hood from his face to reveal his boyish, dark face. It was the Egyptian, the priest of Aphrodite.

Orestes hesitated. The Egyptian held out his hand, fixing Orestes with his brown eyes. Orestes hesitated, doubtfully, and the priest urgently stretched his hand further. Orestes had no choice: he grasped his hand, and the Egyptian lifted him on to the bare back of the horse.

'How did you find me?' he hissed into the heavy cloak of the priest.

'Orestes. I have never left your side.'

The Egyptian spun his horse around, and charged back in the opposite direction. The horse flew over the rough, potholed street; Orestes wondered suddenly how horses negotiated these streets without breaking their legs. There was noise in the alleyways beside them; he could hear Cleomenes' voice calling Spartans to the alert. For a moment, Orestes froze in panic, believing the Egyptian was taking him straight to his enemies, but then they turned into another lane, and the shouts of his hunters grew fainter.

Ahead, racing towards them, was another rider, cloak billowing behind him, the moonlight hitting his face.

It was Hector.

The hoplite reined in his horse as he saw them approach, his eyes shining with fear and amazement. Orestes wished he could leap from the horse and embrace him. But he wasn't sure why Hector was there, or what he would do. Maybe he was looking for the Athenian spy to capture him and hand him over.

'They're looking for you,' Hector said breathlessly. His horse reared up, and spun around, frightened by the excitement in the night. Even in all this danger, Orestes' heart welled with happiness: Hector had chosen not to betray him.

'Quickly,' said the Egyptian. 'You must leave the city.'

Hector quietened his horse, and looked at the priest in bemusement.

'Wait!' hissed Orestes. He looked urgently at Hector. 'We've got to warn your mother.' The Egyptian twisted his body to gaze at Orestes' face. 'I'm afraid for her. They might think she knew who I was.'

Hector stared at him with burning eyes. 'I'll go. They'll be looking for you.'

The Egyptian dug his heels into his horse to ride on. Orestes turned to look at Hector as they passed him: their eyes met, in silent understanding. Orestes watched him disappear in the distance, until he suddenly sped off in the direction of Ariadne's inn.

'What will happen to him?' he shouted as they galloped on.

'He'll find us,' said the priest. He bent his head into the wind, and charged through the dark streets.

Hector raced to his mother's house, leaping from his horse as soon as he arrived. The gate was swinging open: Cleomenes was already there.

He ran into the courtyard to find the Spartan commander gripping his mother by the wrist. Petuna the slave girl was sobbing in a corner; Nekos was remonstrating angrily with Cleomenes but keeping his distance.

Cleomenes spun around when he heard Hector behind him, not letting go of Ariadne's arm.

'Who are you?'

'Hector, no!' wailed Ariadne.

'Release her!' Hector yelled.

Cleomenes drew his sword. Hector stared at the weapon in his hand, catching the starlight. His mother shrank away from it.

Hector's sword was still hanging on the saddle of his horse. But he tossed aside his cloak, and glared in rage at Cleomenes. 'Let go of my mother,' he whispered.

Cleomenes pushed Ariadne away, brutally, and lunged at Hector with his sword. Hector ducked back, reached for a chair, and swung it around to defend himself. The sword crashed through the soft wood, but Cleomenes overbalanced slightly, and Hector seized the initiative. He twisted his body, pulling the sword, entangled with the broken chair, and kicked at Cleomenes' leg. The young nobleman tripped; the sword spun from his hand. Hector dived forward, gripping Cleomenes around his waist, and knocked him backward against the table. The wood cracked under the weight of their two bodies.

Without pausing for breath, Hector landed a punch in Cleomenes' stomach, and rammed his forehead into his nose. Cleomenes cried out in pain – but kicked upward, his knee savagely crashing into Hector's testicles.

Nearly vomiting with pain, Hector felt himself rolled on to his back, the senior man wrestling on top of him, pinning him with his knees. Cleomenes seized Hector's head in his hands and cracked it back against the ground. For a moment Hector saw only darkness. The pain in his groin was excruciating. Above him, Cleomenes' face was a grimace of triumphant fury. He punched Hector brutally in the face, and he tasted the blood which oozed into his mouth. He struggled, trying to free his arms, to gain some purchase with his legs, but Cleomenes was incredibly strong. Through the pain, Hector was aware of Cleomenes' cock surging to erection, digging into his groin, as if, with Hector helpless beneath him, he would savagely complete his victory by claiming the hoplite's arse. Hector strained every muscle in his arms to throw the officer off; but he was getting weaker. As another blow hit him in the face he was losing consciousness.

Then Cleomenes went limp. As Hector's vision hazily returned, he could see Cleomenes' eyes looking down, shocked and glassy; the knees pinning him to the ground trembled, and released him.

The nobleman's own sword had been plunged through his back, its tip emerging, bloodily, from his chest.

Cleomenes toppled over. Behind him, her face white with terror, was Ariadne.

Hector stared up at her. She was trembling in horror.

Nekos ran forward. 'Quickly, both of you,' he said. 'Get out of here.'

Ariadne looked at him, numb with shock. 'What about you?'

'Don't worry, I'm leaving.' He ran to Petuna, who was sobbing uncontrollably, and lifted her from the ground. 'Go on. Run!'

Hector looked down at Cleomenes' corpse, stunned by the enormity of what they had done. They had killed an aristocrat. The punishment for that would be no mere banishment: the penalty was death.

He stared at his mother, who was still staring at Cleomenes' body, numbly. There was blood seeping into Hector's mouth. His groin was throbbing with pain. His head was bashed and bruised. Ariadne threw her arms around him, clasping him tightly. She was terrified.

Nekos hissed at them across the courtyard. 'Get her out of here!'

Hector grabbed his mother's hand, and pulled her out into the street.

Orestes and the Egyptian galloped across the fields, the city behind them, the open countryside ahead. Orestes clung to the priest's body, the wind whipping his face. The earth beneath them flew by, as though they were racing at uncanny speed, the horse's hooves not touching the ground.

Suddenly, the Egyptian pulled in the reins, and the stallion drew up. The priest climbed down.

'Where are you going?'

'Back. Don't worry. Wait here. Hector will join you shortly.'

'How do you know?'

'He'll be here. But as soon as he arrives race like the wind until you reach a little village by the side of a river. You'll find a peasant woman called Alyssia. She'll hide you until morning.'

The Egyptian pulled up his hood and started to walk back to the city.

'Wait,' called Orestes. 'I haven't thanked you!'

But the messenger of Aphrodite had disappeared into the gloom.

A short while afterwards, sitting on the stallion's back, Orestes heard the thud of a horse's hooves on the dusty soil. He peered into the dark, afraid of Cleomenes or his men. But he quickly recognised Hector, his mother behind him in the saddle.

Hector slowed to a canter when he saw Orestes. They reached forward, without leaving their horses, and embraced each other tearfully, kissing.

'You shouldn't have come,' said Orestes.

Hector laughed, grimly. 'No choice now.'

Orestes gripped Ariadne's hand. 'I'm so sorry,' he whispered.

Ariadne looked back at Sparta. 'We should go,' she said. 'They'll be looking for us.'

With a final glance back at the place of his birth, Hector clicked the reins in his hands, and galloped ahead.

Orestes kicked his heels into the stallion's flanks and sped after them. His mind was racing. He couldn't understand why Hector, let alone Ariadne, had chosen to abandon their city and go with him. Something terrible had happened.

The stallion was miraculously fast, and he soon overtook the others, and had to rein him in so Hector could keep up. It was like another magical gift from the mysterious Egyptian. He felt suddenly as if even the stars above were on his side; some supernatural guardian was protecting him, rescuing him from death, and bringing the man he loved to him. Whatever the danger pursuing them, or lying ahead, Orestes was glad, in a way he had never been glad before.

Sixteen

It was still dark when they reached the top of a low hill and looked down at a village: a few huts by the side of a river. The stars were bright overhead.

As they rode down the hill, a candle was lit in the window of a little hut, and a face looked out – an old, wizened face belonging to an ancient woman, a crone.

'We're looking for Alyssia,' said Orestes nervously.

'Come to the right place, then,' the crone cackled. 'That's me.'

A moment later she appeared through the front door, and reached up for the reins of Orestes' stallion to begin tying them to a wooden pole. Orestes, Hector and Ariadne climbed down from their horses, waited while she finished tethering them, and followed her into the hut.

It was a small, wooden cottage, with a fire to one side, which she bent down to light, a metal cooking pot hanging over it. The place smelt of fish. 'I've been expecting you,' she said with a toothless grin. Ariadne, exhausted, sat on a rug of fleece by the fireside. 'Wasn't sure you'd get here, though. But I've made you some soup.'

'What do you mean, you were expecting us?' said Orestes. 'We didn't know we were coming ourselves.'

'Ah,' said Alyssia.

Hector squeezed Orestes' hand, then went to the fire to inhale the thick odour of the fish soup. 'I think the gods are looking after us.'

Later, warmed by the hot broth, they were shown to their beds. Sheepskins were scattered along one side of the hut. Ariadne and Alyssia shared one pile of skins, and Orestes and Hector climbed under another a short distance away. Alyssia blew out the candle, but the fire still smouldered across the room, filling the room with a sombre, red glow.

Soon there was the sound of the crone's soft snoring. Ariadne seemed fast asleep.

Orestes and Hector snuggled closely together under the fleece, Orestes' head nuzzled into the Spartan's neck, his arm draped over his chest. They were warm, and felt safe. Hector twisted his neck, and Orestes lazily kissed him, lifting his knee up Hector's thigh until it gently brushed against his balls. Their faces were flushed in the firelight.

Orestes pressed his erection against Hector's thigh, as the Spartan caressed his hair, touched his cheek. They kissed again, Hector turning his hips so their hard-ons brushed against each other; for a while they stayed like this, mouths joined tenderly, stiff pricks playfully fencing. Orestes murmured sleepily, stroking his fingers down Hector's back and circling his buttocks. Hector reached down and lightly tickled Orestes' cock, carefully gliding the foreskin down from the head, and smoothing a dribble of pre-come over the slit. Orestes gripped Hector's warm erection in his hand, loosely, moving his fingers up and down the tight, stretched skin. They continued this way, indolently, for a long time, each of their cocks growing moist, flexing and kicking in delight at the other's touch.

Orestes moved his mouth to Hector's full, knotted nipples. He took one carefully between his teeth, his hand still loosely holding the Spartan's dick. Hector shivered with pleasure; his cock flexed. He kissed Orestes' tousled hair, as the Athenian bit

195

harder, more urgently, at his chest, circling his tongue around the soft hairs which surrounded the dark circle on his chest.

Orestes moved down Hector's body, kissing every inch of naked, goosepimpled skin, until his face was hovering over the warm, kicking cock. He ran his tongue down its length, tenderly eased back the foreskin, and kissed the cleft by the head where the foreskin was attached. He tickled the sides of the warm shaft with his fingers, stroked his tongue over the tip, lapping the salty juices which were seeping from it. Hector shivered, moaned softly, running his hands through Orestes' hair.

For a while Orestes teased him, caressing Hector's balls so lightly he would hardly feel it, kissing the stiff cock. Then he lifted it with one hand so it was vertical, and covered it with his mouth – still not touching it, just enclosing it with his warm breath. He gripped Hector's balls more tightly, felt the cock throb against his teeth, then closed his lips around the shaft. Slowly, very slowly, Orestes moved his lips up, then down, the thick cock. With his other hand he squeezed Hector's nipple, and the Spartan sighed, arching his back, lifting his cock deep into Orestes' adoring mouth.

Hector shifted slowly, turning his body; the sheepskin slipped from them, but they were warm enough from the dying fire and their lovemaking not to need it. Hector moved so that they could suck each other, side by side. As Orestes continued luxuriously caressing his cock with his mouth, Hector gripped the Athenian's hard, needy dick and stared at it, as if it amazed him. He blew on it gently, on the contracting, hairy balls, then delicately licked the tip. Orestes' cock grew utterly rigid in Hector's hand, and he lowered his face, more forcefully, over the Spartan's hard-on. Hector stared for long moments at the solid shaft of muscle, then sank his mouth down on it, lustfully, absorbing it up to the balls.

Orestes pushed Hector's buttocks gently, rolling him on to his back, as they continued sucking each other. Orestes was over Hector now, his cock pulled back to plunge down into the Spartan's mouth as he hovered over Hector's groin, twisting his head to devour the cock from every angle, gazing down at the luscious balls. Orestes' balls dangled in Hector's face; for a moment Hector released the cock from his mouth to adore them, while Orestes' cock squirmed, slippery and warm on his face. Hector licked from Orestes' balls up towards his arsehole, lathering the firm muscle between his legs with spit; Orestes did the same, gripping Hector's dick in his hand as he lowered his face between the strong thighs and licked, passionately, at his ring.

They sank their tongues into each other's arsehole, their stiff, wet cocks rubbing hard into each other's chest. Both of them were trembling, stretching to force their tongues up into the other's crack, wriggling their hips in delight. Orestes returned to sucking, swallowing Hector's cock with a soft gasp of desire, and Hector twisted his neck to seize the Athenian's balls between his lips.

Orestes licked his finger, and squeezed it gently into Hector's arse. The Spartan gasped with pleasure. Still sucking, harder now, Orestes forced his finger in, stretching Hector's arsehole. Hector spread his legs, adoring the tremulous thrill which shot inside him. He grabbed Orestes' cock and choked on it, swallowing its length greedily.

Hector pushed at Orestes' hips, indicating he wanted him to move. The Athenian turned to kneel over him. They looked into each other's face, flushed and trembling, and kissed, tasting each other's mouth. Hector hitched his ankles over Orestes' shoulders and lifted his thighs, reaching down with one hand to grasp the Athenian's cock, gorged and straining, and to guide it into him.

Orestes pushed, gently forcing the head into Hector's arse. Hector's face screwed up in a brief moment of pain, but he seized Orestes' hips, begging him to enter further. Orestes slowly pushed in the full length of his cock.

Hector looked up at his lover's passion-inflamed face, as he gripped his arse tightly around the shaft inside, which started to pump. His own cock was incredibly hard, rising from his stomach, straining. Orestes spat on his hand and lathered Hector's cock, wanking it slowly as he fucked him. The Athenian bent forward, Hector's feet behind his head, and they kissed: Hector sucked Orestes' tongue into his mouth. Their bodies rocked, and Orestes' dick slid back and forth; Hector clasped Orestes to him, his legs tight around the Athenian's neck as he lifted his hips, flexed his powerful thighs in time with Hector's thrusting. Sweat dripped from Orestes' body on to Hector's. They were sliding against each other, sticky from each other's sweat, their bodies moving faster and faster.

The rocking of the fuck took over. Every muscle was trembling, as the rhythm of their hips overpowered them. Orestes seized Hector's legs for balance, his cock plunging into the tender, eager arsehole. Their faces were contorted in ecstasy. Hector's cock was utterly solid, rock-hard, the thrill of Orestes' dick inside him sending tremors of pleasure through him. Orestes gazed down at his lover's rigid shaft with deep, proud desire. The muscles in Hector's smooth chest were hard, expanding to their limit. The gorgeous muscles in the side of his neck were stretched and rigid. Orestes' chest was heaving, the tendons tight. They each breathed quickly, heavily, in time with the instincts of their hips.

Hector came. His cock bloated, the head swelled, and jets of spunk shot over his chest, hitting him in the mouth, the eye, and landing behind him on the sheepskin. He stifled his sobs of pleasure, as his arse tightened around Orestes' cock. Orestes fell forward, Hector's spunk squashing between their chests as he emptied himself inside his Spartan lover.

They grinned and kissed lovingly, their eyes closed, and Orestes eased out his cock. Hector pulled Orestes down to lie on him, and slowly tickled his back, as they continued to kiss. Their cocks were still hard. As they gazed into each other's eyes, each felt the thrill of his lover's cock, swelling again, digging into his stomach.

'I love you,' Hector whispered.

Orestes kissed him again. 'More than anything in the world,' he said.

Orestes slid down beside Hector, and pulled the sheepskin

around them, laying his head on the Spartan's chest. He could hear the heartbeat, still hard and fast with excitement.

Hector glanced over at his mother. In a low voice, he said, 'Do you think she heard us?'

Orestes shook his head. 'She's asleep.'

Hector stifled a giggle. 'I hope she's asleep.'

Orestes stroked Hector's face. There were tears of love in his eyes. 'Don't worry about her.'

They wrapped their limbs around each other's body and fell, finally, to sleep.

They were awoken suddenly by the sound of horses. Hector's eyes snapped open, and he pushed back the sheepskin. Orestes stirred sleepily beside him as he climbed to his feet.

It was light outside, well past dawn. Hector hurried to the window, and peered out. There was mist rising from the river. In the distance were shapes, horsemen, descending the hill.

'Don't worry your pretty head about them.' Alyssia was across the room, warming her hands by the fire. Orestes was awake now, grabbing his tunic and rushing to Hector's side. Ariadne lifted her head from her sheepskin pillow, fear in her face.

The horses drew closer, their hooves thudding ominously on the turf. Hector seized his sword from where it was leaning by a wall. Orestes threw him his tunic to cover his nakedness. There was the sound of voices.

To Hector's dismay, Alyssia hobbled to the door and went outside.

He crouched down by the window with Orestes, each of them afraid the crone would betray them. Hector waved to Ariadne to keep out of sight. They heard the horses stop, stamping the ground, and a voice spoke haughtily. It was Dionakles.

'Whose horses are these, old woman?'

'Oh, just the men of the village,' she wheezed.

There was a pause. Hector gripped his sword. Orestes had his in his hand. They hardly dare breathe.

'They don't look like villagers' horses.'

'Don't they? One horse looks same as another to me.'

'Who's staying in your shack?' demanded another voice. This was Lyador.

'Nobody.'

'We'll have to look,' said Dionakles. There was the sound of him dismounting from his horse.

Hector and Orestes grasped their swords tightly in their hands. Ariadne, across the room, grabbed a carving knife, and held it, anxiously, by her side.

'Nothing to see,' said Alyssia.

There was a terrible moment of silence, which seemed to stretch on for ever. Hector's heart was pounding in his throat.

'All right,' said Dionakles suddenly. They heard his footsteps returning to his horse. 'If you see anyone . . .' But then he just grunted, and swung back into his saddle.

Amazed, Hector listened as the horses galloped off into the mist.

Alyssia came back into the cottage, and looked at them calmly. 'Bread and olives do you for breakfast?'

'We have to be going,' said Orestes. He found his sandals, and started to tie the straps around his leg. 'Or they'll get to Athens before us.'

'What will that matter?' said Alyssia. 'The only thing that will matter is if they slaughter you on the way. As long as you get to Athens before they have time to hatch their plan, everything will be all right.' She started to break bread on to clay plates for them.

Orestes regarded her anxiously. But Hector wasn't paying attention. The reality of what they were doing, and where they were going, had just fully dawned on him. Of course: Orestes needed to get back to Athens to warn them of the plot. He felt no grievance any longer about this: it was Orestes' right as an Athenian to protect his city. But how could he and his mother – Spartans, and himself a decorated Spartan soldier – go to Athens? What would they do there? Would it not be the most appalling betrayal?

'Who are you?' said Orestes to Alyssia. 'How do you know everything?'

The old woman just looked at him and bared her gums, laughing. 'It's amazing what you can know if you pay attention.'

Hector glanced between Orestes and Alyssia, bewildered. He went to his mother and put his arm around her. Then he looked over at the old woman. She turned to face him, and smiled.

Hector felt as if his heart stopped. For a brief second, no more, the crone's face seemed to change. It was so fast and so ephemeral that he couldn't be sure it wasn't a trick of the light, or because he had slept so little. But it was as if, instead of a crone, wizened and hunched, Alyssia was a woman of the most extraordinary beauty: young, with long, sable hair; eyes like flashing emeralds; lips round and rouged; soft, full breasts in some transparent fabric like woven cobwebs, glinting in dew. He blinked; and the crone was smiling at him again.

But Hector gripped his mother's shoulder. He was convinced he had seen what he had seen. He began to tremble in wonder, because the explanation seemed so clear: impossible, extraordinary, lunatic – but clear. It explained everything, how she knew about them, how she had sent their enemies away and saved them.

He swallowed hard.

Alyssia looked deep into his eyes. 'You want to know if you should you go on to Athens. Am I right?'

He nodded. Of course, she knew without his asking. Hector shivered in awe; his mother gripped his hand, frightened by his suddenly pale, shocked face.

'Look into your heart.'

Orestes was watching them, uncomprehending. Hector glanced at him, then back at Alyssia. He bowed his head, suddenly unsure if he should even look at her.

'Don't be afraid, Hector,' Alyssia whispered.

'Hector, what is it?' Orestes crossed to him, alarmed. Hector looked into his face, his eyes stinging with tears of amazement. Every hair on Hector's body was standing on end. There were thrills of awe, and indeed a little fear, passing over his skin.

'Hector?' Ariadne took his arm tightly in both hands.

He looked down at her. 'Mother. You know we're on our way to Athens.'

'Of course, Hector. I'm not afraid. Orestes will take care of us.'

'I'll take care of you,' Orestes repeated. He seemed suddenly afraid that Hector might choose to turn back.

'Where else could we go?' said Ariadne.

Hector looked back at Alyssia: she went on preparing their breakfast as though the matter were finished. Hector didn't know what to say or do. He thought perhaps he should prostrate himself at her feet. But she seemed again just an old crone, breaking bread with wrinkled, arthritic hands. He moved away from his mother, and took one of those hands in his to kiss it, unsure if this was the right thing to do, but desperate to show his gratitude.

'Oh, stop that!' cackled Alyssia. 'You'll get an old woman all fired up. You wouldn't like that! I might pounce on you.' She laughed, enjoying her joke immensely. 'And then,' she added, slapping her thigh, 'your beautiful lover would be all jealous, and my! I'd be in a pickle.' Slowly she stopped laughing and dabbed her eye with the back of her hand. 'Of course, you wouldn't get this old sack of bones into all sorts of amazing contortions.'

Hector blushed. Alyssia handed him a plate of bread and olives. 'There. Eat up. And then you must be on your way.'

Seventeen

Orestes was disturbed by Hector's silence as they raced across the flat plains of the northern Peloponnese. Ahead of them was the sea, and, to the east a little, the isthmus of Corinth. By evening, at this pace, they would be in Attica.

They stopped to rest for a short while by a river which ran down towards the sea, where they drank the fresh water, and washed their faces.

'What's wrong?' he asked Hector as he knelt beside him.

Hector looked into his eyes, and laughed. 'Do you really not understand?'

'What?'

Hector put his arms round Orestes' neck and kissed him, happily. 'We're blessed, Orestes,' he said. 'Aphrodite's been watching over us since the day we met. I'm sure of it. I can't imagine why. But I'm sure of it.'

Orestes looked at him, his beautiful face and shining green eyes, finally happy after so much sadness. He rested his hands on Hector's powerful biceps, and smiled. His cock swelled to erection, as he bent to kiss those soft, moist lips. They each had stubble, now, which grazed roughly against the other's skin. Orestes scraped his hand down the side of Hector's face. He wanted to take him, abruptly, by the side of the river, like the first time they had made love. The image of Hector lying back, thrusting his pelvis, his cock so hard, his face straining with lust, flashed through Orestes' mind. It seemed incredible that this beautiful young Spartan wanted him so much. Orestes' dick throbbed with desire. The pulse was fast in Hector's neck; his lip was trembling slightly as Orestes lifted away his face.

'I've never felt like this,' Hector murmured, the larynx bobbing in his throat. 'I could make love to you all day. I just have to look at you and my dick gets hard.'

Orestes reached down to see if this was true; and it was. Hector's cock was burning with lust for him. The Spartan bent forward and kissed Orestes' erection through the cloth of his tunic.

'Come on,' said Orestes, his voice husky and shaking. 'We've got to move.'

They stood, laughing at the hard-ons they each had, tenting their clothes, and jumped up and down a bit to get rid of them before they rejoined Ariadne.

'Oh, your cock's amazing,' Hector sighed.

'Stop it!' Orestes laughed, and slapped him lightly on the arm.

'Race you!' Hector shouted. He sped up the bank of the river towards his mother, who was waiting with the horses. Orestes charged after him, but it was no contest. He felt a little ungainly and slow, watching Hector speed ahead, the sun beating down on his neck. When Orestes reached them, Hector was already in the saddle of his horse, helping his mother up beside him.

'You're so slow!' he laughed.

Orestes waved his fist at him, and climbed up on to the warm, bare flanks of the stallion.

The sun had set as they entered fields on the outskirts of Attica. Orestes sighed, happy and relieved to be nearly home. They passed little villages, and heard a few peasants singing songs, accompanying themselves on simple lyres.

He looked at Hector and Ariadne, riding beside him. 'We'll be there soon.'

Hector nodded, anxiously.

'Athens is very beautiful,' said Orestes. He wasn't sure what to say. He understood how momentous this occasion was, for both of them: they were riding into the very capital of their age-old enemy. For Hector, they had been enemies for almost his entire life. Orestes wished there was something he could do to make things easier.

The sea was to their south. Above them, constellations of stars glistened magically in the heavens. The moon was an enormous white ball, reflected in the still, silent Aegean.

And finally, looming in the distance, the city began to appear. The Acropolis was luminous in the moonlight, the Temple of Athena high on the flat-topped hill, the marvel of the world. Orestes' heart beat quickly as they rode towards it.

'It's wonderful,' murmured Ariadne. 'The most beautiful thing I've ever seen.'

Hector kicked his heels and raced faster towards the awaiting city, as though he wanted to get this over with.

It was late, but Athens was still busy with life as they galloped into it. People were out in the street, talking, drinking, sharing carafes of wine. The streets were paved more evenly than in Sparta, although here and there a dangerous pothole waited treacherously for passing traffic. They slowed to a trot, tired after coming so far, so quickly.

Orestes climbed from his horse, and led them into a wide street of magnificent villas, facing towards the sea. He stopped by a low, white-stone building with a garden of roses at the front, and excitedly raced up to the porch. Hector and Ariadne hung back, and he turned to beckon them forward.

A woman appeared in the porch of the villa. She was in her forties, with her hair tied high over her head, and a long pleated dress. When she saw Orestes she cried out in joy and ran to meet him.

He threw his arms around his mother and lifted her from the ground. She wept into his shoulder, gripping him tightly.

Putting her down, Orestes turned to Hector and Ariadne. 'Mother, we have guests.'

They stepped forward, a little apprehensively. 'This is Hector, and his mother Ariadne.'

Frowning, puzzled, Orestes' mother bowed courteously to them both. 'Welcome to our home,' she said.

'Orestes!' A voice bellowed from the porch, and Orestes' father strode casually down to meet him. He shook his son vigorously by the hand. He was a handsome man, perhaps forty-five, with a clean, patrician face, and a red silk tunic edged with gold.

'And this is my father, Archos.'

Orestes quickly introduced Hector and Ariadne, then gripped his father by the arm. 'We have to talk, immediately,' he said.

Orestes' mother, Hermione, led Hector and Ariadne into a huge room and asked them to sit. The room was white, lit by massive candles. There were couches covered in silk cushions. Perfectly sculpted statues stood in the corners. On one wall was a frieze of dolphins playing in the sea.

Hector sat, awkwardly, his mother beside him, as Hermione sent one of the slaves for wine. She said she was sure they must be hungry, and asked what they would like to eat, as if they could order anything they wished. Hector said some bread and fruit would be nice. He was suddenly aware of his Spartan accent: it seemed coarse and provincial in this palace of a home.

Hermione left them to eat, leaving the slaves to serve them, whether because she was shy, and had nothing to say, or saw it as beneath her to entertain foreign guests, Hector could not tell.

There were three slaves to bring them food: different types of bread, an extraordinary range of fruits, most of which Hector had never seen before, and wine served in glass cups. The wine was sweet, much gentler on the throat than Sparta's.

When they were alone, Hector turned to his mother, anxiously. 'I feel like a peasant,' he whispered.

Ariadne smiled, and squeezed his arm. 'We'll be fine, Hector. They seem very nice.'

★

'These people are Spartans?' Orestes' father looked at him as if he was mad. 'You've invited Spartans into our house?'

'They helped me escape, Father. They've thrown their lives away to be with me.'

'Don't tell me that little Spartan farmer is your lover, Orestes.' Orestes gritted his teeth. 'He's not a farmer.'

'Orestes! What are you thinking of? You can't take a Spartan as a lover. It will scandalise the city, my son with a Spartan farmer for a lover. Have some respect!'

'He's not a farmer,' Orestes repeated. 'He's a soldier. And I couldn't care less what people say. Father, I sent a Spartan slave to you. Where is he?'

'I can't believe you would do this,' said Archos, shaking his head and pacing the room. 'I'm a respected citizen, Orestes. I'm running for office. For goodness' sake, I'll be a laughing stock.'

'Where is Theddalus, the helot scribe, father?' insisted Orestes.

Archos looked at him blankly, barely listening. 'A Spartan! Oh, no. He doesn't . . . bugger you, does he? It's one thing to have a Spartan lover, but, by Olympus, if the young thug . . . Orestes, promise me *you* do the buggering.'

Orestes seized his father by the arm. 'Father, Dionakles is in league with the Spartans. They are planning an insurrection to be timed with a Spartan attack. I sent a Messenian scribe ahead with his family, with a letter. Did he get here?'

Archos blinked at him. His face turned dark with fury. 'Are you sure?'

'Dionakles was in Sparta. And Kreon. And three others, at least. I'm not sure exactly who they were, but I have my suspicions.'

'Yes. They weren't at the festival. I wondered where they were. Should have realised. Great plays this year, by the way.' He shook his head.

'They saw me there, Father. They know I know. I imagine they'll want to put their plan into operation all the sooner.'

Archos took a deep breath. 'Yes. Do you know any details?'

'No,' said Orestes sadly. 'When they saw me, I had to run for my life.'

His father tapped him on the shoulder. 'Of course. Glad you did.'

'But Father, you should have received word of this from an old slave – he left Sparta days ago with his family.'

Archos looked at him, and shook his head. Orestes wiped his face, worried in case Theddalus had been caught, or attacked, or some disaster had befallen him.

'Right!' said Archos. 'So Dionakles is a traitor, is he? That'll put paid to his ambitions, the bastard!' He stormed from the room.

Orestes stared after him, bewildered.

Orestes had a large chamber, looking out at the sea, which was not too far away, and a soft bed. He noticed that Hector seemed awkward, and took him in his arms.

'I know it seems strange. But you'll get used to it. I got used to Sparta.'

Hector nodded, uncertainly. 'I don't think your parents like us.'

Orestes laughed. 'They'll get used to you, too.'

'They think we're barbarians, don't they? I suppose we are. I suddenly thought, while I was sitting in that room . . . Your house is enormous! I suddenly thought: what if one of the slaves starts quizzing me on philosophy, or asking what I think about some poet? I know a bit of Homer, but not word for word. Just the stories.'

Orestes laughed again, hugging him tightly. 'Believe me, my father wouldn't know Homer from Hesiod or Sophocles from Aristophanes. Don't worry about that.'

He stared out at the darkness of the Aegean for a moment, anxious about Theddalus.

Then he turned, and looked into Hector's worried face, and kissed him, thrilled by the Spartan's erection, which grew so suddenly and eagerly, digging into his groin. He pulled Hector to the bed, tearing the clothes from his back.

They made love tenderly, the worries gradually emptying from Hector's beautiful face, adoring each other's body in the safety of Orestes' villa. As Hector fucked him, bending over the bed, Orestes thought how outraged his father would be, and smiled, briefly, until the heat of passion overtook him, and his sperm spilt over the silk sheets.

Eighteen

Hector walked with Orestes through the bustling streets, amazed at the colours and smells. The market tradesmen sold wonderful, exotic fruit. Foreigners from all over the world bought and sold their wares. The buildings were high and beautiful, perfect in every way: the smallest house seemed like a palace. Orestes knew a lot of people, and had to stop to greet citizens as they passed. But they were in a hurry: Archos walked briskly ahead of them. There was a chill of excitement in the air.

And Orestes was very anxious, glancing around as if for possible assassins. Several times Hector asked if he was all right; he just nodded and gripped Hector's hand.

They reached the foot of the Acropolis hill, and Hector stared up, awestruck. The temples towered above him, bleached in the sun. The walls of the mount, like cliffs, reached down towards them as if descending from Heaven. Built here, into the side of the rock, was a large theatre, and it was to this that men were anxiously walking. An Assembly was to meet, hastily convened to discuss this urgent matter.

When they reached the edge of the theatre, Archos turned diffidently to his son. 'He can't come in, you know that, of course.'

Orestes nodded, irritated. He took Hector's hand and

shrugged in apology. 'Citizens only in the Assembly.' His father glanced down at their clenched hands and shook his head in dismay. Orestes looked back at Archos. 'I'll catch you up in a moment.'

Impatiently, Archos went inside.

Orestes kissed Hector, in full view of the citizens arriving for the Assembly. Then he nodded up to his right. 'If you want to see, go up there, on the hill. I used to go there as a child to watch the proceedings. You get a great view.'

'Will you be speaking?' asked Hector, unsure if he wanted to be this close to the centre of Athenian government.

'Of course.'

Orestes kissed him again, and joined the throng of Athenians going into the theatre. Orestes had explained that in theory there were literally tens of thousands of citizens entitled to attend the Assembly. In practice only a few thousand regularly took part, and there was a smaller elected council – of which Archos was a member – which met more frequently. Today the messengers had gone out to summon as many citizens as possible. Hector was amazed that such an impressive number was arriving at such short notice.

As he pushed his way through the crowds towards the hillside where he could watch, he had a sudden stab of panic. There, heading grimly for the Assembly, was Dionakles. Hector looked over anxiously for Orestes, suddenly afraid that the general might be planning to murder him before he could speak. But Orestes was inside the theatre now: he could see him, sitting down with his father. Still, Hector muttered a prayer to Aphrodite as he climbed up the hillside. A large number of others, all foreigners intrigued by this Athenian custom, had had the same idea, it seemed. He was jostled by people in strange costumes, with all manner of skin colours. Eventually, he found a place to sit.

There were at least three thousand people crowding the theatre when an old man stood and called them to order. Hector was amazed how his voice carried, and by the discipline with which the assembled citizens fell silent. All at once, the place was a deathly hush, as if the whole city had stopped to pay attention.

'Citizens,' the old man said. 'Thank you all for attending so quickly. Something grave indeed must be discussed today. We have word of a terrible plot to overthrow our precious democracy – from among our own citizens.'

There was a rustle of shocked chatter, which quickly fell silent. Hector leant forward, fascinated by the spectacle.

The old man sat, and across the theatre Archos stood. Orestes stood with him, and they walked slowly down to the centre of the near-circle of stone seats, to the little platform that formed the stage. This was the place, Orestes had told him, where the tragedies and comedies were performed. He imagined that it would be a marvellous sight indeed, the actors in their masks, the musicians playing their instruments, the chorus singing.

Archos stood and faced the assembly of citizens. 'You all know my son,' he said. His voice, little more than a whisper, echoed clearly around the hillside; Hector wondered how they created this miraculous effect. 'A short while ago my son, Orestes, was chosen to go into the heart of the enemy, into Sparta itself, to spy for secrets.' He waited for a reaction, and there were murmurs of admiration. Even though his own city was the enemy here, Hector felt a swell of pride that Orestes was the focus of this moment. 'Facing great danger, he barely escaped with his life. But what he found there was worse than any of us could have expected. He found traitors, plotting our destruction in league with Spartan military.'

There were gasps of disbelief. Orestes held up his hand so he could speak. Hector gazed down at him, adoringly. He was so handsome, so tall and impressive, so at ease despite his earlier anxiety.

'I saw this with my own eyes, citizens,' said Orestes carefully. He was looking around the Assembly; Hector followed his gaze, until suddenly his eyes alighted on Dionakles. 'I saw General Dionakles and General Kreon in the house of a Spartan ephor, plotting to destroy us.'

As the Assembly rippled with incredulous horror, Dionakles

and Kreon leapt to their feet, waving their fists, demanding to be heard. Dionakles, every inch a commander, pushed his way from his seat and climbed down to the centre of the auditorium; Kreon stood in his seat, yelling abuse at Orestes and his father.

Dionakles stood beside Orestes, his face brimming with contempt. 'Citizens!' he shouted. His voice was loud and powerful. The Assembly fell to a hush to hear him. 'Citizens.' Dionakles turned, slowly, as if facing each citizen in turn. 'You know me. I have led our armies in many battles against the Spartans and their allies. I have had my defeats – but glorious victories, too. My family is one of the oldest in Attica. My father's grandfather fought the Persians at Marathon. My grandfather captained a ship at Salamis.'

He lifted his arms like a supplicant. Hector was entranced. The general's performance was riveting.

'And I stand accused of treason?' He glanced at Orestes as if he demeaned himself by looking at him, then focused hatefully on Archos. 'By this man's son?' Dionakles laughed, as if the subject was genuinely amusing. 'Citizens, please. Archos has been my political enemy for years. He is an . . . ambitious man.'

He laughed, inviting laughter from his audience, and indeed there were some chuckles. Hector was tense, afraid for Orestes, because the extent of this general's power was clear to him. There was no one in Sparta like this: nobody with a honey-coated tongue like this, who could freeze the truth with a smile, and snap it in half.

'Ask yourselves. Why would Archos want to accuse me, of all people, of treason? I'll give you two reasons. His hatred for me, and his longing to be seen as some kind of saviour.'

'My son saw what he saw,' said Archos.

'Did he? Perhaps your son can speak for himself. Or is he dumb without lines to read, like an actor needs speeches by Euripides?'

'I saw what I saw,' said Orestes.

Dionakles turned to look at him. Hector couldn't see his lover's face. He thought, If only I had an arrow, I could shoot the monster through the back of his head.

'So tell us!' Dionakles swung round, his arms embracing the crowd. 'What is my terrible conspiracy? What exactly do I plan to do? Or don't you know?'

Orestes stared at him. 'I saw you, and Kreon, and three others, in the house of a Spartan magistrate. His scribe told me that you had earlier written to them.'

'His scribe? And where is he?'

Orestes looked into Dionakles' eyes. Hector was afraid. He knew nothing about the ephor's scribe, but plainly there was something amiss here. Dionakles was very confident, waiting for Orestes to answer him. Hector followed Orestes' gaze as he switched it from the general to his father.

Even from this distance, Hector could see the slight shift in Archos's stance, the shiver of discomfort that passed over his face. What had happened here? Orestes seemed puzzled, or worse – appalled. For a moment he seemed lost for words.

Dionakles laughed, apparently satisfied that Orestes could provide no proof of this mysterious scribe and his evidence. 'Archos's son, you see, can't show us these letters, or even the slave he claims read them. How much longer are we to be forced to listen to this preposterous drivel? Citizens! I and Kreon have been viciously slandered by Archos and his family. Will you entertain their lies a moment more?'

Orestes spun, angrily, from his father, and addressed the Assembly in a proud, ringing voice. 'People of Athens, I may not have led your armies into battle, but I am as honourable a citizen as any of you. Dionakles claims he's been slandered – but what more terrible slander could there be on my father and our family than to claim that these serious charges are no more than a petty political ploy?'

'Prove it, then, upstart!' yelled Kreon from where he was standing. Hector glanced over at him, recognising the swarthy Athenian who had fucked his friend Timos. The image of these two generals in his own barracks, his comrades their helpless playthings, made him blush with shame and anger.

'Prove it!' others were shouting. 'Prove these outrageous charges!'

The Assembly was stirring. Citizens were shaking their fists at Orestes. Hector stared down in trepidation. It seemed Orestes was losing his fight. Orestes was staring in disbelief at Archos, who was raising his arms, trying to calm the multitude.

'Citizens, this is madness!' Orestes' father shouted above the hubbub. 'If you listen to this traitor, you will sell our hides to the Spartans . . .'

Dionakles grinned triumphantly at Orestes. Orestes glared at him, and said something, although Hector couldn't hear him over the shouting. The general shrugged, and the noise around them grew. Hector watched, understanding that his lover had been defeated.

He found himself rising to his feet. He didn't know what he was doing: he felt as if he were looking down on himself, barely able to understand what he said.

'I can prove it!' he shouted.

Orestes looked up. The Assembly fell slowly into silence, as every one of them looked up the hillside. Some of them shielded their faces from the sun with their hands.

Hector ran down the hill, and climbed over the low wall of the theatre, slowly descending the steps.

'Who's this?' yelled Dionakles. 'Is he even a citizen? Are we to allow some foreigner into our Assembly?'

There were a few cries of protest, but most of the gathered Athenians seemed intrigued by the young man walking down to speak to them. As he drew close, Dionakles seemed to recognise him, vaguely, as if he couldn't place him.

Hector stood beside Orestes. Orestes put a hand on his arm, concerned. 'This isn't your battle, Hector. You don't have to do this.'

The Spartan glanced absently at Orestes. He still felt outside his own body: he imagined he was above them all, somewhere, watching the proceedings from the sky.

Then he realised where he was, and that thousands of Athenian eyes were watching him. He felt conscious of his Spartan manners and voice: he'd never addressed a crowd before, let alone one so big, and had none of the Athenians' experience of oratory. He remembered that in this very theatre great poets had their work performed. He was suddenly more nervous than on the eve of battle.

'I'm a Spartan,' he said, his voice cracking. The entire Assembly stared at him in disbelief.

'A Spartan!' howled Dionakles. 'There's a Spartan in our Assembly!'

Hector spun to face the general, and pointed his finger at him, accusingly. 'I was one of the soldiers who were going to assist in this man's treason!' he shouted. 'I saw him, too. Twice. And that one.' He turned and pointed at Kreon. 'In my own barracks.'

There was a stunned silence.

Dionakles struggled to regain the initiative. 'See! It's Archos and his son who are in league with the Spartans!'

Hector laughed, contemptuously. 'Well, if they're in league with a rank-and-file hoplite it's not going to get them very far.'

There was a ripple of laughter from some parts of the Assembly.

Hector held out his hands to the crowd in a kind of peace gesture. 'Look. I'm a mere soldier. Not an aristocrat, not even a full Spartan citizen. I can hardly believe I'm here myself. In all honesty I'm not sure that what I'm saying isn't treason to my own people. But that's more reason to believe me, not less. Me and my comrades were to assist in a rebellion, led by this man. We were told our job was to find the most prominent Athenian citizens and slaughter them in their beds. That's the truth.'

Dionakles seemed suddenly to grasp what had happened and who Hector was, as if the pieces of the puzzle had suddenly fitted. 'This,' he shouted, pointing at Hector, 'is Orestes' Spartan whore! You're surely not going to believe him!' There was a note of hysteria in his voice. 'He's on the run from Sparta for murdering the son of a magistrate!'

Orestes looked into Dionakles' eyes. 'And how do you know that, citizen?'

Dionakles gawped at Orestes, suddenly lost for words. He went pale, glancing up at Kreon.

'Only the Spartans,' said Orestes, 'know that.'

'General Dionakles is condemned out of his own mouth,' boomed Archos.

The Assembly began to hiss with agreement. Hector looked at Orestes. He muttered a prayer to Aphrodite that he had not just sentenced his own comrades to death: if they had set out on their mission, now they might be caught. Around the theatre, Athenians were leaping to their feet, their voices rising in a roar of indignation. Dionakles was struggling to think of an explanation for his blunder.

Hector glanced up to see that Kreon was already leaving, angrily pushing past his fellow Athenians. Dionakles had a look of panic on his face, and abruptly changed tack completely.

'People of Athens, what are we coming to? Our citizens bring back Spartan boys to share their beds . . . Where is our pride?'

This was too much for Hector to stand. He looked at Dionakles and snarled. 'Not too proud to fuck a barracks full of Spartan boys yourself, though, are you?'

Dionakles stared at him, astonished. Hector had not meant to announce to all the world his comrades' humiliation, but, thanks to the perfect acoustics of the theatre, the entire Assembly had heard him; he glanced around, awkwardly, as he heard the buzz of their shock at this fresh revelation. Dionakles was too confused to speak: from the puzzled look in his eyes, Hector thought the general must be trying to remember if Hector was one of the boys he had fucked. The general recovered his composure too late to save himself. The voices around were growing to a crescendo of anger.

Hector wondered what was going to happen. What would the Athenians do with their traitor? Dionakles stared at him, as if unable to grasp how a contemptible Spartan soldier had managed so abruptly to precipitate his defeat.

Orestes took Hector's hand, and whispered into his ear. 'We should go.'

'Are we in danger?' Hector asked, glancing around, alarmed by the extent of the tumult.

'Of course not. But you shouldn't really be here, and my part in this is over.'

He led Hector past the throngs of fist-waving Athenians towards the street. Hector noticed him glance back at his father, who was starting to speak, fully in control of the crowd. Dionakles was gazing up at them, more angry than afraid.

'What will happen to the general?' asked Hector.

'He'll be exiled and his family's land confiscated, I should think.'

'Is that all?'

'If the people of Athens don't rip his arms off first.'

As they walked through the streets, making their way back to his house, Orestes glanced proudly at his lover. He understood that what Hector had done was an enormous leap for him, and that the reason he had taken it was love. Only a few days ago, Hector had run from him, horrified to discover his identity. And now he had acted to save the very Athenian democracy he had trained his whole life to destroy. He didn't know how to thank him. Anything he said would seem trite and feeble. He prayed Hector didn't regret it, now or any time to come. For with his selfless act Hector had burnt his bridges completely.

For better or worse, Athens was now his home.

Nineteen

Orestes turned to face his father, his face red with rage. 'Tell me the truth,' he said.

'About what?' said Archos, picking a bunch of grapes from the table and plucking one with his teeth. They were in a room in the back of the villa, overlooking a hillside covered in olive trees.

'About the Messenian scribe.'

'I don't know what you're talking about, Orestes.'

Angrily, Orestes seized his father by the shoulders. Archos's face darkened. 'Take your hands off me, Orestes.'

'Tell me the truth!' shouted Orestes. 'Where's Theddalus? I promised him his freedom.'

'That was rather a big promise, wasn't it?' Archos glared into his eyes. 'Anyway, it doesn't matter. Your Spartan farmer did the trick.'

Orestes punched him.

Archos fell backward, landing in an undignified heap on the marble floor. Shocked, he felt his lip with the back of his hand. There was a little drop of blood.

'I gave him my word, Father.' Orestes clenched his fists, ready to hit Archos again. 'Where is he?'

'I don't know,' said Archos angrily, getting to his feet. 'I sent him away. He's probably wandering around the hills of Thebes by now, looking for someone to take him in.'

Orestes shook his head in fury. 'Send people out to find him,' he hissed. 'Send as many horsemen out as we can afford to search the whole country until they find him.'

Archos stared at him, surprised by the violence in Orestes' voice.

'If there is any honour in our city, we will find this man and his family and give him everything I promised him.'

'You've got a lot to learn about politics, Orestes,' said Archos in a low voice.

'No, father. I think you do. We needed that Messenian helot to win our case today. If not for Hector, nobody would have believed what I said, and the conspirators would have defeated us. How stupid are you?'

Archos wiped his bleeding lip.

'Find Theddalus, Father.' Orestes strode from the room.

Hector was in something of a daze as Orestes showed him around the city. They had left his mother talking in the rose garden with Hermione; they seemed to be getting on quite well, Orestes' mother fascinated by Ariadne's stories of Spartan life.

They stopped at the agora, the marketplace, where philosophers argued bewilderingly about the strangest things. A small, ugly man with a pug nose, whose name was Socrates, sat on the steps of an elegant building, berating his listeners about everything under the sun. Hector listened, but couldn't follow a word, a little relieved when Orestes told him not to worry, as nobody else could, either.

From there they went to the gymnasium, which consisted of a few low buildings and a piece of open ground not far from the centre of the city. Hector expected something like his own camp, groups of young Athenians practising athletics. It was a little like that: there were a few youths wrestling, a few more tossing discuses. But there were huddles of young men poring eagerly over star charts, 'maps' of the world, or pages and pages of numbers; reading poetry to each other; listening to philosophy teachers explaining the thoughts of a long-dead Thracian who thought the whole world was water, and why he was wrong. Hector thought it was extraordinary: astonishing, but strangely exciting.

Suddenly Orestes gave a shout of happiness, and dragged Hector over to a group of young men, who leapt up in excitement to greet him. These were Kleothon, a stocky Athenian with rippling muscles a little like Gatha in appearance, and, strangely, also an expert at the discus; Albiades, a slender youth with a mop of black hair who looked as if he would break if you hit him; and Drako, wide-shouldered and brawny, a wrestler from the first sight of him.

They clapped Orestes heartily on the back and said how much they had missed him, and shook Hector eagerly by the hand.

'Quite a performance at the Assembly,' said Drako, looking Hector up and down.

'If I go to Sparta, can I get one like him?' asked Albiades, his eyes glinting with unashamed lust.

Orestes slapped him playfully on the back of the head. Hector laughed, nervous to be with Orestes' friends, and worried he would say something irremediably stupid.

They walked together towards the open air, where there was a little semicircular theatre. 'So tell us about your adventure,' said Kleothon. 'Did you narrowly escape with your life, or was it all wine and hoplites?'

Orestes laughed, embarrassed. 'Pay no attention to any of them,' he said to Hector.

They sat in the theatre, and Orestes explained that sometimes the students of the gymnasium, those who especially loved poetry, would recite here for their fellows, and occasionally put on little productions of the great plays.

'I look forward to seeing one,' said Hector. 'Do you do them? Dress up and act, I mean?'

'Me? No, never,' said Orestes sternly.

As the sun began to set, Albiades disappeared for a while, returning with a couple of huge watermelons, some loaves of bread, and five carafes of wine. They were already quite drunk as the darkness enclosed them, leaving just the light of the bulbous moon overhead. Hector relaxed; suddenly he was happy. Orestes' friends were generous and funny, and even if sometimes they spoke quite incomprehensibly, he enjoyed their company. And he was safe, with the man he adored. He was sad that his own friends were so far away, and he would never see them again. With a pang of grief, he realised he wouldn't be able to tend to Epharon's grave, and worried it would be abandoned. He closed his eyes, visualised Epharon's face, and prayed he would forgive him.

Orestes stretched his legs, warm from the wine in his veins, happy to be home. He hoped Hector was all right; and he seemed to be. He was joining in the conversation, and laughing; and his friends clearly liked him. Orestes leant into Hector's shoulder, dreamily, as the talk meandered on around him. Hector poked him, to offer him a slice of watermelon, and he crushed its cool flesh in his mouth.

A little later, Hector nudged him again, and he looked down to see that Albiades and Drako had started to kiss. With a strange detachment he watched his two old friends slowly pressing their tongues into each other's mouth. He looked up at Hector, who grinned at him, amused, it seemed, not at all upset. Of course, Orestes thought, this is a man who has been part of an army of lovers; this is nothing odd to him.

Albiades poured some wine into his own mouth, and teasingly kissed Drako with his mouth full. Red liquid dribbled out between their lips. Albiades slowly lifted Drako's tunic over his head, revealing his broad, tight erection to the moonlight. Hector squeezed Orestes' shoulder; when Orestes glanced down, he saw a mound at the Spartan's groin, which flexed once, pressing up into the fabric. He had a moment of jealousy. Then, suddenly, it aroused him, watching his lover's desire as he gazed at Drako's cock.

Drako roughly pulled Albiades' tunic off: Albiades' dick was long, and rather thin, but hard and succulent. Orestes rested his hand against Hector's swelling erection, and his own cock stiffened deliciously. He looked up into Hector's eyes, and the Spartan just smiled at him again, guilelessly, reaching his hand under Orestes' tunic to gently squeeze his balls.

Kleothon, tossing his clothes aside, dropped his head abruptly into Drako's lap, moving his tongue down the wrestler's shaft until it was shining with his spit. Albiades pushed Kleothon aside impatiently, and sank his lips over Drako's fat cock. Kleothon glanced up at Orestes and Hector, his eyes greedily focusing on their hard-ons.

He stepped towards them. Orestes glanced up again at Hector, who turned to kiss him passionately. Kleothon watched them feverishly as they wound their arms around each other, and darted their tongues into each other's mouth. Hector pulled at Orestes' clothing, dragging the tunic over his head.

In a moment, Orestes and Hector were naked under the stars, each gripping the other's erection in his hand; Kleothon loomed over them, his cock bobbing eagerly. Orestes looked up at him, and then at Hector, who smiled, and shrugged, his dick flexing in Orestes' fist.

Kleothon lowered his face to the Spartan's groin. Orestes watched in a kind of lustful fascination as his friend the discus thrower slowly engorged his lover's cock in his lips. Hector continued to kiss Orestes, his tongue exploring Orestes' mouth; but he grunted softly in pleasure as Kleothon slowly, gently sucked him.

Albiades and Drako looked up, intrigued and excited by what was happening. They joined Orestes and Hector on the steps. Albiades grabbed urgently at Orestes' hard cock, as the wrestler bent beside Kleothon to share the delights of their new Spartan friend. Hector didn't take his mouth from Orestes', as two tongues caressed each side of his slick, rigid dick. Orestes watched, wonderfully aroused by the sight, shifting his buttocks a little as Albiades, grunting, consumed his cock.

Suddenly, Drako was standing over Orestes' and Hector's heads. They each looked up at the thick, pulsing dick, the round, heavy balls hanging below it, the powerful, brawny body which towered above them, the stocky thighs which trembled by their faces.

Hector kissed Orestes again, then turned his head to gently lick under the wrestler's balls. Orestes stared, thrilled by the sight. He touched Hector's head, guiding it up, wanting to watch him suck Drako's cock, wanting to see the lust in his lover's face, astoundingly aroused by the prospect. He felt no jealousy at all; perhaps he was so secure in Hector's love that there was no room for it. He wanted to watch Hector sucking.

But, for the moment, Hector wanted him to join him, and pulled Orestes' face forward to share what Drako was offering. Hector kissed the throbbing shaft, and Orestes kissed it with him. Their tongues slid around the hard cock, and over each other; they paused to kiss, then in unison smothered the wrestler's cock with spit. Drako groaned in pleasure. Hector briefly lowered his lips over the head of the straining dick, then moved aside for Orestes to take his turn.

Drako seized each of their heads; Orestes looked up his wide, hairy chest to see the scowl of lust on his face. He gazed at the dreamy happiness in Hector's eyes. They kissed again, then shared Drako's shaft, tasting each other's spit on it; the cock was gleaming with their saliva. Orestes glanced down to where Kleothon was slowly sucking the Spartan's dick; Albiades was expertly writhing his head around Orestes'.

Suddenly, with a moan of lust, Hector took the wrestler's cock deep into his throat. Orestes kissed his lover's neck as he gorged on Drako: the sight was sending thrills of excitement through him. He took his turn, drawing the wet, hard shaft up to the base, as Hector sat back and watched him, breathlessly aroused. Drako's firm thighs were quivering with excitement. While Orestes continued to run his lips up and down the stiff, hot shaft, Hector buried his face in Drako's balls, smothering them with his tongue until the hairs were matted with spit.

The Spartan's hand was still on Orestes' shoulder, squeezing it reassuringly. But he was slavering hungrily at the wrestler's balls, and thrusting his hips to meet Kleothon's mouth. Albiades' sucking was incredible: gentle, slow, tingling. Orestes stopped what he was doing for a moment to watch Hector suck Drako's balls greedily: he was seizing the tender orbs in his lips and tugging them down, gazing up at the trembling shaft, with a low growl in his throat. Orestes was amazed how exciting it was to see this raw lust in his lover's eyes; but it was. Hector glanced at him, sighing, and kissed Orestes again. Drako's cock oozed a slither of pre-come, and Hector lapped it up with his tongue. The dick was enormous, swollen to its utmost, eager for more adoration.

Hector grabbed Orestes' face, suddenly turning it away from Drako; Orestes looked into his flushed face, as he kissed him again. He wondered suddenly if Hector was as easy with this as he had seemed. Perhaps he couldn't cope with watching Orestes gorge himself on another man's cock after all.

Orestes whispered, 'Do you want to go?'

Smiling, a little shyly, Hector nodded. Orestes had a brief chill of disappointment, because watching his lover sucking had been so thrilling. But he was glad that Hector wanted only to be with him.

Orestes and Hector stood, each of them laughing slightly at the disappointment on the others' faces. Albiades for a moment was reluctant to let Orestes go, and clung with his mouth to his hard-on. Orestes gently removed his head.

'Have a nice time, lads,' he whispered. Albiades gave up and lunged instead for Drako's cock, burying it in his face. Drako shrugged, smiling. Kleothon waved goodbye as he thrust his face in the wrestler's arse; they were going to be happy enough.

Their mouths glued, their dicks rock-hard, Orestes and Hector walked across the theatre towards the dark expanse of the field beyond it. The Acropolis loomed above them on the hill, translucent under the moon.

As soon as they had climbed into the field, Orestes threw his arms around Hector's chest. They fell to the grass, as if they were fighting, lunging with their hips to drive their cocks into each other's stomach. They rolled down the slight hill, their arms wrapped around each other, their legs entwined.

'You liked Drako's cock, didn't you?' Orestes whispered, his voice rasping with excitement.

'No more than you,' said Hector.

'You were sucking his balls like a maniac.'

'You should have seen your face, gobbling at his rough, hard cock.'

They rolled again, briefly stopping to kiss, Hector on top.

'Got a taste for Athenian dick, then?' Orestes said.

'Athenian dicks are wonderful.' Hector gazed down, panting. 'How many Spartan dicks did you suck?'

Orestes flexed his cock, thrilling as Hector's flexed back. He did a quick calculation. 'About nine.'

'Is that all?'

'And a Macedonian. And an Egyptian. And a Nubian fucked me, while a Persian licked my balls.'

Hector grunted, and ground against the Athenian's body. 'Nine including mine?'

'Think so.'

Hector's lips trembled in a lascivious grimace. 'Whose was juiciest?'

They rolled again.

'Yours, obviously,' Orestes whispered.

Hector grabbed his head and sank his tongue into Orestes' mouth. 'You're only saying that,' he murmured, pausing for breath.

Orestes slid down Hector's body to his cock, and roughly stuffed it in his mouth; the Spartan arched his back, grunting. Orestes stopped abruptly and looked up. 'Your captain fucked you, didn't he?'

'Suck my cock,' said Hector, 'and I'll tell you.'

Orestes stared up at him, Hector's cock clasped tightly in his hand. He stuffed it back in his mouth.

Thrusting his hips, burying his dick in Orestes' mouth, Hector gritted his teeth. 'He fucked me like a wild animal. Sank his enormous cock in my arse.'

Orestes paused, gripping Hector's rigid hard-on in his fist. 'Did you love it?' Orestes' dick was utterly stiff.

'I adored it. Biggest cock I've ever seen.' Hector gasped; he was shaking, helplessly, rapturously aroused. 'I just fell on my knees and worshipped it like a god. When – when he rammed it inside me, I came like a maniac.'

Orestes consumed Hector's cock in his mouth, squeezing his balls hard, almost enough to hurt him. The Spartan writhed with delicious pleasure.

Then Hector looked down. 'Did Cleomenes fuck you?'

Orestes took his mouth away, and held Hector's eyes. 'Yes.'

The Spartan pushed him backward, and climbed on top of him. Their balls squashed together. Orestes stared at Hector's cock, the red head glistening with pre-come; his eyes were wide, as if he ached to be fucked by it.

Hector dropped his head and devoured Orestes' dick, dragging down the foreskin and squeezing the bloated head in his mouth. He stopped, breathing hard, a drool of spit from his lips to the head of Orestes' dick. 'Who was the Macedonian?'

Orestes writhed, desperate for him to continue. 'A virgin called Philipus who couldn't get enough of my cock.'

'I don't blame him.' Hector looked down: Orestes' dick flexed, and slapped down against his stomach. The Spartan rolled his eyes with desire, and gave Orestes another hard, frenzied suck. 'Did you fuck him?'

Orestes writhed on the grass, stretching his legs. 'Yes,' he gasped, his cock intensely stiff, dripping with Hector's spit. 'While the Nubian was fucking me.'

Hector murmured. 'Stuck in the middle. I wish I'd been there – to watch.' His lip trembled.

Orestes kicked up suddenly, violently, and knocked him over; quickly he had pinned him to the ground, and sat on his chest, holding down the Spartan's arms with his knees. Hector's heart was pounding under his balls. He pressed his dick against Hector's lips. The Spartan bent forward to suck it, but Orestes pulled it away.

'What was the best fuck you ever had in the army?'

Hector struggled for a moment, gazing up at Orestes with shining, avaricious eyes. But Orestes had him trapped. 'We had a contest. The winner was a hoplite called Timos.' Orestes pushed his hips forward, thrusting his dick into Hector's lips to reward him.

'How did he win?' Orestes demanded, withdrawing his cock.

'Fantastic sucker. Incredible cock. Tremendous. Sweet arse-hole.' Hector stretched his neck, trying to reach Orestes' cock.

'How many of you were there in your company?'

'Ten.'

'And you'd fuck each other every night?' Orestes' shaft was like forged iron, throbbing with lecherous hunger.

'Fuck each other to sleep. Every night.'

Orestes swallowed, hard, and relaxed his grip.

Hector threw him over, grabbed Orestes' ankles, and lifted them around his neck, then fell to hold Orestes' arms down at the wrists. He pressed the tip of his cock against Orestes' arsehole, and the Athenian gasped, needily, his dick lifting and slapping again on his stomach. They were both starting to drip with sweat.

'Who was the Egyptian?'

'You met him. The priest.' Orestes wriggled his arse forward, desperate for Hector to fuck him.

'Him? He was a messenger from the gods.' He pushed the tip into Orestes' arse, slightly. 'I didn't fuck him. I fucked you instead.'

'Fuck me again,' pleaded Orestes, breathlessly. Hector pushed inside, but Orestes' arse was dry, and he moaned in pain. For a brief moment, Hector released him to spit on his hand, and Orestes took his chance to knock him over. They rolled across the grass, until Orestes was astride Hector again, holding him down with his knees. He lathered his arsehole with spit, and lowered it down on to Hector's rigid cock.

'Tell me more about your captain,' he grunted. 'Tell me how much you adored his cock.'

'Uh . . .' Hector's eyes rolled back in his head. 'It was . . . fantastic.'

Orestes pushed down further, squeezing Hector's dick with his arse. The Spartan stared with raw carnality at Orestes' hard

228

cock jutting up between his legs, craving to hold it or suck it. 'You slobbered over his fat cock like a dog,' Orestes grunted. 'And wanked yourself into a frenzy.'

Hector nodded, his chest heaving, his cock pulsing inside Orestes. 'Twice. The second time I fucked him – and his cock spurted come all over his chest.'

Orestes pushed down harder. Both of them gasped with pleasure. Hector's cock filled him, throbbing inside him in time with the rapid beating of his wonderful Spartan heart.

Then Hector twisted his body, and Orestes overbalanced. The Spartan's cock slipped out of his arse; but before he could fight back Hector had grabbed him and rolled him on to his stomach. Orestes wailed, wantonly, in ecstasy, as Hector plunged his dick back into him.

'Did they fuck you like this, those aristocrats?' he whispered. 'Stuffing their hot Spartan dicks inside you?'

Orestes moaned, pushing up with his arms and knees, until he was crouching, struggling for purchase with his feet; Hector gripped his arms under his chest as he ravished him frantically with his cock.

'No one fucks like you,' Orestes grunted, his body convulsing as Hector drove into him.

'No one fucks like you,' the Spartan echoed, gripping Orestes' dick in one hand and savagely squeezing his balls with the other.

'No one's got a cock like yours,' Orestes moaned, dropping his head, nearly collapsing under the weight of the Spartan sinking his shaft inside him.

Almost weeping, Hector whispered into his lover's ear, 'You've got the most wonderful cock . . . the most . . . I love your cock, Orestes, love it . . .'

'I love it inside me . . .' Orestes sobbed.

Hector's hips were raging back and forth. 'I love it when you fuck me,' he moaned. 'I love fucking you . . . Sucking your gorgeous dick . . .'

'I love your balls bashing against my arse . . .'

'Your Athenian arse, tight around my cock . . . Your cock hard in my hand . . .'

'Oh, fuck me, Hector . . .'

Hector wanked Orestes furiously as his hips gyrated, out of control. 'Oh, your cock, your balls, your hard, hard cock . . .' He squeezed Orestes' balls tight in his hand, and bit Orestes' back.

'Your Spartan cock inside me . . .' Orestes fell forward on to his elbow, and reached back with one hand to feel Hector's swinging balls, the shaft ramming into his arse. They could hardly balance; Hector's feet were sliding on the grass; their bodies were solid, taut, trembling muscles.

'Your hard, hard cock . . .'

Their hearts were pounding like drums, beating through their bodies.

'I adore your cock, Orestes, your sweet, tight Athenian arse . . .'

Their voices shook, they could barely breathe or speak. Orestes let out an enormous, passionate wail, and sobbed into the grass, his legs and buttocks trembling, as his hips ground with the rhythm of his lover's hungry dick. Behind him, Hector wailed, sobbing into his back; his teeth bit hard into Orestes' skin.

'Fuck me . . . I love you . . . Fuck me with your wonderful Spartan cock . . .'

'I love you . . . Oh, your balls . . . Your thick, hot Athenian dick . . .'

Orestes' cock was about to explode, held tightly in Hector's fist, which was wanking it faster and faster, the other hand desperately rubbing and squeezing his balls. Hector's balls glided over the palm of his hand: he could feel the shaft, hard and slick, as it pounded in and out of him.

Hector's body tensed in spasm. Orestes felt the cock swell inside him, and it pumped spunk into his arse. His dick burst forth in Hector's hand, covering the grass in spurts of thick, milky liquid.

Exhausted, Orestes collapsed on to the ground, his lover falling on top of him, Hector's dick still inside, throbbing. Their chests heaved together, their hearts beating clamorously and fast.

Hector kissed his neck, gently, over and over, soft little petals against his skin; Orestes flexed his muscles around the shaft still lodged inside him.

There was a moment of pain as Hector pulled out and rolled off on to his back. The Spartan was coated in a layer of sweat, his chest still swelling with passion, but his breathing was starting to slow. Orestes leant on his arm and looked sideways at Hector's flushed, dreamy face.

The Acropolis was resplendent against the skyline behind them. They were silent for a long time.

'I've never looked so hard at the sky,' said Hector suddenly. 'It's beautiful, isn't it?'

Orestes rolled over, and gazed up at the glittering constellations. 'Not as beautiful as you.'

Hector turned on to his side and stroked Orestes' chest. 'Every time we do it, it gets better.'

Orestes grunted softly in agreement. He looked into Hector's eyes, which were glassy with tears. 'It's a pity, isn't it, that our cities have to be fighting each other, when it would be so much simpler to fuck each other's brains out instead?'

Hector laughed. 'I think then you'd conquer us without much resistance.'

Orestes looked at him as if this comment surprised him. 'I was thinking the opposite.'

They were silent for a moment, watching each other breathe.

'But that's the point, isn't it?' said Orestes. 'Nobody would have to win or lose.'

'You're wonderful,' said Hector.

Orestes kissed him, his body shaking with love. 'So are you. My sweet Spartan warrior. So are you.'

They were leaning forward to kiss, when there was the sound of slow hand-clapping nearby.

They spun around, to see Dionakles, sitting on a low stone wall.

Instantly, they leapt to their feet, glancing around for any other traitors who might be lying in wait to kill them. But there was nobody else.

'Most impressive,' said Dionakles. His eyes swept across their naked bodies, and there was a faint smile on his face, pale in the light of the moon. He was dressed in full battle armour, his polished breastplate reflecting the stars. 'Splendid performances. Who would have thought that two such nice young men could be so excitingly bawdy?'

'What do you want?' hissed Orestes.

The general stood. 'I couldn't leave,' he whispered, 'without saying goodbye.'

Hector's body tensed, ready to fight. He glanced down at the sword at Dionakles' side. But the general made no move towards them. He simply stared, contemptuously, at them both.

He addressed Orestes directly. 'We could have brought an end to this senseless war,' he said softly.

'At what cost?' Orestes retorted in a cold, angry whisper.

Dionakles stared up at the Acropolis, wistfully. 'Why do you think we would need Spartans to murder our enemies in Athens?' he said suddenly. He looked back at Orestes. 'Do you really think we have no assassins of our own?'

Orestes blinked at him.

'What does he mean?' said Hector.

Dionakles sighed. 'Why does your family insist on siding with the rabble?' For a moment there seemed to be a look of genuine puzzlement in his face. 'We had made a perfectly simple agreement with the Spartans. An end to the war. Of course, our new government in Athens would have been, technically, their vassals. But it would hardly have mattered. The Spartans are too stretched controlling their own little country to enforce their rule over us. We're a rich state, Orestes. The price they wanted in tribute was absurdly low. We could have paid them and barely noticed the loss to the treasury. And there would have been an end to this anarchy.'

'Yourself as tyrant.'

'Many great men in our history have been tyrants. I would have brought order. What we have now is the tyranny of the

232

mob.' He glanced over at the gymnasium. 'All this prattle. We would have closed down these houses of pointless chatter. Reorganised Athens as a state fit for soldiers. And bided our time.'

'Turned it into another Sparta.'

'Better than Sparta. Richer, more terrible. Eventually, we would have thrown off our temporary masters, and conquered the world.'

Hector stared at him. 'You wanted us to slaughter Athenians in their beds.'

Dionakles laughed. 'As I say, little hoplite. We have perfectly efficient assassins of our own.'

Hector shook his head, baffled.

Dionakles' eyes travelled down Hector's body, and settled on his groin, his penis red and swollen from its exertions.

'What, then?' whispered Orestes.

The general laughed. 'The hoplites were a gift to us from their Spartan commanders. In return for our generous assistance, for transforming Athens from enemy to client state, for our annual tribute, which they seemed to believe was cripplingly high, they gave us three companies, thirty men, of hoplites to be our personal –' his mouth twitched '– bodyguards.' His eyes flashed slightly as he looked again at Hector. 'You were to have been one of them, before you deserted.'

'I don't believe you,' gasped Hector.

Orestes glanced at his lover.

'Our leaders would never –' Hector was trembling.

'Wouldn't they?' Dionakles smiled at him, cruelly. 'We were offering a similar gift in return. Thirty handsome Athenians to replenish the oligarchs' virility. A perfectly simple arrangement. A sign of our deep new friendship.'

Orestes shook his head, and touched Hector's neck. 'They were selling you into slavery.'

'And a delightful prize you were. You have a friend by the name of Timos.' He grinned malevolently. 'I was most looking forward to his services. Gatha: he was enjoyable. And you would have been the most delightful of all. Pity I never got to savour your tight little arse.'

Hector was wide-eyed in horror and disbelief. 'My captain,' he said hoarsely. 'Did he know?'

'Pausanius? A war hero, I believe. Of course he knew. '

'But –' Hector was almost in tears. 'But the dishonour . . . The humiliation . . .'

'Yes. The purest pleasure of all. But you Spartans seem to relish humiliation. Your comrades pleaded to be humiliated.' His mouth twitched into a grim, obscene smile. 'As if there was nothing they wanted more in all the world than to be fucked by an Athenian general.' He laughed softly. 'Pausanius, poor fellow, seemed upset by the whole business. Oh, he shared the desire. But he was, it seems, consumed by guilt. Having to tell such a pack of lies to his soldiers. Telling them what an honour had been bestowed on them when he knew all along they were being sold into a lifetime of disgrace.'

Orestes watched the despair in Hector's face, as tears lined his cheeks.

'So he killed himself. Pausanius. Not honourably. He threw himself into a river.'

Hector buried his face in Orestes' shoulder.

'So,' the general went on, 'the war goes on. The mob continues to rule. And I must leave Attica, an enemy of the people. I hope you're both very happy.'

He turned and walked away, as Hector sobbed into Orestes, who gripped him tightly, frozen in horror at what Dionakles had told them. He watched the general slowly disappear into the gloom of the night, and whispered a prayer of thanks for their deliverance.

Twenty

It was dawn when Orestes and Hector arrived back at Orestes' villa. The sun was rising over the sea, gleaming on the clear blue water in the distance; the stone building looked cool in the morning air.

Archos was sitting on a couch in a chamber inside, anxiously. He looked up at them as they entered. A shadow passed across his face. He stood, and nodded to his son, then awkwardly offered a hand to Hector.

Hector shook it. Orestes smiled, putting an arm proudly round his lover's shoulder.

'I haven't thanked you,' said Archos to Hector. 'For your help yesterday.' Hector nodded, as if unsure what to say in response. 'I appreciate it wasn't an easy thing to do. We are grateful. *I* am grateful. You saved our city from a dreadful fate. A dreadful defeat.'

Hector looked down. Orestes was watching his father's face.

Archos looked at him vaguely. 'The conspirators have been arrested, those of them we can identify, except for Dionakles and Kreon, who have fled the city.' Hector didn't look at him, and he seemed puzzled by his lack of interest. 'We've probably arrested some innocent men, but they'll have their chance when they go to trial.'

Orestes frowned, puzzled by his father's agitation. 'What's wrong?' he asked.

Archos turned away, and crossed to the window. 'We found your scribe. The Messenian.'

Orestes took a deep breath. 'Thank the gods. Where is he? I need to explain everything. Get someone to draft documents giving him his freedom. And we must discuss finding a piece of land for him. Somewhere fertile, with olive groves . . .'

Archos turned to face his son. Orestes looked into his eyes, and was sick in his stomach. He knew what Archos was going to say.

'He's dead, Orestes.'

There was a long silence. Hector touched Orestes' hand, but he barely noticed. Nothing could diminish the horror he felt in this moment. 'What about his family? He had a wife, a son – his son's wife, and their daughter. Did you find them?'

'All dead.' Archos looked down.

Orestes pulled away from Hector, and moved forward as though he were about to hit his father again. But he held back, fists clenched in anger, tears of horror and shame in his eyes.

Archos cleared his throat. 'Evidently they were found by Kreon's men.'

'After you turned them away.'

'Yes.'

'And they still had my letter.'

Archos nodded, taking a deep breath. He glanced at Hector, as if he had forgotten he was there.

'Did you read the letter?'

'No,' said Archos. 'Orestes –' He stepped forward, pleading in his voice. 'Listen to me. I am told an old man on a cart, with his whole family, is at my door, saying he is a Spartan my son has promised land to. What am I to think?'

'You refused even to see him.'

'He could have been an assassin.'

Orestes laughed, bitterly. 'They weren't Spartans. They were Messenians. Helots.' He looked into his father's eyes in fury.

'What about me, father? I might have needed help! I might have been desperate to get word to you.'

Archos glanced awkwardly at Hector, who was staring at him. 'I was angry with you,' he said to his son. 'I thought, What is he doing making promises to Spartan slaves about freedom, sending them to my house? My house.'

Orestes looked at his father in contempt and shook his head. Then he turned to Hector. 'Welcome to Athens,' he whispered. 'Glory of the world. Centre of civilisation. The city of poets and thinkers.'

They slept for a long time, entwined in each other's arms. Hector awoke sometimes, from troubled dreams, to gaze into his lover's sleeping face. He would kiss it, tenderly. Once he awoke to find Orestes' erection pressing into his back, and turned, hugged Orestes to him, his own cock instantly hard. Another time, Orestes was lazily sucking him, still half asleep, and Hector drifted into more pleasant dreams, comforted by the warmth of the Athenian's lips. In and out of sleep they wound their legs around each other's body, rested their hands on each other's balls, drowsily kissed.

His dreams were haunted by Pausanius. He understood, now, what had destroyed his captain. It wasn't simply his lust for Hector. He had been given a terrible task – to deliver his finest soldiers to the outsiders. It had eaten up his soul, poisoned him, until no dishonour was too terrible, anything was thinkable. Poor, tragic man, after a life of glorious combat choosing to drown in a river.

Then the warmth of his lover beside him comforted him, and his dreams became sweeter, erotic dreams of Orestes. In his sleep he moaned, and pushed his legs apart, dreaming of his lover filling him with his beautiful cock. Unsure if he was still dreaming, Hector found Orestes was indeed on top of him, his cock inside him, where it had been carefully slid, without waking him. Orestes was quite still, except for thrilling pulse of his cock, as though he had fallen asleep again. Hector's hard-on dug down into the soft, silk sheets, and he sighed, closing his eyes and floating back down into the clouds of slumber.

Orestes found Hector later, staring out of the window at the turquoise sky. There were gulls sweeping down towards fishing boats out at sea. From somewhere nearby drifted the sound of a musician practising modes on a lyre, singing along wordlessly in a low, male voice. It was a mournful melody. Hector was naked, the sun framing him. Orestes gazed at his wide back and narrow hips, his thick legs.

Hector looked at him. 'What will happen to us?' he said softly.

Orestes didn't speak for a while. 'We're blessed, remember?' he said eventually.

'But I'm in a city that hates Spartans like cockroaches,' Hector whispered. 'Which would like to see all of us exterminated.'

Orestes put a hand on his shoulder. 'Maybe some of them do,' he agreed. He thought with a chill that this might indeed be true. 'But most of us don't. Most of us are reasonable people who just want a quiet life. Like most Spartans.'

Hector smiled, hopefully.

'It wasn't always like this,' said Orestes. 'Greek against Greek. It won't always be like this.'

They gazed out at the dazzling azure of the sea.

'I think history will look back at us,' Orestes said. 'At our world. And be amazed by it. They'll think your people and mine weren't so very different.'

They dressed and went out into the rose garden, where Ariadne was sitting with Hermione. Apparently the two women enjoyed each other's company, finding much to talk about.

Ariadne looked up and smiled at them. 'Where have you been?' she laughed.

Hector kissed her. Hermione asked them to sit, and sent the servants for food and fruit juices.

'Athens is wonderful,' said Ariadne to her son. 'I'm going to like it here.'

'Tomorrow,' said Hermione, 'we're going looking for an inn

for Ariadne to buy. Your father's agreed to lend some money which she can pay back over – oh, as long as it takes. I told her, she can have the room overlooking the quadrangle if she wants, but she says she prefers working.' She looked at Hector. 'Will you be living with your mother, or moving in with Orestes?' Hermione smiled happily at her son. 'He's terribly handsome, Orestes. The whole city thinks so. You should hear the talk! How you brought home this lovely young Spartan who saved us all from a grisly death.'

Orestes laughed, grinning at Hector. 'What do you want to do, Hector?'

Hector looked out at the brilliant, blue sea, then back at the vast villa, gleaming white in the sunshine. 'I want to join the gymnasium,' he said finally. 'Maybe I'll learn something about philosophy. Or try my hand at some poetry, even.'

Orestes laughed again. 'Well, then. I'll see what I can do.'

They were still sitting there, listening to Hermione and Ariadne talk on, as the sun began to set behind them, and the Aegean grew dark. Orestes and Hector were on the lawn, Hector's head resting in the Athenian's lap, and Orestes stroking his hair.

Hector looked up when he heard the sound of horses, and wheels clattering over the paving stones.

A cart was approaching, a burly, heavy man at the reins of the horse. The women stopped their conversation, and Hector peered into the gathering gloom, trying to see who this was.

He realised his mother had stood. Slowly, she walked down towards the cart: the man stepped out, a young girl at his side. Ariadne suddenly broke into a run, and threw her arms around him.

It was Nekos, the burly sailor, and Petuna, Ariadne's slave girl.

Hector climbed to his feet and, Orestes beside him, waited for Ariadne to climb up to the house. She seemed tremendously happy.

Nekos nodded to them. Hector frowned, extremely puzzled.

'Can't believe I've spent all this time without a ship,' the sailor grunted. 'Trundled over hills in that damned cart for three days.'

Ariadne seemed suddenly a little nervous. The sailor faced Hector as if he owed him an explanation. 'Sparta was scandalised by the death of the ephor's son,' he said. 'But I soon found out who Orestes was. And, well, I guessed you'd all be here. I have to admit, I thought it would be harder to find one Athenian in a whole city. But it turns out you're quite a celebrity, Orestes – and you, Hector, although someone will have to explain to me what the hell has happened. I asked in the market, and here I am.'

Hector looked at his mother, and grinned, suddenly understanding. 'I had no idea!' he laughed, turning to Orestes. 'Did you?'

Orestes shook his head.

Hermione seemed a little worried, as she walked down to meet them. 'And is this . . . another Spartan?' she asked, tentatively.

Orestes broke into laughter. 'No, mother. This is Nekos, a sailor from Pylos. And, apparently, Ariadne's lover.'

Looking down from the Acropolis, a hooded figure turned to the old crone beside him. The sky above them was full of stars.

'The war's not over,' said the Egyptian.

'Oh, no,' she agreed.

'Who will win?'

'Sparta. But it will hardly matter. Before long all of Greece will be conquered by the King of Macedon. And then his son will conquer the world, his handsome lover at his side.'

The Egyptian nodded, thoughtfully. 'But they'll be happy. Orestes and Hector.'

Alyssia nodded. 'Of course. I've taken a special interest.'

The goddess Aphrodite raised her arms. Her body straightened, her dirty rags disintegrated, becoming instead delicate, beautiful feathers, as her arms spread wider and wider, and she transformed into a white, ghostly eagle.

Then she flew up, circled the Acropolis, and sailed out over the sea.

IDOL NEW BOOKS

Also published:

THE KING'S MEN
Christian Fall
Ned Medcombe, spoilt son of an Oxfordshire landowner, has always remembered his first love: the beautiful, golden-haired Lewis. But seventeenth-century England forbids such a love and Ned is content to indulge his domineering passions with the willing members of the local community, including the submissive parish cleric. Until the Civil War changes his world, and he is forced to pursue his desires as a soldier in Cromwell's army – while his long-lost lover fights as one of the King's men.

ISBN 0 352 33207 7

THE VELVET WEB
Christopher Summerisle
The year is 1889. Daniel McGaw arrives at Calverdale, a centre of academic excellence buried deep in the English countryside. But this is like no other college. As Daniel explores, he discovers secret passages in the grounds and forbidden texts in the library. The young male students, isolated from the outside world, share a darkly bizarre brotherhood based on the most extreme forms of erotic expression. It isn't long before Daniel is initiated into the rites that bind together the youths of Calverdale in a web of desire.

ISBN 0 352 33208 5

CHAINS OF DECEIT
Paul C. Alexander
Journalist Nathan Dexter's life is turned around when he meets a young student called Scott – someone who offers him the relationship for which he's been searching. Then Nathan's best friend goes missing, and Nathan uncovers evidence that he has become the victim of a slavery ring which is rumoured to be operating out of London's leather scene. To rescue their friend and expose the perverted slave trade, Nathan and Scott must go undercover, risking detection and betrayal at every turn.

ISBN 0 352 33206 9

DARK RIDER
Jack Gordon
While the rulers of a remote Scottish island play bizarre games of sexual dominance with the Argentinian Angelo, his friend Robert – consumed with jealous longing for his coffee-skinned companion – assuages his desires with the willing locals.

ISBN 0 352 33243 3

CONQUISTADOR
Jeff Hunter

It is the dying days of the Aztec empire. Axaten and Quetzel are members of the Stable, servants of the Sun Prince chosen for their bravery and beauty. But it is not just an honour and a duty to join this society, it is also the ultimate sexual achievement. Until the arrival of Juan, a young Spanish conquistador, sets the men of the Stable on an adventure of bondage, lust and deception.

ISBN 0 352 33244 1

TO SERVE TWO MASTERS
Gordon Neale

In the isolated land of Ilyria men are bought and sold as slaves. Rock, brought up to expect to be treated as mere 'livestock', yearns to be sold to the beautiful youth Dorian. But Dorian's brother is as cruel as he is handsome, and if Rock is bought by one brother he will be owned by both.

ISBN 0 352 33245 X

CUSTOMS OF THE COUNTRY
Rupert Thomas

James Cardell has left school and is looking forward to going to Oxford. That summer of 1924, however, he will spend with his cousins in a tiny village in rural Kent. There he finds he can pursue his love of painting – and begin to explore his obsession with the male physique.

ISBN 0 352 33246 8

DOCTOR REYNARD'S EXPERIMENT
Robert Black

A dark world of secret brothels, dungeons and sexual cabarets exists behind the respectable facade of Victorian London. The degenerate Lord Spearman introduces Dr Richard Reynard, dashing bachelor, to this hidden world. And Walter Starling, the doctor's new footman, finds himself torn between affection for his master and the attractions of London's underworld.

ISBN 0 352 33252 2

CODE OF SUBMISSION
Paul C. Alexander

Having uncovered and defeated a slave ring operating in London's leather scene, journalist Nathan Dexter had hoped to enjoy a peaceful life with his boyfriend Scott. But when it becomes clear that the perverted slave trade has started again, Nathan has no choice but to travel across Europe and America in his bid to stop it.

ISBN 0 352 33272 7

SLAVES OF TARNE
Gordon Neale

Pascal willingly follows the mysterious and alluring Casper to Tarne, a community of men enslaved to men. Tarne is everything that Pascal has ever fantasised about, but he begins to sense a sinister aspect to Casper's magnetism. Pascal has to choose between the pleasures of submission and acting to save the people he loves.

ISBN 0 352 33273 5

ROUGH WITH THE SMOOTH
Dominic Arrow

Amid the crime, violence and unemployment of North London, the young men who attend Jonathan Carey's drop-in centre have few choices. One of the young men, Stewart, finds himself torn between the increasingly intimate horseplay of his fellows and the perverse allure of the criminal underworld. Can Jonathan save Stewart from the bullies on the streets and behind bars?

ISBN 0 352 33292 1

CONVICT CHAINS
Philip Markham

Peter Warren, printer's apprentice in the London of the 1830s, discovers his sexuality and taste for submission at the hands of Richard Barkworth. Thus begins a downward spiral of degradation, of which transportation to the Australian colonies is only the beginning.

ISBN 0 352 33300 6

SHAME
Raydon Pelham

On holiday in West Hollywood, Briton Martyn Townsend meets and falls in love with the daredevil Scott. When Scott is murdered, Martyn's hunt for the truth and for the mysterious Peter, Scott's ex-lover, leads him to the clubs of London and Ibiza.

ISBN 0 352 33302 2

HMS SUBMISSION
Jack Gordon

Under the command of Josiah Rock, a man of cruel passions, HMS *Impregnable* sails to the colonies. Christopher, Viscount Fitzgibbons, is a reluctant officer; Mick Savage part of the wretched cargo. They are on a voyage to a shared destiny.

ISBN 0 352 33301 4

THE FINAL RESTRAINT
Paul C. Alexander

The trilogy that began with *Chains of Deceit* and continued in *Code of Submission* concludes in this powerfully erotic novel. From the dungeons and saunas of London to the deepest jungles of South America, Nathan Dexter is forced to play the ultimate chess game with evil Adrian Delancey – with people as sexual pawns.

ISBN 0 352 33303 0

HARD TIME
Robert Black

HMP Cairncrow prison is a corrupt and cruel institution, but also a sexual minefield. Three new inmates must find their niche in this brutish environment – as sexual victims or lovers, predators or protectors. This is the story of how they find love, sex and redemption behind prison walls.

ISBN 0 352 33304 9

ROMAN GAMES
Tasker Dean

When Sam visits the island of Skate, he is taught how to submit to other men, acting out an elaborate fantasy in which young men become wrestling slaves – just as in ancient Rome. He must learn how to win and how to lose. Indeed, if he is to have his beautiful prize – the wrestler, Robert – he must learn how the Romans played their games.

ISBN 0 352 33322 7

VENETIAN TRADE
Richard Davis

From the deck of the ship that carries him into Venice, Rob Weaver catches his first glimpse of a beautiful but corrupt city where the dark alleys and misty canals hide debauchery and decadence. Here, he must learn to survive among men who would make him a plaything and a slave.

ISBN 0 352 33323 5

THE LOVE OF OLD EGYPT
Philip Markham

It's 1925 and the deluxe cruiser carrying the young gigolo Jeremy Hessling has docked at Luxor. Jeremy dreams of being dominated by the pharaohs of old, but quickly becomes involved with someone more accessible – Khalid, a young man of exceptional beauty.

ISBN 0 352 33354 5

THE BLACK CHAMBER
Jack Gordon

Educated at the court of George II, Calum Monroe finds his native Scotland a dull, damp place – so he relieves his boredom by donning the guise of a dashing highwayman. But a more sinister fate awaits Calum in the Black Chamber, where he has to endure humiliations and dark pleasures at the hands of his guardian James Black.

ISBN 0 352 33373 1

WE NEED YOUR HELP . . .
to plan the future of Idol books –

Yours are the only opinions that matter. Idol is a new and exciting venture: the first British series of books devoted to homoerotic fiction for men.

We're going to do our best to provide the sexiest, best-written books you can buy. And we'd like you to help in these early stages. Tell us what you want to read. There's a freepost address for your filled-in questionnaires, so you won't even need to buy a stamp.

THE IDOL QUESTIONNAIRE

SECTION ONE: ABOUT YOU

1.1 Sex (*we presume you are male, but just in case*)
Are you?
Male ☐
Female ☐

1.2 Age
under 21 ☐ 21–30 ☐
31–40 ☐ 41–50 ☐
51–60 ☐ over 60 ☐

1.3 At what age did you leave full-time education?
still in education ☐ 16 or younger ☐
17–19 ☐ 20 or older ☐

1.4 Occupation _____

1.5 Annual household income _____

1.6   We are perfectly happy for you to remain anonymous; but if you would
      like us to send you a free booklist of Idol books, please insert your name
      and address

      _____

      _____

      _____

      _____

SECTION TWO: ABOUT BUYING IDOL BOOKS

2.1   Where did you get this copy of *The Greek Way*?
          Bought at chain book shop   ☐
          Bought at independent book shop   ☐
          Bought at supermarket   ☐
          Bought at book exchange or used book shop   ☐
          I borrowed it/found it   ☐
          My partner bought it   ☐

2.2   How did you find out about Idol books?
          I saw them in a shop   ☐
          I saw them advertised in a magazine   ☐
          I read about them in _____
          Other _____

2.3   Please tick the following statements you agree with:
          I would be less embarrassed about buying Idol
          books if the cover pictures were less explicit   ☐
          I think that in general the pictures on Idol
          books are about right   ☐
          I think Idol cover pictures should be as
          explicit as possible   ☐

2.4   Would you read an Idol book in a public place – on a train for instance?
          Yes   ☐   No   ☐

SECTION THREE: ABOUT THIS IDOL BOOK

3.1   Do you think the sex content in this book is:
          Too much   ☐   About right   ☐
          Not enough   ☐

3.2 Do you think the writing style in this book is:
Too unreal/escapist ☐ About right ☐
Too down to earth ☐

3.3 Do you think the story in this book is:
Too complicated ☐ About right ☐
Too boring/simple ☐

3.4 Do you think the cover of this book is:
Too explicit ☐ About right ☐
Not explicit enough ☐

Here's a space for any other comments:

SECTION FOUR: ABOUT OTHER IDOL BOOKS

4.1 How many Idol books have you read?

4.2 If more than one, which one did you prefer?

_____

4.3 Why?

SECTION FIVE: ABOUT YOUR IDEAL EROTIC NOVEL

We want to publish the books you want to read – so this is your chance to tell us exactly what your ideal erotic novel would be like.

5.1 Using a scale of 1 to 5 (1 = no interest at all, 5 = your ideal), please rate the following possible settings for an erotic novel:
Roman / Ancient World ☐
Medieval / barbarian / sword 'n' sorcery ☐
Renaissance / Elizabethan / Restoration ☐
Victorian / Edwardian ☐
1920s & 1930s ☐
Present day ☐
Future / Science Fiction ☐

5.2 Using the same scale of 1 to 5, please rate the following themes you may find in an erotic novel:

Bondage / fetishism ☐
Romantic love ☐
SM / corporal punishment ☐
Bisexuality ☐
Group sex ☐
Watersports ☐
Rent / sex for money ☐

5.3 Using the same scale of 1 to 5, please rate the following styles in which an erotic novel could be written:

Gritty realism, down to earth ☐
Set in real life but ignoring its more unpleasant aspects ☐
Escapist fantasy, but just about believable ☐
Complete escapism, totally unrealistic ☐

5.4 In a book that features power differentials or sexual initiation, would you prefer the writing to be from the viewpoint of the dominant / experienced or submissive / inexperienced characters:

Dominant / Experienced ☐
Submissive / Inexperienced ☐
Both ☐

5.5 We'd like to include characters close to your ideal lover. What characteristics would your ideal lover have? Tick as many as you want:

Dominant	☐	Caring	☐
Slim	☐	Rugged	☐
Extroverted	☐	Romantic	☐
Bisexual	☐	Old	☐
Working Class	☐	Intellectual	☐
Introverted	☐	Professional	☐
Submissive	☐	Pervy	☐
Cruel	☐	Ordinary	☐
Young	☐	Muscular	☐
Naïve	☐		

Anything else? _____

5.6 Is there one particular setting or subject matter that your ideal erotic novel would contain:

_____

5.7 As you'll have seen, we include safe-sex guidelines in every book. However, while our policy is always to show safe sex in stories with contemporary settings, we don't insist on safe-sex practices in stories with historical settings because it would be anachronistic. What, if anything, would you change about this policy?

_____

_____

SECTION SIX: LAST WORDS

6.1 What do you like best about Idol books?

_____

6.2 What do you most dislike about Idol books?

_____

6.3 In what way, if any, would you like to change Idol covers?

_____

6.4 Here's a space for any other comments:

_____

_____

_____

_____

Thanks for completing this questionnaire. Now either tear it out, or photocopy it, then put it in an envelope and send it to:

Idol
FREEPOST
London
W10 5BR

You don't need a stamp if you're in the UK, but you'll need one if you're posting from overseas.